T0158776

Grace *and* Favors

Grace *and* Favors

Dolores Palà

iUniverse

GRACE AND FAVORS

iUniverse books may be ordered through booksellers or by contacting:

iUniverse
1663 Liberty Drive
Bloomington, IN 47403
www.iuniverse.com
1-800-Authors (1-800-288-4677)

Because of the dynamic nature of the Internet, any web addresses or links contained in this book may have changed since publication and may no longer be valid. The views expressed in this work are solely those of the author and do not necessarily reflect the views of the publisher, and the publisher hereby disclaims any responsibility for them.

Any people depicted in stock imagery provided by Thinkstock are models, and such images are being used for illustrative purposes only. Certain stock imagery © Thinkstock.

ISBN: 978-1-5320-0724-8 (sc)
ISBN: 978-1-5320-0725-5 (e)

Library of Congress Control Number: 2016915693

Print information available on the last page.

iUniverse rev. date: 09/19/2016

For Juan, then and now and forever. With thanks.

Acknowledgements

Kathleen Grosset has taken the trouble to weed out the brambles of my manuscript for the third time running. And, with Thierry Mignon elegantly designing its setting, she has brought it to life.

Ailsa Paterson has joined them in editing my prose and imposing the proper use of punctuation, an element I am not always at home with.

I thank them from the bottom of my heart.

Cover design "The Perfect Straight Line", Joan Pala, 1990

That day, Marisa Short had been in Paris for exactly five months. She decided that the occasion called for a treat. She was to have twelve months as a student in Paris, her junior year abroad. The treat should be something cushy and self-indulgent—perhaps even a tad expensive.

Despite her five months abroad spent secretly trying to acquire a continental touch, she looked as American as she had the day she'd sailed from New York Harbor. With her long legs, long strides, high cheekbones, full mouth, and mop of dark hair that did not take to French hairdressers, she was instantly recognizable as American. Her wide china-blue eyes and their frank gaze only confirmed it. That irritated her a bit, for she had nurtured the idea that a few months in Paris would alter her look and perhaps even her perceptions.

Her horizons had widened upon traveling through Europe—but only in the sense that now she saw all its warts. She no longer melted at the visions she had acquired while growing up during World War II in New York, in a neighborhood that had been forever altered by an influx of persecuted Europeans.

She no longer romanticized the free French either. She had come down from her cloud of good and evil, but she was left ill at ease with what appeared to be the naked truth. She had expected to find two easily identifiable extremes from which she could choose. She felt she deserved that. Her only brother had died in the battle for Rome. But now she had come to view his death as a sacrifice to geopolitical insanity, because today, on the verge of 1950, the half-century mark, working for a true peace was a subject that had slid off the horizon. Peace was now everyone's goal, but it meant different things to different sides.

During her French university term vacations, of which there were an amazing number, she'd managed to visit several Eastern Europe cities behind the Iron Curtain. Most were beautiful, such as Prague and Budapest. Compared to Paris, they were all a trifle sad, yet none gave off a sense of fear and tyranny lurking behind the traffic lights, as she had been led to expect. The notion of venturing behind the Iron Curtain sounded daunting. Westerners were geared to reject Communism and deplore the cruelty inflicted on the hostage populations who lived under it, the people of countries that Americans were told to call the Captive Nations.

The docility of those nations' citizens might have been explained in part by the preceding war years, which had inculcated fear as a way of life. That explained their furtive glances as well as the half-empty store windows on seldom-crowded streets throughout Central Europe.

The Nazis had set the tone by occupying Europe in the first place. The Communists had inherited a mind-set: they just had to snap an ideological whip in order to control people. Prague, an exquisite monument to grace and harmony, was now iced over and distant. No one smiled on the streets. On the contrary, averting one's eyes seemed to have become a national characteristic. Marisa had come to believe that the war was not over; it was just living through a change of rules.

She had spent a September week in Vienna and explored its charming outskirts on local buses. With her heart in her mouth, she'd watched the Allied jeep patrolling the occupied city nightly with four military policemen aboard—British, French, Russian, and American. They'd driven along slowly in silence. She'd shuddered, half in despair and half in apprehension.

Marisa spoke fairly decent French by then but no German, yet she managed to connect with the people she got to talk to. The Germans tended to speak English more often than not. Also, she discovered that much to the irritation of the prickly French, English had become the universal language since the war, not French.

There was nothing German about Austria, she'd come to find, to her surprise. She had known that Austrians claimed distance from Germany, but to find the distance to be true amused and relieved her. She liked Austrians; there was a fey quality to Austrian conversation. When one young man in a Vienna café had tried to describe the chasm between Germans and Austrians, she'd reminded him that Hitler was Austrian by birth. At that point, he'd leaned back in his chair and laughed, saying, "Yes, but look from where!"

She'd realized then and there that it would take more than a year abroad to understand Europe. Since she had nothing else to do and no one waiting for her at home, she decided she would stay in Europe to find out more once her school year was over.

Marisa Short came from the top edge of Manhattan. Her playground was Fort Tryon Park, which had opened its gates when she was a little girl. She had gone to Catholic schools within walking distance of her home, and she and her brother, Peter, and their large crowd of playmates referred to the rest of New York as downtown. Few had much to do with the other boroughs, unless one counted the Staten Island ferry rides their parents took on Sunday afternoons. Their families were second- and third-generation Americans for the most part, and they were comfortably installed. Most of her friends' fathers had fought in the First World War. One was badly disfigured, and her own father had been in the army but not overseas.

Her parents were marginally different from the others. Her father was a postman, a small gray man who walked with a funny slope, probably from carrying a mailbag over his right shoulder for so long. He had thinning gray hair, pale blue eyes, and a face that became gentle when he smiled. He came from a tiny Catskill town called Cairo. It was pronounced "Kayrow," but he liked to lead people to think he was from Egypt, and he pronounced it almost with a foreign lilt. The town was something of a resort, yet he never suggested it as a place to visit, let alone a place to spend their summer holidays. Marisa and Peter never got a clear answer to their questions regarding why he did not visit his hometown. It was as though both their parents had been born only once they got to Manhattan. Anything that had happened before didn't count.

Peter and Marisa's parents had sent them to a summer camp out on Long Island for the children of city employees. It was a flat, anonymous, and unlovable place. Both of them would confess later that they dreaded their summer vacations, because aside from swimming, there was little they could find to enjoy. Other kids in the neighborhood came back from their two weeks at the beach or in the country with tales of adventures, such as climbing mountains, sailing boats, and cycling overland to visit farms or forests. However, the Short kids did nothing more than wait for the tide to come in.

"If they don't play with the other kids, it's their own fault," their mother said, scowling, always ready with a chastisement. At times like that, they would catch her looking at them stonily, as though wondering how they'd come to be there at all—and how long they were planning to stay.

The children would comfort themselves with make-believe tales they concocted while in bed at night, tales wherein they had been found in a mailbox and their amiable father had taken them in over their sourpuss mother's objections. They were only half joking.

Agnes Short saw her children as unruly burdens who had thwarted her small-town girl's ambition to make it in Manhattan. What she'd planned to make it as was never specified. Whatever it might have been, it did not involve taking care of children.

She too came from upstate New York, somewhere near Troy. Her maiden name was Rhinebolt. Her parents were German, and though she seldom admitted it, she spoke German fluently. She never suggested a visit to Troy. It was as though she'd never had a life before landing in Manhattan and meeting Smitty in a diner downtown. The children grew up without any extended family. In New York, however, that in itself was not much of an oddity. New York was, by nature, a city of transients.

Agnes Rhinebolt met her husband, who was called Smitty, though his name was Joseph, at the downtown diner where she worked, near the main post office on Thirty-Third Street. One of the other girls behind the counter had gone out with him, and she told Agnes he was harmless. "He'd be good for a movie and a speakeasy drink after but not much more," she said. One dull night in 1927, he asked Agnes to join him at a new speakeasy in Greenwich Village, where they could have a bite and a drink. She fancied the idea of going to the Village, so she said yes.

They started out that way, with her looking for something he might be able to offer her. Not long after, he invited her uptown to visit his new apartment. It was all the way at the top of the island. "A little bit more and you drop into Spuyten Duyvil," he told her, making her laugh, which was something of a feat. She accepted his invitation.

The neighborhood was new, fresh, and full of greenery. Amid the woods along the river, a new city park was being fashioned at the location of a great fort used during the War of Independence, where the views of the Hudson were stunning and unexpected. It would soon be on the new subway line. "The A train," he told her. It sounded promising.

His building turned out to be an attractive six-story redbrick structure with a front portal made of fancy wrought-iron grillwork over thick glass. It hinted of safety, and that caught her eye. The building was called the New Orleans, and it had an elegant dark green canopy in front and a uniformed elevator man inside who addressed Smitty as Mr. Short. Its funding had something to do with the post office, so he had a preferential deal, he told her cockily. He actually owned the apartment. She took note.

The building was at the crest of a hill and had a sweeping view of the parkland all around. The Palisades nipped the sun, which changed the color of the rock formations in front of her eyes on the other side of the river. There were tennis courts just down the hill to her left, and she could see the extensive landscaping going on to her right in what was to be a vast new park where there had once been a vital fortress in the American Revolution. "George Washington had his headquarters right here, where he beat the hell out of the Hessians, who were the British army's hired hands," Smitty told her with great pride. Agnes liked that. Her parents had come from the Frankfurt area of Germany. They were Hessians.

Her grievances against her parents touched heavily on their German accents. During the First World War, their guttural vowels and harsh consonants had been a burden she could not forgive. Thus, the super American Firster she had become pricked up her ears. She treasured reminders of America's might over its European colonial masters. The fact that Upper Manhattan was the scene of so much native victory made her look around with pleasurable interest. She smiled at Smitty, who took it personally, knowing nothing about her prickly patriotism—or anything else of her past, for that matter. She did not invite questions, much less offer confidences.

He told her that the Rockefellers were giving the park a real French cloister with a chapel and a famous tapestry showing a lady and a unicorn, and it was all being assembled stone by stone to make it special. There would be different kinds of gardens around it, even a garden with just herbs, such as chives and rosemary. She had read about that in the newspapers, and she now peered at the odd construction site. It looked something like a giant toy—an erector set castle for grown-ups. She smiled at Smitty again, this time with real interest. He was agleam with anticipation.

His new apartment turned out to be bright and sunny. There were four large rooms, including a big eat-in kitchen with a roomy new refrigerator—not an icebox but an electric refrigerator. The views were bewitching from all the rooms. They were on the fourth floor and seemed to be perched over a vast parkland with a river racing through it and a toy bridge being built girder by girder under their noses. She smiled. It was the George Washington Bridge. She liked that.

Smitty was enchanted though a little surprised at Agnes's reaction while looking around his yet nearly unfurnished domain. He had been afraid that this unusually attractive but oddly unsmiling girl would complain about the distance or say something sour, such as "Once a hick, always a hick," which another girl had already done, cutting him to the quick. Quiet to the point of surliness, Agnes seemed almost happy in his new apartment. He watched her move through the empty rooms with grace, and he savored her amazing figure, including the smooth curve of her hips and a breathtaking pair of breasts that he thought made up for her lack of smiles.

He felt sorry for Agnes, though he was not sure why, except that she was visibly unhappy. She also gave him a serious case of the hots, as he put it, and he wondered how he might approach her. Now he led her to the bedroom, where he had a new double bed and a dresser that had been delivered the day before. He was planning on moving into the apartment this coming weekend.

She looked at the bed and paused for a second. Then she turned to meet his eyes. Smitty and Agnes were the same height, so they were nose to nose. She tilted her head to one side and kissed him. Then she began undressing, not slowly but carefully, folding her dress and underwear but kicking her shoes to a far corner and smiling as they flew by.

Smitty nearly died of bliss and astonishment. After what seemed a long time to him, she reached out her hand and tugged him down to join her on the bed. She kissed him and ran her fingers lightly along his sides while he melted. "Where did you learn to do that?" he managed to croak.

She pulled away and snapped, "Don't get any ideas, buster. I am my own boss. And guys are not the only ones who can enjoy this, you know."

She glared at him. His astonishment got to her, though.

"Okay," she said, sighing. "No, I guess you don't know. Well, maybe you can learn." She sank back onto the bed.

"Maybe we can become friends?" he ventured.

She thought about it for a bit. *Friends?* She had no friends. Eventually, she met his eyes and quietly agreed. "Maybe," she answered. Maybe it was time, she thought. "I will be twenty-nine in November," she said in a low voice.

He laughed. "Hell, I'm forty!"

"Okay, but you are not me," she answered, and for the first time, he heard a softness in her voice, the hint of a need, a reach for help. He propped himself up on his elbow and gazed down at her.

When her face was relaxed, she was pretty, not pinched or closed. More than that, when she was lying with the fading sun playing on her naked body, she was beautiful beyond measure. Her long legs were perfect, her breasts were like fruit, and the curves of her hips were a constant enticement. "Marry me," he blurted out, "and I'll make you laugh. I promise. I'll make you want to laugh."

First, she stared at him as though he had lost his mind, and then she frowned thoughtfully. She reached down to the floor for a cigarette, matches, and an ashtray with the words *Pennsylvania Diner* on it, the place where she worked. She grunted when she saw it. The words *marry me* echoed in her ears. *Marry Smitty the postman?*

Why not?

Why not?

Agnes was surprised that the poky hick was so good in bed. He even seemed to know a few things she didn't.

Agnes liked making love and was disconcertingly frank about it. She had liked it since the first time, when she'd been cornered in the back garden by the older brother of her schoolmate Peggy. He had pinned her down between two rows of trees. Halfway through, he'd realized she was enjoying it, and he'd pulled back for a second to look at her carefully. She'd opened her eyes just enough to meet his and whispered, "Is that all?"

He'd laughed out loud, astonished. "No, that is not all. Just hold on," he'd whispered. "This is going to be historic." A few minutes later, she'd nearly fainted with pleasure.

Lying quietly on the mossy grass afterward, she'd smiled at him like a satisfied kitten in complicity.

"So that's what all the fuss was about," she'd murmured, turning to him. Silently, she'd made up her mind that she would be like the boys around her, not the girls. She savored her pleasure and her command over that pleasure, and she would take it just as she deemed fit. *Like they do,* she'd thought. *Just like the guys.*

Except she had the upper hand because no guy would ever expect it. She had the last laugh, and she found almost as much pleasure in that as she did in the act itself—almost.

Agnes's affair with that first lover might have gone on for years had he not been graduating from college that spring. He'd been booked to leave for a job in Rochester right after.

He'd toyed with the idea of taking this strange girl with him, this kid who was so taciturn and who seemed to ask for nothing but a diet of milkshakes and burgers, a double bill at the local movie house, and an endless exploration of her senses and his. She would try anything; she seemed to have taken over his whole body with a strange, new silence he could not bear to leave. She'd frightened him, yet when he'd had to let her go, he'd cried.

She'd smiled at that and promised to write—which, of course, she never had.

She'd come to the city when she was twenty-two, after her father had retired from his hardware store because of ill health. Her two brothers had left for Chicago for jobs on a building site. Her parents had asked her to stay at home because they needed her help. It was then that she'd taken a Greyhound bus to Manhattan. She'd left them a note on the kitchen table.

If they'd ever made an attempt to find her, she'd never heard of it. She would later say that she never looked back.

She'd been instantly stirred by the anonymity of the city; she liked its bigness. She found comfort in crowds. There was no need to pretend interest in others. There was no need to pretend anything at all. *No one knows you here,* she thought, exhilarated. Furthermore, the city had an endless amount of movie houses where she could dip into other lives to her heart's content. No one asked her questions, and she could choose a lover the way she chose a speakeasy—with no strings attached. All this made her heady with independence. She was free.

Then Smitty had come along, and the skinny little guy turned out to be a devil in bed. They saw each other regularly. She had been living in the city long enough to know how to pick her partners and how to ditch them as well. She was not ready to settle down, and she seemed to have been born knowing never to mix sentiment with sex.

Agnes was about fifty years ahead of her time.

The downside was that her cavalier attitude did nothing to help her make female friends. On the contrary, other women avoided her. They feared her, misunderstood her freedom, and mistrusted her scorn for the rules of the game.

Perhaps if she had had more insight into herself, she would have avoided the pitfalls that scarred her life and the lives of those around her.

After a few months of visits to the uptown apartment, she discovered she was pregnant. At first, she was furious, indignant, and bent on an abortion. It was Smitty's fault; they both knew that. She screamed and threw things till she was exhausted. Then, slowly and coherently, he talked her around.

He could offer her a nice place to live, a place she liked. He had a steady job with a good pension, and he was offering her relative freedom, he said while looking straight into her eyes. He did not mean she could go off on the speakeasy circuit or screw anyone she fancied, he told her, his eyes digging into her. But everything was relative.

She understood what he meant and what he often said: "What I don't know won't hurt me." That day, he caressed her hair gently while she cried like a wounded child in his arms and agreed to marry him.

Smitty wanted a home, not a furnished room, and he wanted a family. He wanted what everyone wanted: a pretty wife, a couple of kids, and something to look forward to. He told her that and saw something snap in her eyes. Having something to look forward to was a concept she had barely ever thought of. Anyway, he went on, he liked her a lot. Liking someone was not all that common. Was it? And what the hell? It was time to settle down.

After a while, she shrugged and murmured something he took for assent. She was almost smiling, he noticed.

She was twenty-nine that year. "What the hell?" indeed.

Peter was born in February 1927. Agnes found, to her dismay, that she felt little maternal instinct. She was bitterly ashamed of herself for that and had to fight back her conviction that it was the baby's fault. She knew it was not. He was a pretty little boy with blond hair and big blue eyes, and he smiled and gurgled just the way he was supposed to do. She did not hate him; she just decided to keep him at bay—to a certain extent at least.

Nonetheless, she refused to nurse him. There was no one she could talk the question over with—there never was for her—so she sank deeper into her distance and made no attempt to bridge it.

To make up for having to walk around the park for the baby's good health in the icy winter winds, she took to having a couple drinks with Smitty when he came home from work. They resumed their lovemaking, now improved thanks to the booze and the return of her hormones. Three months later, to her horror, she found she was pregnant again. She screamed and threw things at him. She cried and neglected Peter, but Smitty calmed her down.

The main reason Agnes kept the baby was because she was scared of a kitchen-table abortion, not because she considered it immoral. She was afraid she would be sexually crippled in the process. All sorts of stories went around about botched abortions, the most common of which was that the procedure could leave a woman so scarred inside that sex was torture forever afterward.

Don't take that away from me too, she cried silently, keeping Smitty eternally confused about her reasons.

Marisa was born in February 1928, a year and a day after Peter.

Agnes had her tubes tied before she left the hospital, though she never told a soul. She paid $250 for it. They were her tubes after all.

The children would be her burden and Smitty's delight till his death. They grew up with the new and beautifully landscaped park as their backyard, and the bells of the Cloisters were their private timepieces. The schools they went to were also brand new. The neighborhood had the feel of a small, pristine Hudson River estate, despite the arrival of the huge and handsome George Washington Bridge just down the road. Beneath it was a landmark lighthouse that both children took to their hearts, their private totem. When one would run away from their mother's shrill calls to "Come here, dammit," their refuge would be the red lighthouse. Their handy playground was, of course, the stone cloister from Aquitaine, complete with its tapestry of a lady and a unicorn and a model fourteenth-century herb garden to scent the air.

Marisa remembered sniffing the varied scents of the herb garden plant by plant with enchantment while her father watched, minding her tricycle, while Peter whizzed around on his new scooter.

Though their mother was crotchety and their father foot weary when he came home at night, they were not unhappy children. No one beat them, and no one was an alcoholic. No one did much of anything. They spent their after-homework hours either at other children's apartments or downstairs by the park's entrance, peacefully playing street games in a safe environment. They built snow-packed fortresses in winter and held majestic snowball battles around them, and they sold lemonade to passersby for a nickel a paper cup in summer. They did their first Communion and confirmation together because the fees were lower that way.

They were told to be careful with money, but they lacked nothing. They were taught to say please and thank you, but above all, they were told that nothing was due to them. "You have to earn it," their mother told them, "so make sure you are smarter than the others."

"And get yourself a college education," Smitty added.

"Get a scholarship, get good marks, and go to college," their mother advised bitterly. "Then you won't have to sling hash for a living. You won't have to give up before you even get started," she added in a stinging tone.

Her voice made them shiver. They loved her because children instinctively loved their mothers, but they felt no joy in their hearts for her, and they did not know how to deal with that. "She makes it hard for you to show her that you love her," Marisa told Peter one night in the darkness of their room.

He muttered something in assent and then added, "As long as we feel it's true that we really do love her, I guess it's all right. But suppose one day you don't really mean it? What happens then?" he asked.

"That will never happen," Marisa assured him, knowing full well it had happened already a long time ago.

Agnes would stand to one side if Smitty was talking to them about the future, but she often managed to add a curt little note reminding them that their parents were under no obligation to send them to college; she and their father would be doing it only because their father wanted to—in the event they both got good marks and were given scholarships for their expensive Catholic high schools. Though each had special friends, there was a bond between the two siblings that had to do with their closeness at home. There were no aunties, uncles, or cousins their age in their lives, and the family infrequently had guests.

They were a first-generation New York City nuclear unit. It was unfortunate perhaps but not unusual; there were lots of others in their midst just like them, but those families were not American born, as the Shorts were. The Short family was "differently different" according to Peter, who had a way with words.

Agnes took on her job of mother much as she had taken on her job at the diner. She did what was expected of her, no more. She performed but clearly did not enjoy it. Worse, she did not participate.

While in grade school, the children had to show her their homework, which they did with each sitting at one end of a big desk in the room they shared, before being allowed to listen to the radio or open a book for pleasure. They did not question the routine—not only because they never questioned anything she ordered but also because a certain docility came easily to them.

Both were excellent students, except in math, in which they had problems. She never offered help but was fair with her comments. If their papers were sloppily written, she would have them rewrite them, leaving no room for dissent. As she expected, they worked more carefully as a result.

It never appeared to bother her that there was a lack of love in their dealings, as well as a lack of affection or even pride in their accomplishments. Both children skipped grades in primary school, and both graduated from high school at sixteen, a year apart, as in everything.

Smitty was a proud father. Agnes just nodded. She gave them tennis lessons as graduation gifts—but with another teacher, not herself. Naturally, both excelled. Smitty was proud of their strokes and their sleek young bodies. He did not seem to notice that their mother, who was a good player herself, never once suggested a game, nor had the children expected him to notice it.

He cherished the pleasure his home offered him and did his utmost to maintain it. "What you don't know won't hurt you" was his lodestar. At the end of the road, there would be a good government pension. What more could a boy from the boondocks ask from the big city? Smitty looked at his wife's ass as she moved from the table to the bedroom at the end of his favorite radio program and smiled to himself. *Indeed, what more?* he thought.

In their teens, Peter and Marisa reached out for special friends, confidants to go with their changing lives in adolescence. Lots of little things changed in their lives without their noticing. They still shared a room and still chatted before turning the lights out, but they were going down different roads.

Both acquired new best friends.

Marisa's was Lane Berger, who lived a couple of buildings down the street. They went to different schools because Lane was Jewish, but they walked down the hill to the bus stop together every morning, and since it was the top of the line, they scurried for seats together on the upper deck.

Marisa went to St. Catherine of Sienna, a small but scholastically advanced girls' school to which she had a full scholarship. She got off the bus at the third stop. When Lane did not show up, she walked to school. She only took the bus to be with Lane, and she paid the fare out of her pocket money. Her mother did not think a bus was necessary, as the school was within walking distance. Her mother had no idea what this friendship meant to Marisa. How could she? She had no friends.

Lane went to Ethical Culture, which was farther downtown. They had fallen into one of those early friendships that nourished and sustained youngsters more than might have been the case at any other age. They told each other almost everything, within a certain space. They discussed everything about boys but not everything about their lives at home. Lane did not go into detail about the Battle of Stalingrad; her mother's enthusiastic support of the Soviet Union in general; or even her interest in the American labor movement, free medical care for the poor, support of home relief for the unemployed, and other worthy concerns that a girl who went to a convent school and had a grouchy mother might not be prepared for.

Lane cherished Marisa's carefree air and wanted to keep her friendship. She didn't want her mother's concern for higher issues to mess it up.

Marisa, over the years, saw only that Mrs. Berger was a pretty woman who always seemed late for an appointment, spoiled her girls with Saks Fifth Avenue clothes, and had a certain touch of glamour about whatever it was she was doing, no matter how potty it seemed to others. She was busy with causes, and she wore hats with ribbons and even a fur-trimmed cape in winter. No one else wore capes. She went to lectures at the Jefferson School on industrialism and factory-floor abuse, though she did not insist her daughters accompany her.

None of Mrs. Berger's doings made much sense to Marisa, who was unfamiliar with foreign politics or social unrest but viewed Communism as an enemy not only of the Constitution but also of the Holy Roman Apostolic Church. There was that.

She refrained from asking too many questions about these points for fear of endangering her friendship with Lane.

She did know, however, that the good lady had been something of an activist long before the war. She had been a union organizer in the book trade, and she was well known around Fourth Avenue, where the choice used-book shops were clustered. She'd then gone on to collecting funds for the Soviet Union during the war and had taken a few courses at the Jefferson School, which had become a prized target for Senator McCarthy's ferrets.

As a result of the rampant anti-Communism that had shot up around them immediately after the war, Lane and her older sister had been cautioned never to discuss their parents' politics with their school friends. Discretion came naturally to them, but when anti-Communism had grown to be a major industry, with victims ranging from Hollywood stars to the hapless Rosenbergs, the stakes had become higher still. Recognizing the shrill hysteria that was sweeping over the land, though she was not particularly involved herself, Marisa watched it warily.

Marisa was not drawn to participate, though she clearly stood on the side of freedom of opinion. She instinctively disliked the sound of the word *un-American*, and McCarthy's face and voice insulted her nervous system as well as her brain.

Beyond that, the two girls had enough to bank their friendship on, including school results, an increased interest in boys, and the relative merits of B movies over Hollywood moneymakers, to get too involved in world issues. Closer to their hearts was what colleges they might aspire to attend.

Lane kept her counsel about her mother and subversion, and Marisa never thought much of anything beyond hoping the war ended before Peter got drafted or joined the paratroops, which he had mentioned one night before going to sleep.

She had been alarmed at the idea and told him so. Mildly, he'd told her to calm down. He'd promised to go for the navy and asked her to please forget he'd even mentioned jumping out of airplanes. They'd gone to sleep on it.

Not convinced, however, she went to the Forty-Second Street Public Library to look up casualty rates among paratroops, and she nearly fainted at what she saw. She copied the figures onto the last page of her notebook so as not to forget them.

That was the day he enlisted.

She went ice cold when he told her. "Who's going to kill me?" he scoffed. "It's almost over anyway. By the time I'm trained, we'll all be dancing in the streets of Paris." He laughed her off.

Adolescence was a time of far-ranging fragility. Marisa depended on her friend Lane for the kind of solace she sorely lacked. Her reliance on her brother was enormous, in equal parts with the oddness of her family. She needed Lane's complicity; she needed her strength almost as much as she needed her brother's protection of her.

Peter graduated from high school in June and went away on a summer job on the Maine coast, working on a holiday schooner running up and down the New England coast. It was an off-beat job with a touch of glamour, like everything he did. He looked gorgeous when he came back with his golden suntan and new sun streaks in his blond hair. The girls on the block would have died for his hair when he returned at the end of August.

Instead, she thought, he'd enlisted without warning. He'd done it surreptitiously, she felt. Marisa was stunned. She felt almost betrayed. She was hopelessly apprehensive as well. Several local boys had gone missing in action, and two boys from the building had been killed in the gory Pacific theater. She began to hate the Japanese and then chided herself, for she knew that hating anyone was the wrong way to go about solving problems. Her teachers at St. Catherine's were educated women with wide interpretations of the world that was falling apart around them.

Marisa shared all the raging patriotism of the time and the same ardor in defending what was visibly a just cause, but she was terrified for Peter's life. She could not bear the thought of his being injured or captured as a prisoner of war. Her mind recoiled at even the hint of his being killed. It was out of the question.

How long will it last, this hideous massacre? she railed, going cold inside when she was forced to face his vulnerability.

She was alone in their shared room now. She could not stop the sobs. What was wrong with the world that wholesale slaughter could go on and on like this, with devastation the only winner?

Once he left home for boot camp, however, she settled down to pretend she was brave. She kept her sobs to herself and wrote him funny letters almost every day. His answers said he was fine. He told her stories about guys from bizarre places, such as North Dakota or Arkansas, and asked her if she knew how to spell Mississippi. He reminded her that they would go skating in the park when he got home on leave, as they had done every year all their lives. He pretended that nothing had changed.

Neither of their parents had seemed overly horrified or even particularly frightened when Peter enlisted. Marisa, however, remained devastated. She sat back and allowed all her friends to cajole her into believing he would be fine. Maybe he would be an officer too. He would look great in an officer's uniform, wouldn't he?

With Peter in it, the war was no longer far away, no longer an abstraction on Pacific islands or a scene of manic destruction in the fairy-tale corners of Europe she knew only from illustrated books. Now the war had become a snake pit in their fortress bedroom.

She did not feel patriotic now that he was in danger; she felt fearful. Her brother was her anchor, her protector, her sanity. He made up for her mother's chill indifference and her father's pretense of living in a normal family.

Marisa was too frightened for him to be proud of his daring. Once he was sent overseas, though, she did not admit that to anyone but Lane.

When the telegram came from Vice President Henry Wallace, announcing her brother's death in the battle for Rome, she sat utterly still, knowing that her heart had been sliced in two. The half that had been his would be buried with him. She would be alone from now on.

She did not sleep that night. She felt sick in her classroom the next day, and someone took her to the nurse. Halfheartedly, she told the nurse what had happened. The nurse sent her home in a cab with an envelope containing two pills to help her sleep. Just two—she would not need any more, the nurse told her, because she would come to learn that no one and nothing would be able to find balm for her wound. It would come by itself, because that was the way it was.

The nurse was a nun who seemed at ease with hopelessness. Marisa was grateful to her, for her words were precisely what she needed to hear.

Get up and walk.

Peter had been her guide from birth. He'd been her protector and her mentor in everything from playing hopscotch to managing life with their mother. Now Peter was only alive inside her head, and she would have to live for both of them. She would have to learn how.

Her father was shattered by his boy's death. The world as he knew it crumbled. He lost his markers, the reasoning he had leaned on all his adult life. His boy was dead, and that senseless death rotted the foundations of the world he had constructed so painstakingly. "This house, this woman, these children" had been his motto, but his happy home lay smashed at his feet now, and his will to live crumbled in its wake.

He took sick leave, and the months dragged by. He stopped eating at the table. He picked at bits and pieces from the fridge but left the kitchen when Agnes or Marisa came in. He did not bathe until he could no longer stand his own stench. After a time, his health failed. He sat at the window listlessly.

When the war eventually came to an end, he barely noticed. He listened to the radio woodenly. A year went by in silence.

That was how Smitty coped with his son's death.

Agnes was different. She became more silent than ever, but now her silence seemed an affront to Smitty, a willful slight to his loss. He watched Agnes travel further into an orbit of her own and ignore his pain. When neighbors tried to console her, she would turn her head and say, "I don't want to talk about it." Smitty glared at her in motionless silence.

He vented his anger on Agnes and was consoled.

He would cradle Marisa in his arms, sharing her confusion and her sense of Peter's absence, offering her what little comfort he could spare.

One night Smitty moved out of his bedroom and began sleeping on the living room couch. Thin and wraithlike now, he would walk through the living room door, burdened with pillows and an old army sleeping bag, and then switch off the overhead light as soon as he could. Wordlessly, he sought a solitude Agnes could not intrude upon. He left her in the most hurtful way possible. She begged him to talk to her, to explain why he punished her for the boy's death.

As soon as Marisa left the apartment in the morning, Agnes would confront him and beg him to return to her bed or at least give her a reason. Marisa sometimes could hear her mother's voice while waiting for the elevator on the landing outside their apartment. She could hear her mother's sobs and her father's muffled refusal. "I gotta work it out myself," he would tell her. "I gotta do it alone."

One chilly morning, Marisa came out of her room into the silent, dark living room, where her father lay asleep. She tripped over his shoe but broke her fall by banging into an armchair, only to knock over a standing lamp in the process. Her father did not move. Not a sound came from the couch, but her mother burst into the living room, livid at the noise. "Can't you look where you're going?" she said, and then she stopped abruptly.

"Smitty?" she said in a funny voice, standing over him by the couch. When he did not answer, she pulled back the sleeping bag and shrieked, "Smitty! Godammit, Smitty!" She fell to her knees, emitting horrible sobs.

Marisa had not moved, petrified. When her mother's half-crazed voice screamed for her to call the post office, she just stared and shook her head. *No,* Marisa was saying wordlessly, *you call the post office.* She stepped back into her empty bedroom, the room she had shared with her dead brother all her life. She closed her door. Somehow, the hours passed.

No one called an ambulance. Their doctor, who lived in the next building, came and called a funeral home.

Marisa left the apartment, fleeing her mother and Smitty's dead form on the couch. She had no destination in mind till she realized she was almost in front of Lane's house. She looked at the ground-floor windows, and half dazed but in terrible need of the comfort only Lane might offer, she went inside and rang the bell at the ground-floor apartment door. Almost at once, the door of the apartment next to it opened instead.

Mrs. Goodman, their neighbor, said, "They've gone. They left early this morning. They went on a ship. All of them. They only took suitcases—a bunch of suitcases but nothing else. Like the spinet, that little piano they had. The long couch too. Everything is still there. They left. Maybe to Europe. I don't know. Just like that, as though they were going to the Catskills for the weekend."

Marisa was dazed. The woman's words were like slaps to her face, stinging her but waking her at the same time. Was this possible? She could barely believe she was losing Lane too.

Going to Europe with her family, literally at a moment's notice? At this particular moment's notice?

Marisa stared at the neighbor, who showed her incomprehension and a mounting suspicion about what was going on. "Who runs away like that, taking their two teenage daughters and a couple of suitcases? On a moment's notice? And the day before, Mr. Berger was running after a cop in the street. I don't believe it. It's a crazy story," Mrs. Goodman murmured with a shake of the head.

Then, pointing to the apartment door, she said, "Mr. Gumper, the super, has the keys, and he has the name of the lawyer who is taking care of everything. But no one is to go in without Mr. Gumper or the lawyer. Not even you." She looked at Marisa steadily. "Lane said that to me—that you would be upset because you had been so close since you were little kids."

She was silent for a second, not knowing how to react to Marisa's pallor. She shook her head sympathetically and reached out a hand to stroke Marisa's cheek.

"But there you are. I'm sorry I have to tell you all this," Mrs. Goodman added uncomfortably, edging into silence. After a moment's silence, Marisa nodded and said good-bye, thanking the woman politely. It was as though there had been a death in their midst. It was that kind of silence.

She had no idea what to make of the Bergers' disappearance. Mrs. Berger was a bit fluffy but not certifiable, she thought, dazed. Mr. Berger was a businessman and not at all fluffy. *What is this all about? And why today?*

She walked down the street to the gates of the park behind her and entered the small church that had always been part of her life. Tears burned down her face, and she gave in to desperate fear.

Marisa was well tutored in religion, but today she sought solace with God, a comfort that would be deeper than the formality of prayer.

She was asking for help. She felt she was plummeting downward through the darkness beyond her limits, and only Lord Jesus Christ could intervene now. A rush of sobs wracked her body till, exhausted, she straightened up and began to breathe evenly again, in and out softly, rising once more into the light.

There in the softness of the church, she was strengthened once more, able to return to the edge of reality, reaching out to a trace of her Lord, who seemed to have forsaken her, letting her plunge to near destruction.

Marisa firmly believed in the God the nuns and priests of her childhood had assured her of, and she believed in his sanctity and his care of her, but she had been overwhelmed by the cruelty of death in her midst and now, incomprehensibly, the punishing absurdity of her friend's disappearance. Her faith had faltered. She begged for forgiveness and implored help in the absence of her own fortitude.

I am falling, she longed to cry out, imagining herself plummeting down from great heights to the hard ground below, unable to rise again.

Yet now she was rising slowly, shivering from the touch of the cold stone floor. She was not healed, perhaps only numbed, but that would do for now. She began to walk home.

Her notion of time had blurred. The notions of time and death twisted in her memory so that she was to remain confused about that day's order of events forever after.

The day of her father's death had begun crisply and brightly, but it had clouded over and was hazily damp by the end of the afternoon.

Still groggy from what had happened earlier, she suddenly decided she needed to escape into a walk on her own through the familiar scrub near the edge of the river. She headed down the rocky path amid the scratchy grass and weeds that had torn at her ankles when she was a little girl. She walked along the river, well beyond the landscaped lanes, reclaiming their almost forbidden trail through scrub and sharp-edged rocks. She and Peter had not been allowed to venture there as children. Perhaps for that reason, it had become their favorite secret patch later on.

She'd had her first kiss there at the age of fourteen, when Frankie Lopez had pecked her awkwardly on the lips, making her wonder if she was now expected to marry him. The more sophisticated Lane had confused her the next day. When Marisa had told her, she'd asked, "Did he put his tongue in?"

Horrified, poor innocent Marisa had almost vomited.

Today she was seeking refuge in this same rough-edged incline, full of the memory of their innocence, in a place where she had been safe before.

As the daylight faded, she headed closer to the water's edge, where the streetlamps, higher up now, shone better on the path.

It was there that she saw the body. She froze. She knew instantly it was dead—not drunk and not injured but dead. It was half covered by weeds, brush, and stalks of dead tall grass, but it was there.

She did not question who it was or why it lay there half hidden, almost obscene, on the ground. She questioned none of that, nor what it had to do with her on this death-encrusted day. She knew only that she must flee from it— now, urgently. She must run away fast, away from the river and up to the street, for it would only bring her more harm and further sorrow on this terrible day of her father's death.

She ran back up the path away from the river, her long legs racing along the rough narrowness, and finally reached the street and then her house and its ornate wrought-iron front door. At last, she was safely inside in the warmth of the building.

It was dark outside now. *How long was I running?* she asked herself wildly, her mind in disarray. The freight train tracks, not much used these days but still sometimes dotted with passing hobos, as they had been when she was a child, gleamed below in the evening light. She shuddered. Instead of taking the elevator, she ran some more, this time up four flights of stairs to the apartment where her father lay dead and her mother would probably be waiting to curse her for having disappeared, for having bolted from the darkness within.

Surprisingly, neighbors and Smitty's buddies from the post office were in the living room, so her mother just nodded as she slipped inside, skirted the living room, and headed to the bathroom, where she scrubbed her face, combed her hair, and washed her hands finger by finger. When she emerged, her mother looked up and said, "You should go to bed now. Tomorrow is going to be a long day." Her voice was almost kind.

Marisa went into her room and closed the door, trying to make sense of what had been a day of nightmares.

From then on, all she remembered was that once she entered the apartment, where her father still lay lifelessly on the couch, a vague impression of the faceless body on the damp ground by the river began to fade. It was as though it had been part of a nightmare about death and flight. It would grow dimmer once she closed the door of her bedroom, with its floor-to-ceiling bookcase dividing the space between Peter's side and hers, providing them with half a haven each, where both would always be safe.

There couldn't have been a dead body near the tracks and near the river, she told herself at length. She dismissed the thought and told herself she had been hallucinating. Hysteria—that was all it was. *Because my father made himself die.* She went to sleep, exhausted—a sleep that would help her heal and force her to learn to accept loss as the personal enemy it would always be.

Marisa and Agnes got through Smitty's funeral, and then they took up their lives and reentered the time and space that had governed their ways till then. They were calm and careful with each other.

Agnes bridged the distance between them only to the extent that she made sure her daughter was eating properly, going to bed at a reasonable hour, and doing well in school. In June, Agnes went to see Marisa play the lead in the senior class school play.

She also went to Marisa's high school graduation and took her to a fancy restaurant in the Village afterward. It had once been a speakeasy, she told her daughter. Smitty had taken her there in those days. She gave Marisa a gold watch and a Parker pen-and-pencil set. There was a truce between them.

Marisa sorely missed Lane, for only Lane knew how odd her mother was. Lane had been her confidante, especially in Peter's absence. Now she had no one to fill the breach, no one at all.

Her English teacher, sensing the extent of Marisa's losses in such a short time, had the idea of casting her in the senior play as the narrator in a dramatized version of *A Tale of Two Cities* that the teacher had adapted herself. It was cleverly paced and colorfully staged.

Marisa, with her long legs and attractive voice, would be a fine figure in dramatizing the visual pageantry the play called for. At first reluctant, Marisa finally accepted, realizing that the teacher was attempting to help her.

Everyone in the class figured that out, except one girl, the sore loser who had thought the part hers and who did not give up easily. Her name was Patricia Conway, and she showed little grace in being overlooked for the lead. No one paid much attention to her sulking, however, and Marisa promptly forgot her.

The whole of that year and the two that followed moved by as though wrapped in cotton wool, motionless and deadened to both sound and feeling.

The body in the park had received no mention in the press, or if it had, she had missed it. No one around her seemed aware of a mystery in the neighborhood, so the incident faded from her memory, a fly speck on the image of her father dead in a sleeping bag on the living room couch.

Marisa won an excellent scholarship to NYU to study journalism, which made her mother raise an eyebrow. "A reporter," she said, trying the word out. "Yeah. I would have liked to do that," she added, surprising her daughter, for she seldom voiced anything that might have given insight into her own dreams.

For the next two years, they coexisted in the apartment without closeness but without clashes either. Then, one day at the end of Marisa's second year at NYU, Agnes was waiting for her in the living room when she came in. She asked Marisa to sit down because she had something to tell her. Marisa was first intrigued and then astonished.

"I am going to California. I have some cousins there who have a timber business, and they want me to come out."

"Cousins?" Marisa blurted. "I thought you were the world's most complete orphan."

"Yeah, well, I'm not. I have these cousins, and they are offering me a life out there, so I'm going to go. They are only talking about me for the time being, so I'm going to go alone, and if I think it would suit you, you can come out later.

"Now, listen carefully; this is important. The apartment stays in our name because I am a post office widow, and I can keep it till I die, but if you ever want to move someplace else, you can rent it out, and the bank will take care of the details, like seeing that the rent comes in regularly. The apartment is a sort of co-op. I have worked all that out with Mr. Murtagh at the bank, and he knows what to do. You just go in, talk to him, and sign the papers, and it will all run smoothly. He expects you."

She paused and then looked at Marisa carefully. "I want you to understand that your father did this as security for me and for his children. This apartment was a stroke of luck that Smitty deserved. Till then, it's yours. I signed the papers. I have given it to you. Take care of it."

Then she looked hard at her daughter to see if she had understood.

Marisa leaned back in her chair, white faced. She let the silence sit with them. Then, looking up at her mother, who was wearing her eternal frown, she said, "Did you ever love any of us?" Her voice was calm; there was no accusation in it. She might have been asking about the weather.

Agnes looked away from her, still calm, letting the frown fade. She almost smiled. "Smitty knew how to get around me," she answered, ignoring her daughter's slow blush. "And the kids weren't all that bad. I'm sorry it ended so."

A silence fell, and Agnes rose to her feet. "Wish me luck," she said quietly, and she headed for the door.

Marisa stared after her. "You mean now?" she cried out, aghast.

Two large suitcases were waiting behind the coatrack in the hall, where Marisa had not noticed them.

My mother is staging an escape, she thought wildly. *An escape from being my mother. My mother is running away from home.* She was speechless and, for a second, terrified.

Agnes opened the front door, picked up her suitcases, and let the door close gently behind her.

Marisa remained seated there in the living room, watching the front door for some time. She had no idea what to do, and she was too stunned to be frightened. She slipped into a numb state that was to cling to her like a shroud for some time.

The next weeks went by quietly, evolving into a curious pattern almost by themselves. She called on the few friends who would be in a position to help her, including one whom she knew to be what her father had called a family lawyer.

A portly man in his forties, he had worked briefly at the post office while going to law school at night. His name was Bill Irons, and his wife was called Cathy. They lived a few blocks away, and they'd often met with her father on weekends in Fort Tryon, when the park people, as she called them, came out to their favorite benches and took up conversations left off the previous nice weekend. Fort Tryon was that kind of park. It catered to its regulars.

When Mr. and Mrs. Irons met Marisa at their favorite bench, the couple listened to Marisa's tale, at first making little sense of the situation. Marisa tried to soften the truth, but it still appeared too grotesque for them to grasp at first. "Agnes has left home? She left an underage daughter on her own?" Bill said.

"Is that even legal?" Cathy blurted out, incredulous.

Bill looked blank and then admitted he wasn't sure it was. However, Marisa was not thinking along those lines. She just wanted to get away from New York, the apartment, her mother, Peter's absence, and her father's ghost lying stubbornly on the living room couch.

"No," she said, trying to make them understand, "I was planning to do a junior year abroad in Paris anyway, and I have a scholarship to cover the costs, but I need someone to help me figure out what to do and how to do it." Slowly, she explained. Just as slowly, they began to understand. They were kind but cautious, and they took their time in putting the whole proposition into legal order.

Thanks to their kindness and to the bank's dispatch, Marisa was ready to take up a scholarship for a year in Paris with arrangements to stay at the American house of the Cité Universitaire. She would have a stipend of ninety dollars a month for her expenses, plus travel by ship in tourist class, beginning in June and returning by September the following year.

Bill assured her that the dates were flexible, and if she wanted to change them either way, that could be negotiated. The Irons did all in their power to give her the feeling that her mother had sought to cover all contingencies and was still looking after her. It just did not look that way.

They assured her that once she got settled in Paris, she should feel free to ask them to send her whatever she needed, such as, Cathy whispered ominously, sanitary napkins.

"I hear they use rags. I had a friend who was there last year and nearly died of embarrassment—and she had to rip up all her pretty slips in the bargain. Europe is very far away, you know. If you can't stand it, don't hesitate to come back running. A whole year of tearing up your pretty slips is a lot to take for a walk down the Champs-Élysées."

She gave Marisa a warm hug and a wink that said "Just between girls." Marisa thought she would probably never be able to thank her for that particular kindness, which had filled the razor-edged absence her mother had left behind.

Perhaps that was why she could not hate her mother. She only wondered what had been so awful in their lives together to make her run away so fast and far. How little she had known her mother, she realized. How deeply dependent she had always been on Peter and on her father's kind concern. How dazed she was now without her father, she realized, thanking the Irons as they saw her off on the SS *Nieuw Amsterdam*, the Dutch ship she'd found passage on for early June. Along with the Irons, a few college friends saw her off. She waved good-bye to them at the ship's rail.

It is all up to me from now on, she thought to herself as she felt the ship slowly edge away from the docks. She liked the sensation and stared hard but fondly at New York, as though to memorize it, as she began her voyage far from its shores.

She strolled around the decks that afternoon, watching the skyline fade from her horizon, while Katherine Hepburn, who was also a passenger, played tennis on the first-class court in charming white shorts.

Marisa smiled. Katherine Hepburn had freckles.

Marisa had planned to be a journalist from the time she'd understood what the word meant. She would do all she could to stay in Europe after this junior year abroad. She'd made up her mind about that only weeks after arrival in Paris. She had no intention of returning to New York to finish college. Journalism was not like biology, a subject that could be taught step by step. Beyond a few dozen basics, a knack was what was needed. Marisa knew she had that.

In the five months since arriving in Europe, she had been living at the Cité Universitaire, a green and gracious campus on the south edge of the city. She lived at the American house—not because she sought out other Americans but because in those spartan postwar days, it was one of the only houses that had hot water available all day.

Wartime restrictions were still on. Hot showers were either rationed or nonexistent in the other houses. Food and fuel rationing was still in place in France and was to stay in place in the United Kingdom for another several years. Europe was rising from its ashes, but the process was slow. The black market was a parallel way of life she eventually learned to live with, however uncomfortably.

She made friends of all kinds, including Europeans, several Egyptian graduate students, exiles from Central Europe, and other Americans. She came to see that she would need more than just a single student year in Paris to make sense of this century that was now half over but apparently still hell-bent on self-destruction.

Atomic warfare was no longer just a comic book option; it had already happened. She was uncomfortable with the fact that her brave and handsome country had dropped the bomb—twice. Marisa discovered she had a political conscience. France was an ideal place in which to sharpen its edges.

Early on, Marisa had discovered ideology, and she enjoyed the world of choices. She realized that in order to come to terms with the world she lived in, she had to unravel what *East* and *West* really meant and what the word *free* revealed in its many differing contexts.

But there was more. All her wounds had not just vanished on that lovely week of sailing across the Atlantic to the shores of the wise Old World. For starters, she had not yet managed to gather the courage to visit Italy; her scars were still too raw for that.

She managed to visit Holland, Belgium, and both East and West Germany by the end of the summer, and thus, she got a glimpse of the varying paths to postwar reconstruction. She even spent a week in Prague, which was marking its first year as a people's democracy.

Prague, she found, was a study in holding one's breath. It was an in-between world that she feared would grow gray and barren under the harshness of Communist rule. Its fading beauty made her sad as well as wary about slogans too hastily adopted.

Crossing the imposing bridge over the Charles River, with the spires of the city at her fingertips, she thought of Jan Masaryk, who had chosen to throw himself out of the palace window rather than serve as a puppet for a clumsily imposed Communist regime. Suicide was the ultimate admission of defeat. Defeat before the imposition of a rule over the land entrusted to one, in the eyes of the son of the creator of that land, was unendurable. Jan Masaryk was an important icon in Marisa's eyes. She left Prague having learned a vital lesson: in contemporary affairs, gray was an uncomfortable middle.

She had learned quickly not to rush to judgment when it came to defining liberty and justice for all on the banks of the many rivers she crossed in Europe. Understanding Europe was not achieved in six easy lessons, but she made it her priority.

Living at the Cité Universitaire offered her a social life she could participate in or ignore without going out of her way. There were things going on that any resident could dip into as she chose.

Thus, Marisa was on chatting terms with a handful of interesting other students. She was not at a loss for casual chums for a movie on the Champs-Élysées or in the Latin Quarter or a meal out at a Left Bank bistro, but she was too busy trying to understand Europe and the temperature of its peace to make much of an effort for deeper relationships.

She danced with half a dozen young men on weekends, for there was always a dance going on in at least one of the many pavilions. She also went to lectures and expositions with a few politically inclined others, but no one had caught her eye.

Predictably, she had fallen in love with Paris, perhaps even Europe as a whole, but not yet with any particular European. She wasn't in a rush, she told Ann Wallace, a graduate student she'd come to know in the American house. "I'm not in a rush to jump into the musical comedy bit," she said, shrugging. She was too busy falling in love with Paris for the moment, she told Ann. "All in good time."

That particular November day was unusually bright and sunny, and she was in a carefree mood, strolling down the Left Bank under an unusually clement sky.

Along the quays of the Seine, she stopped at one bouquiniste stall after another, browsing, sniffing, and enjoying the touch and texture of old books no matter what their subjects or even their languages. She was tempted by an ornate volume of Gérard de Nerval's poems but decided it was too bulky to carry around that day. *"Un autre jour,"* she said, smiling at the stand's owner, who smiled back.

"Attendez, ma jolie," he said with a glint in his eye, and then he deftly pulled out a paperback edition of the same book from under a pile of others and presented it to her with a magician's bow. She laughed delightedly and, of course, bought the book.

She walked up to the Boulevard Saint-Germain, to the Café Flore, which had become her home away from home. She had classes on either side of it, at the École des Sciences Politiques, known as Sciences Po, up a few blocks to the left and at the Institut des Affaires Internationales on the right, just around the corner from Les Deux Magots. Geography had pampered her.

At her first glimpse of her European education's location, she'd had the distinct impression she had taken a giant step toward heaven, because her college building at NYU was a tall woebegone office building on Greene Street, better suited to insurance companies than budding pundits.

She glanced lovingly around the Boulevard Saint-Germain that day, grateful to no one in particular for its sense of urban beauty—or perhaps grateful to the spirit of Jean-Paul Sartre and Simone de Beauvoir, whose unquiet minds would haunt this blessed crossroads forever. She imagined herself to be a witness to the genius and grace of the current time. *Its grace and favors,* she thought, secretly pleased with herself.

She was twenty years old, and her Paris was a set of magic streets jumbled up in a photomontage of her unbridled imagination. She was young and confident, and no one knew anything else about her. She was on her own. She loved the feeling of total anonymity it diffused in her.

That day, she walked into the Flore and took a favorite table down on the right, where she had ample leg room and a window ledge on which to put her packages. *If it isn't school books, it's shopping bags,* she thought, but she was never empty-handed, and her pockets inevitably bulged. She dumped her burdens onto the ledge, took out a copy of the *Village Voice* she had bought at the corner kiosk, and settled back on the banquette to browse through Gérard de Nerval, whose poetry she had only just discovered.

She was entranced by his imagery as well as by the knowledge of how he had hanged himself out of unrequited love. Marisa might have been a noisy liberal and a marcher at the first cry of protest against any form, hint, or, particularly, color of injustice, but she had a heart made of butterscotch. Gérard de Nerval brought tears to her eyes in a matter of minutes.

She barely looked up when someone settled in at the corner table next to her, and she did not notice when, after a while, he poked at the *Village Voice* so he could read its front page from where he was sitting. "*Permettez?*" she heard, and she reluctantly looked up.

"Please," he repeated. "If you don't mind, I just wanted to find out if the Rienzi is still there." He smiled.

Marisa had been almost annoyed when she looked up, but within seconds, she was taken aback. He was stunningly handsome, with a finely molded face, dark eyes, and an aquiline nose like an El Greco. *That's it, an El Greco. Yes, but no. There is something else. The boy on the dolphin,* she thought.

He was dressed in a navy turtleneck and gray trousers, though at first she had half expected to see the lace-trimmed ruff and velvet breeches of El Greco. *Or fins for the dolphin,* she thought. She tried to breathe normally and averted her eyes from his olive complexion. She jumped a little when he spoke to her again. She did not hear what he said.

"No, please. You are welcome to read the paper, of course," she finally blurted out with a voice suddenly shrill to her own ears. "Go right ahead."

She was embarrassed now and realized she must sound manic, but it was true; he looked like one of those Greek sculptures of the boy on the dolphin. She pictured the beautiful long-limbed body and exquisitely shaped head, always depicted as glistening wet from the sea, gracefully straddling the smooth, playful dolphin. The stranger had brown eyes, an amazingly elegant nose, and a chin to go with it under a lot of straight black hair.

She forced her eyes back to the page of her book but barely made out the print. She thought the silence would deafen her. He broke it blessedly when he said, "I am so sorry I interrupted you. I didn't see you were reading Gérard de Nerval. I love his work. Have you been to the theater where he hanged himself?"

"In the sea?" she said. Then, realizing the absurdity of what she had said, she shook her head and said, "No, no, I don't know that much about him except that I love his images."

"Yes, he hanged himself at the Théatre de la Ville," he said, as though knocking at the door of her memory. "You can go around the alley and look up, or you can go inside, and on the entresol, there is a plaque commemorating his— well, his life. So if the play you are seeing is good, it is an even more moving experience."

She had lapsed into a silent stare now, too mesmerized and unnerved to answer with anything more than another roll of ums, this time in a different key. Undeterred, he went on enthusiastically. "And if it is a bad play, it will make it better, so you will have won anyway. No?" he concluded, not sure she understood a word he had said. "My English is upside down. I get it mixed up with French now."

Your English is not the only thing that is upside down, she thought. She felt amazed—but at what? She cast about wildly. *What is it? His beauty?* She shook her head, in conflict with her options. *Beauty* had to be the wrong word, yet he was beautiful, and there was nothing feminine about it. "The boy on the dolphin," she wanted to say out loud, but she checked herself just in time. She also had forgotten whatever it was he had asked her by then, so she just nodded vigorously. "Yes, of course. No, no, it's fine. I was just trying to imagine where the theater was—that's all. I get historic suicides mixed up these days."

She colored. She could not believe she had said that. "I mean, that's not really what I ..." She was suddenly afraid he would lean back and hide behind her *Village Voice* or stop talking to her. Or worse, he might vanish. Or even worse, he might go sit next to the blonde who had been eyeing him since the beginning from two tables away.

"Excuse me," he said. "I have intruded. You were thinking of something else. Can I introduce myself? My name is Riccardo Rinaldi, and if you prefer to read, I won't be offended." Then he made a face and corrected himself. "No, only perhaps disappointed a little." He laughed, seemingly at ease.

He had thrown her a lifeline, and she smiled out of real joy. She reached out mentally and caught it. She managed to collect herself and shook her head vigorously. "No, no, please. Of course not. I mean yes, I enjoy talking too. Sometimes," she added inanely, which made them both laugh.

"You are, of course, American." He took up casually, either unaware of her disarray or else the world's best actor. "I was there for a year in the Village, on Bleeker Street. In New York, I mean. I am a painter. I went to the Art Students League for a while. My grandfather thought I should polish my English, so I chose an Italian neighborhood just in case. You know New York perhaps?"

His words were like a blow with a sharp knife. At the mention of his nationality, her heart snapped in two. She froze. He caught her eyes. "You would have preferred South American or a Spanish bullfighter? I thought that by now, Roberto Rosselini had shown you that not all Italians are in the Mafia," he said mildly, but the laughter had switched off in his eyes.

"No," she protested, raising her hand like a traffic cop. "No, please, wait. Forgive me. I do know Rosselini, and I don't much worry about the Mafia, but how can I say this? My brother was killed in Italy in 1944, and I don't know quite how to get around it. In Europe, that is. I mean, Italy is right here. His death is no longer remote the way it seemed to be in New York, where I could avoid its presence. But now it's sort of just around the corner in a place that is recognizable." Her voice broke off, and she looked away.

He had been leaning back, his eyes dark with a closed expression that she read as something between pain and anger—or just dismay. They had been talking for only a few minutes, yet there was something taut, almost precious, between them, something that had instantly disconcerted her and that she wanted to salvage and explore.

Riccardo took a cigarette slowly from a pack of Benson and Hedges and let his eyes open doors to her, silently asking her to hear him out. He offered her a cigarette, which she took. She felt oddly comforted that it was English.

He was no longer just a young man with romantic good looks chatting up a pretty girl in a Paris café. He was one stranger reaching out to another, bridging the darkness between them. More, she thought, he was offering her a further dimension into herself and a measure of peace—a truce of sorts that she clearly needed. He seemed to understand her dismay and was pointing her toward coming to terms with Peter's death. The revelation was happening without fanfare, quietly, between two young people who were living on.

She banished the tears that had welled up in her eyes. He watched her do this and then said, "My grandfather is Carlo Rinaldi. You may know about him. He is a writer, an anti-Fascist from the very beginning. He was one of those intellectuals Mussolini put into internal exile on remote islands when they got too noisy. That was in the 1920s, after the Fascist march on Rome. They were writers, artists, journalists—all kinds of noisy intellectuals who made trouble.

"So they arrested him and sent him to Santini in 1925. Alone. Santini is off the coast of Genoa. It's very small and has no smart villas, as Capri does. Only fishermen, a few chickens, and goats. And us.

"His son, who was my father, lived in Genoa with my grandmother. They were not exiled. They were not even allowed to visit him on the island. My father went to the university there, and he met and fell in love with a beautiful Serbian student of architecture, Gabriela Ivanovich, and they had a little baby. Which is me. They could not get married, because she was only twenty years old, not of age, a foreigner of a different religion, and so on.

"Anyway, one warm day, a bunch of students, including my parents, were sitting on the grass in the university park, enjoying the sun, when a squadron of thugs—what you call a goon squad, I am told—stormed into the park and machine-gunned everyone in sight. Everyone except the baby. The pram drifted off out of their range, untouched.

"All the students who had been peacefully taking in the sun were dead—eighteen of them. Mussolini said it was an accident and insisted that it had nothing to do with his Fascisti. He said the gunmen were all Albanians. Whatever. There was an international scandal. It was terrible—a wild international fuss. The League of Nations, the Vatican—everyone objected, but the act was done. It was done.

"My grandfather was then given care of me, and my grandmother was allowed to join him on our island. We lived happily ever after till the Allies came and rescued us. My sweet grandmother died when I was six, unfortunately, but my nonno managed to survive with the help of a big lady called Severina, who is the regent housekeeper of our lives and who runs us like an empress.

"When he has time to work, he manages to be one of Italy's major voices in today's European Left, as well as being the center of my whole world. No, please, don't look sad. No, please. Living on Santini was not a hardship in many ways. Look what happened in other places. No, it was like a suspended but charmed life, and Santini, the island, is a secret little piece of rocky heaven. Perhaps you will visit it one day.

"So you see, nothing is black and white anymore, but I am very sorry for your brother, and I know that kind of pain."

He looked at her quietly as though they were friends, and she was infinitely touched by this confidence. *Friendships are made without regard to time,* she thought. By then, her feelings had gone well beyond his fine eyebrows. She had listened carefully to how he used words and how strong his desire for her to understand was.

"The war is over now. We—you and me and people like us or, more importantly, people not like us—have to take care of what is left," he said.

He was watching her, waiting for her reaction. He watched her shake her head, which he recognized now as an attempt to hold back tears. He put his hand out as though in an offering. She took it, managing a smile in return. She sat back on the banquette and breathed out, shaking her head.

"I was warned that it would be hard to stay mad at Italy," she said.

He smiled slowly at that but did not answer for a bit. "Oh, I'm not sure," he said finally. "Wait till they pinch your bottom on the bus." He laughed, not giving away any secrets. "But now you must tell me who I am making speeches to. And maybe we are friends already?"

She had listened to him carefully, watching the play of his words reflected in his eyes. She'd watched the frowns, quick smiles, and hard shock and heard the purpose in his voice. The elegant cast of his face gave measure to his words as he spoke. She had long since gone beyond his good looks, when she'd caught flickers of pain as he'd evoked his parents' grotesque deaths. She'd also registered the darts of affection in his eyes when he'd talked about the island.

When he talked, he used his hands and his shoulders too. He was a study in small movement. His accent was distinct, but his English was fluent, as though he spoke it often. The way he spoke it would never alter now. She somehow knew that.

He was a finished product.

She was shaken by her reaction to him. It was as though she had been waiting for him to lean over and explain himself to her, spreading out before her eyes a precious offering, one she had been missing all her life.

After a while, she told him about growing up in the top corner of Manhattan, within the sound of the bells of the Cloisters in Fort Tryon Park. She told him of the tapestry of the lady and the unicorn. She chose her words carefully when describing her family. She did not discuss her mother, nor did he prod. He was familiar with moving sands, she sensed. He would not ask, but he would listen carefully when she was ready to tell.

"I went to NYU to study journalism, and I'm here on a scholarship to spend my junior year abroad. But," she said, turning to him with a serious frown, "to tell you the truth, I'm not sure I am going to go home after it's over, as I was supposed to do. I think I will try to get a job here and forget the college degree. Studying journalism is not really the best way to become a journalist. For that, you should study history and literature and learn a bunch of languages. The rest you catch up on as you go along."

She looked up at him, almost as though she were asking for his approval. She guessed that he probably had an army of beautiful Italian models already groping for his approval.

"You know," he said after a pregnant pause, "I would like to paint you. I told you that I am a painter. Has anyone painted you? You have something in the eyes. In addition to the pretty blue, you know?"

She laughed, charmed. "No, I don't know, but thank you. And no. No one has ever painted me. You would be the first."

She nearly choked on the sound of those last words. She would have liked to fall off the rim of the earth at her clumsiness.

She was surprised to see he was moving with a flurry of quick gestures, rattling his chair while gathering his coat and her *Village Voice*. Then he turned to her. "What do you say we go for a walk on this beautiful afternoon? Like the old friends we have suddenly become. I would like to show you some of my favorite streets, and perhaps they are your favorite streets too. Up by the Luxembourg Gardens? You must not waste good weather in Paris, you know. There is not that much of it."

Too surprised to think twice and half mesmerized at what was happening, she let him lead the way. He seemed to be unaware of his unusually good looks, the grace of his hands, or the elegance of his profile. Best of all, he was pretending not to notice the effect he was having on her.

With her heart pounding, she followed this pied piper into the sunlight of an early winter day.

She was pleased to see that the blonde at the other table was watching them go with an irritated little pout.

Their long shadows would be engraved on the sinewy streets of the Left Bank, a place of magic, among the ghosts of poets who'd died of unrequited love. He flung her bag full of books, with the *Village Voice* sticking out, over his shoulder as though he were carrying her books home from school, as if they were both fifteen years old.

Why is it so easy to romanticize Paris? she wondered, trying to keep up with his long strides and his seemingly endless store of anecdotes about the route they were taking.

"This is a boîte you might know, le Prince Paul," he said, pointing to a narrow doorway on the rue Monsieur le Prince. "An excellent Russian painter sings here with a Serbian student priest. They sing tender songs of young lovers, and they play melancholic melodies on guitars. People put money into a deep Russian hat, so my friend Sergei can keep painting during the daytime.

"Perhaps you will come here with me one evening? Do you like painting, Miss Fort Tryon Park? Or will you say you don't know anything about modern art but know what you like?"

"Exactly," she said. "I love Picasso's blue period. It goes with my dunce's cap. But what about you? How do you feel about the Treaty of Locarno or the strike in the Asturian coal mines that the Spanish Falange are trying to squelch right now?"

He stopped at the corner, his eyes laughing back at her. "I know all about the Treaty of Locarno and even more about *el Fascista* that got away, Miss Intellectual New Yorker, and if you want to know something more about modern art, my studio is just across the Boulevard Saint-Michel and a couple of narrow corners beyond. So if you would like to, I can show you what I am talking about. Who knows? You might even like it. I favor blues too."

They were standing at the corner in front of the Luxembourg metro station, where the train that went to the Cité Universitaire ran. She could leave him now and take the train home. She hesitated, conscious of the fact that if he so much as touched her, she would catch fire. *Yet*, she thought wildly, *if he doesn't, I will cry my eyes out.*

Marisa had little sexual experience, less than most others in her circles. Too many rough edges of her life had taken up her time. She'd had a few groping boyfriends who never lasted and the inevitable crush on handsome boys who were, for a variety of reasons, unavailable. She tended to be dazzled by physical beauty—she recognized that. One boy she'd been attracted to had proven to be homosexual. Another had been engaged to someone else and Jewish. He too had been dark and brooding and looked like a poet. He had backed away from her reluctantly. She'd been eighteen then, and she'd cried herself to sleep. Shortly after that, Peter had been killed, and there had been no place for anyone else afterward.

Now she was standing as still as a pillar of salt on the corner while Riccardo watched her carefully, waiting for her answer. His eyes were telling her that the decision was strictly up to her.

"Yes," Marisa said, putting a lightness into the word, though she was half choked with its implication. "I would love to see your studio. Actually, I have never seen an artist's studio." She felt as if her voice were working on its own. She finally raised her eyes to look at him. He was smiling gently.

"All the more reason then," he said mildly, taking her elbow to steer her across the street. "This way."

Two blocks into the maze of street markets of the rue Mouffetard, they came to a halt in front of a shabby squat storefront with the name Cordonnier in faded letters over the door. "Shoemaker. I have to have the front painted one day," he said with a shrug. "But I call it the Shoe House. For the moment, I am the young man who lived in a shoe house." He opened the door and said, "*Benvenuta*, la Signorina Marisa."

Riccardo switched on the lights much the way a magician would have done on a stage. The Shoe House was now light and roomy, with a pleasant sense of space.

Its counter at the rear, instead of holding heels and soles or laces and nails, was a zinc bar, the far end of which was crammed with American cooking gadgets perfect for an adolescent: a rotisserie waiting for a chicken, a malted milk shaker, and a waffle iron. The counter also held a basket of fruit. Garlic and sun-dried tomatoes hung like rosaries on one wall. There was a designer fridge to one side of the window. An English-looking teapot, creamer, and sugar bowl sat on the fridge—incongruously, she thought. Next to the fridge was an antique china cabinet with an array of pretty dishes. A pair of leather-topped barstools seemed to be waiting for someone to pour. She turned to him, delighted. "It's wonderful," she said.

"If all else fails, I can always open a pizzeria." He grinned. "I bought this house a year ago, and I have felt like a prince ever since. Come see the rest of it. It gets better."

Beyond the counter was a white couch along one wall, flanked by the latest thing in the New York look: a pair of canvas sling chairs. She burst out laughing in recognition.

"I love them, and they are great for reading. I brought them back from Bleeker Street," he explained. The coffee table was long, low, and covered with newspapers and, oddly, a pile of *New Yorker* issues. He saw her looking at them and smiled self-consciously. "I grew dependent on Peter Arno and 'Onward and Upward with the Arts,'" he said, grinning. "It makes me laugh, and it's good for my English."

She realized then that despite his remarkable good looks, he was shy.

There was a door slightly ajar, which she took to be his room. He shook his head. "No, it is my grandfather's room.

He deserves his own room when he comes to Paris. He paid for this after all."

Surprisingly, the walls were bare except for one large dark painting of a woman in blue leaning her head on a scrubbed wooden table, her face averted. Her body was almost formless, yet there was a sense of delicacy about her, a touch of grace at odds with her supine shoulders, which otherwise suggested defeat. The colors, dark blues and black strokes like claims of finality, were what mattered, she thought, not the fact that the subject was a woman. There was an engagement with color and space that struck her, surprising her.

She had not expected to feel anything. Her visits to New York's Museum of Modern Art had been mostly to the downstairs cinema, where she saw intriguing foreign movies from time to time.

"If you take out the shape of the woman, you are left only with space and color. Is that what they mean by abstract art? Or have I said the wrong thing, the dumbest thing you've ever heard?" she asked, making a face.

He was staring at her, perplexed. "You told me you knew nothing about art, but you must, or you would not have asked that." He seemed genuinely surprised.

She shook her head. "No, it is just that you have taken out almost everything but the reason for the colors. Or have I got it all wrong?"

He stared at her for a second longer than he intended to and then said, raising his eyebrows, "I am not sure. Come up to see the studio, and then you will tell me."

A short flight of stairs took them to his studio, which was the full length of the building and gave off a wonderful sense of spaciousness. There were bookshelves on one wall, but more books were stacked with rows of paintings. A variety of tables held paints, smudged palettes, and oily rags. Brushes stuck out of jars, and two easels, plus a long trestle table, stood against the far wall. Her eyes caught a big double bed covered with something that looked like an antique tapestry at the far end of the room.

Unexpectedly, she saw that half the ceiling was made of glass, which explained the illusion that the room had seemed moonlit before he'd switched on the lights.

A short flight of stairs by the bed led up to what she assumed, with amazement, must be a roof garden. She pointed to the steps. "I can't believe you have a roof garden right here in the middle of the Latin Quarter. Rick, this is fabulous!" she cried with delight.

"Perhaps," he said, wincing. "But please don't call me Rick. And we can talk about painting up there too. But first, let us go see what is going on in heaven. Wait. I will go up the stairs ahead of you to open the door. First, we will discuss art, and then I will make us a cup of tea."

Tea? He was full of surprises. She had expected Asti Spumante at the very least. *And "Don't call me Rick"?* She wondered why.

He brushed by her while heading to the stairs, and she felt her heart pound, not only with the charm of his studio or the power she had seen in the blue painting. She felt a physical sting she barely recognized. Half enchanted and half embarrassed, she moved back a step to let him by.

"Follow me," he said. "We will see Paris by fading afternoon." He reached out his hand to help her up the narrow metal steps. If he noticed her confusion, he did not let on.

The beauty of cityscapes was something special to the New York child she remained, and she gasped at his little rooftop heaven. They stood in silence at first. The view was of falling shadows, lights, and lamplight, flickers of the new neon Paris now sported. Fingers of trees dotted the horizon. Traffic inching along the bridges amid the domes and spires of this most romantic of cities played out before her, and she held her breath. Honking horns, oddly endearing in Paris, were muffled in the background, and she stood still, hoping he would not notice how breathless she had become.

He led her over to a white garden table with four chairs and helped her choose a chair so that she looked out toward the lights of the Right Bank. Sacré-Coeur, like toy bubbles, rose in the distance. Notre Dame and the Hôtel de Ville were palaces of the middle kingdom now in the inching night.

His rooftop garden was a secret eagle's nest, reigning over the web of streets below.

They were quiet and at ease, relaxed in each other's silence. It was, she thought, like the moment before a cloudburst or a sudden gust of wind. She turned to say something to him, but he stopped her. He reached across the table and put his hand up gently to her lips to still her. "No, don't. I want to say something to you, something difficult but precious. I think you know that something unusual has happened to us today. I know you know. And I think you also know I would like to make love to you," he said softly. "But if you don't want me to, tell me now, and we will be friends like before."

She held his eyes, shaking within. "Oh no," she said, half choking. "I mean yes. I mean yes, I know." Before she could straighten out her words, he laughed and rose from his chair. He stood before her, took her hands in his, and drew her up to him. He looked at her gravely and then slowly and gently kissed her, his mouth tender yet firm on hers. She knew then that she was drowning.

When he drew away from her, they seemed to be weaving slightly on the pebbled ground. The perfume of the flowers at their fingertips rose in the new air of dusk: hydrangeas in varying tones of pink; long, low rows of potted hellebore that made her think of love and Shakespeare; and rosemary for remembrance.

"This is enchanting," she whispered to him.

He nodded. "It is now," he said, his arms holding her closer again, his hands pressing gently on her back, making her shiver under his touch. "You can't be cold," he said teasingly. "It is still Indian summer up here."

She shook her head. "Yes. No. No, I am not cold." She laughed but then held her breath while Riccardo slowly and carefully took the three most important steps of his life as he moved her to the glassy stairwell, where he then helped her down the stairs to the studio and to his bed.

"I would like to make love to you. You know that. Not only because I think something very special has happened to us today but also because I think it is something new and unexpected—something all the more precious for being unannounced. Do you understand? There is another word for you: *disarming*. In fact, to make a terrible confession, I have wanted to make love to you since you first couldn't tell yes from no in the Flore." He laughed lightly.

Finding the answer he wanted in her eyes, he kissed her hair and then her neck and circled her breasts with his hand. She let out a faint cry and whispered in a small, unsure voice, "Please be patient. This is the first time."

She glimpsed his smile as he said, "I know."

That was a Thursday.

On the following Tuesday, they admitted that they must get dressed and go down to the shops. There was no more coffee or tea, and even the pasta had given out. They giggled like truant children and went hand in hand down the colorful market street, which looked as though it had been put there only for added effect.

"Or to remind young lovers," Riccardo said, "that the other thing you do in Paris is eat."

Years later, Riccardo would say he'd wondered then whether his words would make her blush. But they did not. He told her this a long time afterward and went on to confess that at that particular instant, there on the rue Mouffetard amid radishes and camemberts, he'd wanted to marry his young Marisa of Fort Tryon Park to keep her next to him forever. *Forever*—the word was momentous to Riccardo. It was a word that held all his fears as well as his one need. *Forever* denoted a state of permanence for the child he remained in his own eyes.

Judging by the way she looked at him, he imagined she would say yes. However, this time, she would say it right away.

As they walked around the colorful streets that day, he stopped here and there to say hello or, in special cases, introduce Marisa to the vendors or his neighbors. He called her *mon amie,* and she threaded her way through the passages with her heart ready to burst.

"You have your place here now," he said to her. "They know how I like my camembert and which oranges have the best juice, my Marisa." His eyes were bright with the simple joy of sharing. "This is the first chapter, my angel. Now come meet Beatrice, who saves fresh eggs for me, as well as some butter without ration coupons, because she thinks I am too thin. And after that, we will have something to eat over there." He pointed to the restaurant near the lovely church of St. Médard at the bottom of the market street. He was showing off his kingdom. She savored every moment.

The market stalls began closing up for the long afternoon break, a custom Marisa could not get used to. No New York child could understand closing food shops at meal times— or any other shops, for that matter, for half the afternoon. "It borders on economic insanity," she said.

"Yes, I know. Nothing ever closes in New York, but Europe is a slower world. It eats meals, not snacks, and there are two hours for lunch. The European midday meal is a tradition Europeans will go to war to defend. God knows they've already gone to war for less. You will have to learn to live with lunch here on La Mouff, or they will give you yesterday's eggs or tomorrow's tomatoes, and you will have problems forever. The French shopkeeper is king. In Italy, you will find that life is more adaptable. Someone will always find you mozzarella if you're hungry, especially if you smile like you're smiling at me right now, my Marisina. But I hope you won't do that, because I am very jealous.

We must not forget our national clichés. Just try me." He grinned at her teasingly.

"Are you?" she asked seriously.

"Um, not till now. But everything seems to be different today."

She pondered that for a second and then said in a low voice, "I used to know what everything meant—up until a few days ago. But things have gone into a spin, and the rules are written in a foreign language," she confessed.

"I will teach you the language," he said in a low voice, turning her around to face him. She was next to a market stall piled high with fragrant herbs: thyme, basil, chives, oregano, and, dearest to her heart, rosemary, a symbol remembrance.

There was a sudden note of urgency in his voice and in his eyes when he spoke again. "Don't go back to the Cité Universitaire now. Not now, Marisa. Come to the studio with me, and we will talk about the paintings." He saw that he had startled her and let go of her arm. He began again, making light of his move. "I will start a drawing of you today. Please."

She was about to laugh, but then she saw his urgency and was suddenly taken aback. In an instant, he'd laid bare the crux of his whole being till he had caught himself up again and tempered everything he had revealed in that brief instant.

This was the way of a young man who had feared loss all his life.

During their heady days together, she'd mused over the fact that there were no signs of anyone else already installed on the left side of his bed. When she'd asked him lightly, as though it were just a matter of curiosity, he'd shrugged and evaded a real answer, though he'd admitted there had been a few women. "But no one with eyes the right shade of blue." It was not an answer but a way of avoiding one.

Now, in the middle of the street market, braced by the familiar scents of her childhood herb garden, she looked at him seriously and said quietly, "Riccardo, there is just one little thing I would like to say to you seriously. Please? It is this: I promise you that I will never do anything to deliberately hurt you. If that sounds pretentious—"

"You are younger than I am, my Marisa. You don't know."

She saw that her words had fallen short of the mark. God knew what it would take to convince him otherwise.

She tried to read his expression, but his eyes had closed to her. For a second, she feared he might break away and run across the square, out of sight. Her voice rose slightly.

"Riccardo, listen. Come back with me to my room at the American house, and help me collect my books and the stuff I really need. At the same time, you can see where I live."

He stared at her from what seemed to be a freezing distance but then relented. After a minute, he even smiled. However, she had found it a dangerously long minute.

"And then, when you have collected your stuff, you will come back to the studio? For the portrait? It might take months, you know, perhaps even years. Maybe I will have to write a poem to go with it and then a sonata to go with the poem. And after that, perhaps a sculptured wall to keep them all safe inside? Maybe. You never know. Maybe. It is only the beginning after all."

His smile was relaxed when he added, "First, we will have lunch with Giorgio. He is the first on the list concerning me and my welfare in Paris. He is from Santini and is my grandfather's secret agent. I eat there regularly, and so will you, I hope. I love him; he is like a grandmother to me."

Smiling quietly, he edged her toward a restaurant on the corner. As they walked in, a burly, broad-shouldered man with a mop of curly black hair and a sailor's gait rose from a rear table and came to welcome them, speaking in rapid Italian.

This is his home away from home, his surrogate guardian, his anchor, she realized. She noticed that Giorgio examined her for a second longer than he might have done, but that did not bother her.

She guessed that Riccardo had told him on the phone they would be coming by, and she was secretly pleased. A few minutes after their arrival, a short, dark young woman with a mop of black hair piled high on her head came out of the kitchen and made for their table, half hidden by a huge apron. She kissed Riccardo on the cheek, taking him by surprise, and reached her hand out to Marisa. "*Sono Anna*," she said, as though that explained everything. Then there was a great scrambling of chairs as she settled in while Marisa waited for footnotes.

Giorgio patted Anna's hair, poking the pinned-up left side and making it slide down, deliberately covering her face, which in turn made her cry out in protest. Her hands flew to pin it back as Riccardo nearly choked in laughter while Anna went on in rapid Italian that Marisa lost after the first three words. The scene was warm, funny, and surprising, and Riccardo was tempted not to explain, but Anna stepped in and said in unexpected English, "I am Anna from Santini, the wife of Giorgio and the sister of Mario." Then she sat back and scowled. "And I watch over him," she said, pointing to Riccardo.

For the first time in many months, Marisa felt warm inside.

"And will someone tell me who Mario is?" Marisa said expectantly.

"No, not till after lunch. Mario takes up hours to even imagine, let alone describe," Riccardo said with a sigh. He reached across the table and poked Anna's hair, making it fall again. He then took her fingers in his hands and kissed them one by one. He added, "Fettuccini?" in a loud stage whisper.

Giorgio murmured, "*Non, oggi non. Carbonara.*"

Riccardo sighed. He turned to Marisa, who was visibly entranced by the whole scene, and explained, "This is an extension of the island, and they are my family here. Mario is my best friend, and you will love him. I will tell you all about him, which will take the rest of my life." He sighed as though resigned.

He was opening the gates for her to enter into his realm, where she would be welcomed by people who believed from birth in the sanctity of friendship and the power of love. She could only faintly imagine the way such affection and shared concern for each other's well-being was lived beyond the pages of a novel.

Or in a Pirandello play, she mused.

Riccardo had been in Paris long enough to have his own schedule and his own little world. He was not pressed to sell his work, because he had a modest income. It was a pension, the postwar Italian government's war-crime-retribution damages for the murder of his parents. He told her he had accepted it only after his grandfather convinced him it was the least the successive Christian Democrat governments could do for him, considering.

Riccardo wanted above all to absolve his grandfather of any need to help him financially. Although foreign royalties on Carlo Rinaldi's considerable volume of work allowed for a comfortable income, Riccardo did not accept being his charge. In the unlikely event that he would have chosen to be a dentist, no one would have made all this fuss about his finances, he pointed out. Choosing to be a painter and only a painter was a life-determining decision for him. It was his responsibility, not his grandfather's, he maintained sternly, his jaw firm.

There could be surprising determination—and sometimes icy anger—visible in his face despite the beautiful eyes and elegant nose, a trait that made him look like a classical sculpture come to belligerent life. She liked the dichotomy she had picked up on during the first amazingly long weekend they'd spent together. Even then, he had gazed down at her firmly, as though he were staking a claim, one that might well last the rest of his life.

She sensed that he was sure of himself, not of her. She feared nothing more than breaking the spell. She was to fear that forever.

She asked him where he had learned his English while they had lunch at Giorgio's. "Surely not just in the time you have spent on Bleeker Street."

"No." He laughed. "It goes way back. My grandfather had a prized possession: a long-wave radio one of the fishermen smuggled in to him. We only listened to it at night, when the caribinieri were off the street; otherwise, one of them might have confiscated it. He decided that on weekends, we would only listen to the BBC. And he would try to speak to me only in English. Otherwise, I would end up like the other Santini children, speaking an island dialect only the other islanders understood. Anyway, on weekends, we spoke English. I learned it from him, and of course, he has an Italian accent. *Capito?*"

She thought of the vast discrepancies in their backgrounds and was apprehensive about what he would make of her mother or her sad father. However, she soon learned that he judged people not by their family crests but by what they did. He was indulgent of others, she noticed, and found excuses for their circumstances. She clung to that trait, for she recognized it as generosity of the most vital kind. He proved to be idiosyncratic to an extreme in most things, but he never once lacked generosity of the spirit.

That day, she caught a glimpse of their reflection in a store window on the corner of the rue Gay-Lussac, and she smiled secretly. He was several inches taller than she, and the navy jacket he wore flattered his litheness. Next to him, her New Look blue-checkered skirt showed off her small waist, and its short jacket made her look slimmer than she was. She wore Capezio ballerinas because she hated high heels and had never learned to walk in them.

The reflection in the window startled her, for she saw herself and Riccardo as a couple, well matched, walking casually to catch the train to the Cité Universitaire, where she would introduce him to her friends and gather a few things to take back to what he called home. He was bringing her home with him to stay. She glanced over at his Dolphin Boy profile and felt the smoothness of his stride, and then she said a silent thank-you to whomever arranged improbable love stories in romantic settings amid the ashes of the Second World War. *A cupid with a wry sense of the absurd,* she thought.

They entered the American house at the Cité Universitaire, and she looked around the downstairs hall to see if anyone she knew was there. Almost immediately, she caught sight of Ann Wallace coming toward them, wearing a cheery smile.

"Hi. Did you get my message?" Marisa called out. Ann was several years older, a doctoral candidate doing a thesis on James Joyce's Paris years. She was a Café Flore bench warmer too. Today she was wearing a sly little grin. "Gabriel told me you had not been to the Flore since last week," she said, letting her glance slide over to Riccardo and back again to Marisa's blush. As gracefully as possible, Marisa introduced them.

"Marisa talks about you," he said, bowing slightly. "I feel that I have already met you," he added, taking her hand.

"Yes, well, Marisa is my window to today. With a big *T.* When I get tired of digging around the ghosts of the thirties, she takes me on student protest marches and to the Sorbonne to hear Sartre describe the future to a student body ready to sanctify him. She is my key to today, and she comes from New York, which is always a blessing. I'm from Brooklyn, so we're practically cousins. Only I am nine years older, so that gives me an edge. And you are Italian?" she added with a question mark hanging in the air.

He was about to answer, when two young men joined them. One, a spindly creature with thick glasses, messy fair hair, and an odd voice, was François de Quinsalle. Marisa introduced him after the ritual kisses on both cheeks.

"François is at the rue d'Ulm," she said, as though that would explain everything. And it did.

Riccardo nodded and raised an eyebrow. "Bravo," he said, and he looked as though he meant it.

"And this is Jeff Booker, who is my newsman chum," Marisa said, giving Jeff a peck on the cheek. He looked like a news photographer; he wore a Leica camera hanging from his shoulder as though it were part of his wardrobe. They all edged over to a corner where there was a round table with a few empty leather armchairs around it. Marisa left them settling down for a chat while she went to her room to get some stuff—without specifying what stuff or where she was going with it. She managed the whole performance without a single blush.

My life in sin, she thought, *is getting easier and easier.*

Her heart was pounding as she left Riccardo well installed in a leather armchair, talking comfortably to Ann, her new best friend, and her buddies Jeff and François.

She was impressed at François's career. Sartre and Simone de Beauvoir were products of Normale Sup, as it was known in Paris. Many French intellectual leaders—much of the backbone of government, industry, and finance—were products of these elitist schools, called les Grandes Écoles, whose tuition was minimal but whose standards were high. Their students came almost uniquely from the monied middle class, whose schooling trained them in passing what were probably the most stringent exams in Europe. Being a good student from nursery school on was a matter of class in France, in a system as rigid as it had been since the demise of the monarchy, which it had replaced.

However, her friends cautioned, even that was changing. The war had shaken French class unity: collaboration with Nazi occupants had shaken its self-respect—for the time being at least. The present-day end of empire was being acted out in Indochina's war for independence, a hopeless and unpopular venture in what had become an inevitable period of decolonization for European powers, and a surge of new national identity in former colonies in Africa and Asia.

L'École Normale Supérieure was a breeding ground for ideologists. Marisa, to whom this brand of higher education was new and seemed almost miraculous in its scope, was fascinated by what she learned through François.

All the currents of postwar ideology were in the process of noisy rethinking, and through her friends, this change became accessible to her. Through them, she saw how Europe was coming to terms with its past and its rocky present.

Marisa glanced over her shoulder and caught sight of them; they were already deep in conversation. She was pleased to see her almost ephemeral young man entering into her sphere with ease and with a common language shared by her friends—a part of her dowry, she thought with a smile.

She soon filled her duffel bag with paperbacks, notepads, her best skirts, and a couple of sweaters she could mix and match, plus a batch of undies and a cache of girlish goodies, including deodorant, which was then almost unknown in France, to her consternation.

Personal hygiene was a hostage to the continental divide, she'd discovered when she'd first arrived in Paris. There was no deodorant on sale anywhere. She had a healthy American horror of body odors, so once her initial supply ran out, she began carrying around a little spray of eau de cologne, which she thought did nothing more than make her feel sugar coated. Finally, she wrote to Cathy Irons in New York. Cathy and her husband considered themselves her surrogate family. She asked if Cathy would be kind enough to send her a year's supply of Arrid. It was then that Marisa decided being European was far more genetic than one ever imagined.

She joined the little group at the table and was enchanted that they were chatting like old friends. All of them knew Carlo Rinaldi by reputation, Marisa learned—all but she, it would seem. On the other hand, she was a lot younger than the others. She sat back and felt what had to be happiness color the air around her as she watched Riccardo talking comfortably with her Paris friends.

In my house, she thought silently. *In my house too.*

Step by step, they came together, not cautiously but as though each step obeyed a natural law. Giorgio, Riccardo's guardian angel, and Anna, Giorgio's wife, looked after him at a respectful distance but with all the keen-eyed interest that guardians were known for. Anna was often busy in the kitchen when they first met, but Marisa could see the careful scrutiny she eyed her with, and she saw the warmth that slowly became evident in her eyes as the days and weeks went by. Giorgio and Anna became her world too.

As the days went by, Riccardo's neighbors among the vivid food stalls and bistros of the rue Mouffetard included her in their conversations with Riccardo. She realized how lucky she and Riccardo had been in coming together so easily with no barriers, constraints, or even embarrassments.

She found him so strikingly beautiful that she would have kept him naked all day if it had been possible. He found that hilarious and wondered what those New York nuns had done to her modesty button. She claimed he did not understand; she was speaking of aesthetics. He agreed he did not understand but said, "God bless it."

They laughed easily, and they talked easily. It was as though they had been waiting for each other to knock on the door.

His work schedule was erratic and private. Despite all his ease with her and his apparent need to unfold to her, there was a time when he closed the door and needed to be on his own. He did not have to spell this out. She felt it instantly and was quick to respond. She went to her desk, which had become a little corner on its own, cut off from the living room space by a chair cleverly placed and a standing lamp turned either one way or the other. She had found her niche. There was also a café down on the Place de la Contrescarpe where she learned to savor Europe's most civilized element, the café terrace.

On the rue Mouffetard, the world she watched going by from that café terrace was colorful and busy and served Earl Grey tea.

Riccardo's grandfather had made it easy for him to find hospitable friends in Paris when he first arrived. Some were Italian, but most were French or other foreign intellectuals. There were a lot of for foreign intellectuals, she knew. They were like a special nationality of their own: newsmen, writers, observers, and Paris watchers left over from the fabled prewar days.

Carlo Rinaldi had become an icon in the world of anti-Fascism in the immediate postwar period. He had written copiously both about and during his exile, and he was published widely. His voice was one of the most listened-to voices among observers of the new world order.

Like his grandson, he was extremely handsome, even at seventy. With a full head of white hair and a Roman profile, he cut a compelling figure on the international forums they read about in the press. He still lived in Genoa, in a house built by an earlier Riccardo Rinaldi around the time when Genoa and Venice were vying with each other as to which was the most beautiful world power. It was a four-story stone house, which was typical of Genoa, though not of the rest of Italy.

Genoa had an odd history. It was as independent as Venice and as Mediterranean as Barcelona, which was a continent away from the south of Italy. Mazzini was born in Genoa. The unity of Italy was designed there on those quayside streets with narrow houses more reminiscent of Morocco than of Rome. It was the cradle of modern Italy, yet it was distinct from the rest of it.

The Rinaldi house was on one of the narrow streets in the old town. It had wrought-iron balconies bordering the sea front. At the rear was a patch of garden with orange trees and oleanders leading to an atelier built for an earlier Rinaldi who also painted but who was an architect in the mid-nineteenth century: Don Carlo's grandfather, another Riccardo.

Marisa was fascinated by the chronicle of past Rinaldis, all of whom seemed to have been called Carlo, Riccardo, Lorenzo, or, occasionally, Lucca, such as Riccardo's young father. Most of them were architects or sea captains, with a banker here or there to maintain good order. They all had the same nose, she saw with interest, and the long-limbed grace that went with it. Many had left their portraits behind for good measure. Marisa came to love that house and its storybook history, primed by the way Riccardo told her of his odd childhood on their rocky island somewhere on the route to Corsica. She listened carefully, trying to picture it. His childhood was so different from hers, and she was captivated by the romantic overtones of life on the Mediterranean.

At first, she was apprehensive about the class divide between their different backgrounds.

"My dad was a postman," she murmured to him one afternoon early on in Paris, holding Carlo Rinaldi's picture up to catch the right light.

Riccardo raised an eyebrow. "The Pony Express perhaps? That will be very impressive in Genova," he mused. "Anyway, you are a rich American; they will see that as soon as we arrive. And they will be very pleased for me," he added. "Beautiful and rich," he murmured, nodding in mock satisfaction. "Riccardo deserves as much."

She spun around. They were at the counter in his living room downstairs, having a sort of lunch before she left for an afternoon of classes at Sciences Po, where she was the only foreigner in a course given by the fascinating philosopher Gabriel Marcel, a Catholic of the French left who enjoyed provoking his students with his tolerance for sharing the world with the Soviet Union without coming to nuclear blows. "When we arrive? What do you mean 'when we arrive'?" she asked.

He swiveled around to face her, delighted. "Will you do me the honor, or pleasure, preferably both, of coming to Genoa to meet my grandfather for Christmas and New Year's and the new decade and the new beginning of the new half of the twentieth century? And what else? Ah, yes, and to be the first one in the Cathedral of San Lorenzo on the first day of Holy Year, which is what 1950 is?

"By the way, are you a Catholic? I keep forgetting to ask. Perhaps you are a Baptist? Or maybe a Mormon? No, you would have sung me spirituals by now if you were a Mormon. *Non e vero?*"

She stared at him. He was wearing the special grin he kept for clowning, and it melted her instantly. "Not a Mormon, and they are not the ones who sing spirituals. But they do have several wives, so you might take a fancy to them. And yes, I am a Catholic. I went to Catholic schools. I told you that; you've forgotten me."

He kissed her lightly and nodded. "I love to tease you. Will you come to Genoa so I can tease you through the Christmas break? So you can meet my world? And even the island?"

She saw that he was doing two things: telling her of this wonderful Christmas that would bind them even more and, while he was at it, avoiding the painful subject of her family. She thanked him silently for that.

Early on, she had given a sketchy outline of what her home life had been like while growing up. He had listened to her carefully, making an effort to hide his incomprehension of her mother's role.

"Fort Tryon Park was not just another continent; it was another planet," he whispered to her as he cradled her like a battered child. "And you have left it far behind." He said that firmly. "Far behind."

He could barely imagine Marisa's background, and he sought to keep her ghosts at bay.

It suddenly dawned on her that he had worked out the Christmas holidays without asking her if she had other plans. However, he knew she had no other plans, not for Christmas or for the rest of her life.

Furthermore, he knew instinctively she would be happy to go home with him. As if to illustrate the point, he took her face gently in his hands and whispered, "My Marisa," over and over. "You will love my house, my family, my Christmas. It will be part of you forever. Don't you see that?"

Then he abruptly moved away, dismissing any objection she might raise.

"Que sera sera," he said, giving her a sidelong glance. "To coin a song."

She wondered once again where he had learned his English beyond the BBC weather report.

One step after another, he led the way. They slipped into their own permanence, sharing the corners of each other's lives, of loving each other in little details.

She was afraid he would tire of her and find her inadequate because she knew nothing of his European art world. She was afraid her relative otherness would be too much of a burden and a barrier.

He scoffed at her reticence on the few occasions when she admitted to it. "You are my princess, my American beauty, and you come from the top of Manhattan with a private unicorn in your garden. I will tell everyone who asks in Genoa. Everyone will know that il Riccardino loves a *principessa* with blue eyes and a French cloister in New York."

She laughed at his clownish teasing while more of the new little tears he created welled up in her eyes, unbidden. Like everything else he had brought her, weeping was new in her experience. He had the gift of making her cry with joy.

"You are going to bring me to meet your grandfather? And you haven't even told me? Are you sure?" she said softly.

He jumped off his barstool and reached over to kiss her brow and taste her tears in passing. Then he climbed back onto the stool, frowning. "Otherwise, he will come here. And anyway, I want to go home for Christmas like everyone else. Carina, don't you want to meet him—to show him that you love me? Or don't you think you love me?"

Now he was frowning clownishly, as though he were discussing a bizarre, alien concept. He was half on and half off his stool. She put out her arm to steady him, which made him giggle.

"Oh no! That's the big, big word, and we agreed that we would not use big words for some time," she said, swiveling to face him with a warning in her voice, trying hard to keep up with his lightness. "It has only been seven weeks, Riccardo."

He held her at arm's length and looked at her intensely, as though memorizing all her features. "No, no. You made that rule, not me. I only remember saying, 'Come here, my vestal virgin; let me unlock the heavens for you.' And so I did, as I recall. *Non e vero*? And later on today, as soon as you come back from philosophizing about accommodation with totalitarian ideologies for the good of humanity— ouf!—I will remind you of what I meant." He hopped off the stool and walked toward the stairs, lightly kissing the corner of her eye where the tear had been on his way. "I am going to work on my portrait of you in the blue shirt for his Christmas present."

She watched him go up the stairs, hoping he would not look around, because the tears of happiness flowed freely down her cheeks now, and she couldn't do a thing about it.

They went to Italy. On the train, he reminded her that Genoa was not far from the border; she could always run away on foot, or she could swim to Corsica or stow away on any one of the many ships in the harbor. The sailors would be only too happy to help.

In his mind, Riccardo linked Peter's death with his own parents' senseless murders. He told her that she and he both were survivors of tragedy, but they were strong and armored, bred in sacrifice. They created a new kind of strength. They could do anything together precisely because they had the armor of survivors.

"The war was criminal, a vile insanity. But it is over. We are in new circumstances today with new options. We are creatures of the postwar in the eyes of the new historians. Victims, yes, but also survivors of the old world. We are responsible for today, and we are the architects of tomorrow. Neither your brother nor my parents would want it otherwise. Trust me, Marisa."

His voice was so firm that she did just that—she trusted him.

She leaned against his shoulder and watched France go by outside the train's window.

It was a silver-tinged, bright winter day in Europe.

Suddenly, Riccardo scowled as though he'd just remembered something vital. "Ah, Severina. Severina—how could I have forgotten to tell you about Severina?" He widened his eyes.

"Who is she?" Marisa prompted, fearing the worst.

"Severina is the housekeeper. She is the queen of Santini. She brought me up and came with us to Genoa when the war was over. She is the most generous, the most loving, the most everything woman in the world, and she has only one child. That is me. If you think my nonno might be hard to please, don't bother. Wait till you see my Regina Severina, and watch out because she will be watching you too. Ah, yes, I brought her a book of pictures of Paris by an Italian photographer from Genoa, Mario Dondero. I signed the card for you, Marisa. You will love her. I know it."

Seeing the ill-concealed dismay on Marisa's pretty face, he stopped teasing her. He took her hands in his and bent over to kiss her ear. "My Marisa, you should be happy that I have only two persons to please; most Italians have two dozen. Tell me you are happy. Tell me." He was only half teasing. He had a special look when he toyed with her like this, and she adored it, but it scared her as much as it pleased her.

How easily my world could be damaged, she thought, *on Riccardo's roller coaster.* She feared that one day, he would forget to care about what she felt—or no longer felt.

For the rest of her life, she would remember every detail of that first visit to the Ligurian coast, to Genoa, and then to the exquisite little island of their exile, Santini, where everyone would come out to see Riccardino's fiancée.

The great man himself was waiting at the station for them with a bouquet of red and white carnations for Marisa and wide-open arms for his *ragazzo*. Riccardo and Don Carlo rattled on in Italian before switching to English to include her, and she was amused to find that the eminent Don Carlo made the same mistakes in English that Riccardo did. She was forced to conclude that mispronunciations were genetically transmitted.

Don Carlo, true to the photos she had seen, was handsome and distinguished, but he was also tender and attentive to her position among them. A delightful storyteller, he had a quick wit that went over well in both languages. He welcomed her with a benevolent eye but remained watchful nonetheless, she sensed. His first interest was, of course, his boy, though he made it wordlessly clear that as far as she was concerned, he was hoping for the best.

He liked her from the moment Riccardo introduced them at the railroad station, when she hesitated and then suddenly reached up and pecked him on the cheek, saying, "And Merry Christmas too." He was instantly disarmed.

He had made his love for the boy eminently clear from the start. The kiss was to show him she recognized that.

"My love, my life, my child, my only fortune," he said at dinner on their arrival day when he looked down the long dining room table and reminisced over beautiful china and heavy family silver on their Christmases past.

One of the patriarchs of Italy's non-Communist left was vividly describing scenes of wartime deprivation with a touch of pratfall ridicule that colored those horrors with a redeeming scent of farce.

She listened to him tell about making the Christmas after Riccardo's grandmother died into a happy one despite her terrible absence. He'd needed a special toy for Riccardo, a wagon to pull around the rocky hills, but there were no real stores on Santini, and there was no one clever enough to make a wagon.

Then he'd thought of the carpenter from San Stefano, a neighboring island to the north that was bigger than Santini, who could make a wagon with wooden wheels. He'd managed to get word of the request to the carpenter through Mario's fisherman father, who asked the carpenter to do it for a reasonable price.

"Tomaso, the carpenter, agreed, and he even found some rubber wheels that were a perfect fit, so he made it, and he painted it red. And that was Riccardo's merry Christmas when he was six. He was in heaven and zoomed all over the hills on it for years afterward. When he grew too big, he gave it to another little boy who did the same thing. And so on. Sometimes even now, I see it on the hills, still zinging along, making a terrible noise on the pebbles, always with a bunch of little children running after it."

He laughed while remembering and glanced over at Riccardo with wordless love in his eyes. Then he turned to Marisa and said, "There is much I want to say to you, my dear Marisa, and much you probably guess at already, but even after so short a time as this, I want to say I am happy Riccardo found you. There is something I can see. Perhaps it is the way you look at him or just the way you look at all of us—the way you walked in here to a country with perhaps not the best associations for you, and yet you let your eyes see without judgment.

"That is very bad English, I fear, but I think you know what I am trying to say. You had great loss in terms of Italy, and no one can ever repair that. But you can also see that Italy is more than a misguided people. The quisling phenomenon came from measured Scandinavia, not Calabria. So it was in the air at the time, a virus, as though the evil in all of us had been harnessed and then suddenly released in pure havoc. Do you know how many Russians died?"

He shook his head. "The devil is strong, like the holy pictures show us. But the angel is stronger still. That is where vigilance comes in. The good angel must keep the devil locked up. All over Europe, you will see primitive frescoes with the angel standing with one foot placed victoriously on the devil lying on the ground. The avenging angel? You will see one in the island's church. We used to look at it often when Riccardo was a little boy. It meant a lot to him. It still does, I hope."

Marisa hesitated in answering him. She had too much to say and too much to ask, she thought. There was still too much to learn. "I just want to tell you that Riccardo is like no one I have ever known. And now I know why. I can see how precious he is to you—and not only because of his talent and the way he responds to that talent, the obligation he feels so strongly. I understand that, and I want you to know, at the risk of sounding pretentious, that I will do everything in my power to encourage him to work."

She leaned forward slightly and went on in a low voice. "And I think I love him a little more now that I have seen him at home with you and, of course, with Severina and this house full of your past—Riccardo's world. Who could resist this beautiful house and your affection? I can only thank you for opening the door for me," she said, which made him smile gently and in relief.

They enjoyed their Christmas dinner. They all talked freely, and she was included in the conversation in a mixture of Italian, French, and a lot of English, which made it both amusing and accessible to her.

This has got to be the most complete display of hospitality and welcome on record, she thought to herself. *How they must love their Riccardino, their miracle child who survived a massacre.* Despite the warmth of the room, she shivered at the image the word *massacre* evoked.

Later on, Don Carlo took her on a tour of the top part of the house, which had tall windows looking down over the sea and the ships in the harbor. It was a very Genovese house, built for a family who lived by and for the world beyond and to whom the sea was an open boulevard. Once upstairs, he looked at her to see if she was enjoying the view, which she was, and then he went beyond it to show what the city meant in terms of its past. They stood at the windows for a second in silence, and then, as though having come to a decision, he nodded and invited her to sit down.

They were in a big informal sitting room on the top floor of the house, looking out on the picturesque harbor. From there, the view was breathtaking. "Will you give me a capsule course in Genoa's history?" she asked, smiling.

Don Carlo shook his head. "Yes, but later. First, I want to try to describe what Riccardo has been through, so you can understand perhaps who he is now. He came to us as an infant, and we loved him as only grandparents know how to love. Someone should write a sonnet on the love of grandparents; it is the purest and least trammeled of any other. And how we came to have this baby in our care, the loss of our Lucca, the difficulties in tracing where Gabriela came from and who she was—did Riccardo tell you about this?" he asked, watching her surprise.

"No, he just said he doesn't know much about them, about her people." Marisa looked puzzled.

He nodded. "No, he doesn't talk easily about his parents. But that is at the core of the matter. He was a happy little boy but a quiet one. We loved him enormously. We loved to play with him, see him grow, teach him things, and watch him learn to do things—talking, walking, playing, learning. We both tried our best to reach the odd little reticence he showed from the time we found him, but we both saw an innate holding back, as though he feared to trust."

He leaned over toward her, frowning. "Think of a tiny baby with beautiful, big eyes but with what we called a slow smile. How can I explain? It was a matter of seconds. He would open his eyes and look at us, but instead of smiling instantly, instead of recognizing our goodwill instantly, he hesitated, and his eyes would look at us for several seconds before he would smile, laugh, or even gurgle the way babies do. Recognition came, but it did so a fraction later than with others—there was a hesitation before the trust.

"Some people said I was imagining it. Even my wife was not sure. She admitted it was there, but she said it had something to do with his eyesight, not his experience with death and fear in infancy. I managed to have him sent to a children's eye specialist, who confirmed his eyes were fine. Remind me another day, and I will tell you how the prisoner of Zenda, which I was, managed to get him to a mainland medical specialist. But not today—later. Anyway, the specialist said he was a healthy baby; nothing was wrong with his eyes.

"So I let it go. Veronica was convinced she was right, and I let her be right. Thank God my poor beautiful wife died too soon to see that I was right: his sight is more than fine; it is his reluctance to recognize that is not.

"Perhaps I should tell you, since I am telling you everything today, she died suddenly in the garden on Santini. She was fifty-six and had a massive heart attack, which no one had seen coming. And of course, it was the boy who found her. He ran out to ask her to peel an orange for him, because he was making a mess of it. She didn't answer, and he started crying—screaming even.

"One of the *guardia* heard and went to see. Some of the guardia were gentle with us because of the little boy, but not all. That was one of the nice ones. He saw what had happened and then ran back and fetched me. I was not let out of the house in the afternoon between two o'clock and six—don't ask why—but he told me to go to her, and of course, I guessed there was something. Well, almost. I thought she had fallen or something but not that she had died.

"Then Riccardo hid behind a chair in the sitting room and crouched there, making no noise—no cries, no sounds. As though he had vanished to what he called in his storytelling No-See Land. He had invented this story place, No-See Land, and then he would hide behind something.

A tree or a chair—anything. If there was no place to hide, he would put his hands up to his eyes and close them hard, crouch down, and rock back and forth slowly, hardly moving.

"And that is what he did then next to his grandmother; he scrunched up in a little ball, not seeing. But he screamed and kicked when I went to pick him up. I insisted and held him harder, and eventually, he calmed down. He breathed deeply, opened his eyes, laid his head against my shoulder, and whispered softly so only I could hear him, 'Nonno, Nonno.' Others came into the room. I kept him in my arms while talking to the caribiniere, and Riccardo only consented to let go of me when I whispered that I had to make a pee-pee. He let go for that—reluctantly. But he stayed close to me for days after.

"And it was then he made his first portrait, by the way. He drew a picture of her that is amazingly recognizable for a six-year-old child. I will show it to you; it is in my room. But in a drawer, not hanging on the wall."

He leaned back and looked at her gently. He had not planned on telling her all that; it had just come out spontaneously, somewhat to his own surprise.

"Marisa, I am glad to be able to talk to you so frankly and to find you so open to what I have told you. He is fragile, my Riccardino, but he is also reluctant to admit to being fragile. In New York, there was a young woman— quite charming and even well meaning—but she wanted him to see an analyst. Everyone in New York sees an analyst now. It is actually a bit tiresome. On the other hand, an analyst might have done him something positive. If he had accepted it, of course. But he did not accept it then, so that was the end of New York and of that particular, um, young lady. Perhaps I can now add 'thank heaven' out loud," he said with a nice little grin for her.

He rose from his chair and walked by her to open the window to air out the room after his half dozen cigarettes, which he'd smoked nervously as he told her all that she had not known or even guessed about Riccardo.

She now understood Riccardo's reluctance to go into detail about his parents' deaths, but she had not guessed the ramifications of their tragedy, nor had she imagined that a baby that young might be so marked by the violence involved. *An analyst was a logical piece of advice,* she thought. *Odd that it was so roundly rejected.*

She went on to wonder what else the young lady in New York had gotten wrong. *Thank the Lord for whatever it was,* she mused, *because she sounds like an uncommon adversary.*

Riccardo did not talk about the girls in his life. If a story he was telling required an allusion to one, he just identified the person as a friend. She had caught on to that but had not pursued the point with him. He was as light as a clown on the surface, but underneath, he was as taut as a wire—a breakable wire, a thin gold filament.

Riccardo knew all about the art of closing doors, yet he had opened what was, in his eyes, the essential part of himself to her. He'd let her know how much he loved her for accepting his fragility and his otherness.

"I am not a big Wild West rider on a horse who knows which mountain to climb, my Marisa of the Unicorn. I am more like that dolphin rider you seem to fancy, trying hard to not fall into the sea. Do you know that?" He'd looked at her with a distance she was not expecting.

After a second, she'd said quietly, "I will try to remember the rules, the warning signs, and the caution. I hope you will be as patient with me."

When she'd glanced up at him, she'd been startled to see how pale he had become.

Now Don Carlo, stretching out his hand to her so they could go downstairs to join the others, said to her, "Thank you for listening so attentively. Another time, I will tell you about how we went to Yugoslavia after the war to try to trace Gabriela's parents or brother. We learned that her parents had died when a small village where they had taken refuge was burned to the ground by the Germans. The Germans were particularly brutal with the Serbs; their war crimes were horrendous. I am not sure why, unless it is because they are a particularly creative people, the Serbs, and they did not make easy victims.

"We knew she had a brother, though, because she talked of him. He was a few years older and was studying medicine in Belgrade when the baby was born. But he did not come to see his sister. I don't know why. I suppose there was no rush. No one could have foreseen the massacre that was waiting for us. No one could even imagine a war, for that matter. Anyway, there was no trace of him beyond that.

"At that time, remember, I was already in internal exile, a sort of prison on my island. I was unable to make formal requests about the beautiful foreign girl my son did not quite marry. I never stopped writing letters, but after the German invasion of Yugoslavia, it was as though her phantom brother had vanished. Yugoslavia fought a valiant war. Perhaps you don't know that. It was torn apart, massacred by the Nazis. Almost anything could have happened to him. Perhaps one day we will find out. Perhaps he will come back after many years in Argentina or New Zealand with a family of little Gabrielas to meet us.

"We saw only one picture of him, this young man called Niko, and he looked like Gabriela—elegant and dark, with an open smile. Riccardo looks very much like Lucca, by the way. And like me a little. At least I like to think so."

He was right, of course.

Don Carlo fell silent for a moment, gazing out over the majestic port that had seen so much of his family's history. She felt as if she had been allowed entrance into a privileged chamber, an unscheduled brush for her with the wider world beyond the Cloisters' windows.

"Let us go for a walk and count the seagulls," he suggested. "I have burdened you perhaps, but you should know beforehand that ..." His voice trailed off.

"That he is special?" she said. "I know that. I knew it from the first. And I give you my word—"

He interrupted her. "I don't need your word; I see it in your eyes. You have the same look that Gabriela had, my dear, only you are living in more humane times. *Benvenuta, mi* Marisa," he said, not knowing that he was echoing his grandson. "And tomorrow we will talk about you. I don't know anything, er, about your family, come to think of it," he said apologetically. "I gather they are not Italian?"

"No, not Italian at all. Well, next time," she murmured, passing through the door to the elegant staircase.

"I love New York, you know, so I am always happy to talk about it. And even Fort Tryon Park and the Cloisters," he told her encouragingly.

She had grown nimble about avoiding the subject of her family but knew that a modicum of frankness was called for. She stopped on the landing and said, "There is not much to tell. My parents came from different corners of upstate New York. We were very much the tiny New York City nuclear family, just ourselves. You don't often see that in Europe, I gather. My father died after Peter, my brother, was killed in the battle for Rome. Yes, the awful battle for Rome."

She paused and then went on, her voice almost tired now. "My father was a postman. He was nice and gentle and happy—sort of, until Peter was killed. He couldn't cope with the unfairness. He felt that he had never asked for much, just his children, yet his boy was taken away by a world he no longer understood. He had worked all his life with Italian Americans. None of them dared to talk to him when they heard. Italy, even with Mussolini, was different in their eyes from Germany. So losing Peter had a touch of evil about it. It was hard to live with that."

She looked over at Don Carlo. His elegant features were locked into a recognition of hopelessness. He just nodded, and they were silent for a bit on the curving staircase. It was as though her words put them into some silent recognition that there would always be questions left unanswered— questions that were, in themselves, the ultimate dregs of war.

Then, brightening, Don Carlo rose. "Let us go for a walk down to see the cathedral. Riccardo can join us there, and then we will see what happens next. You must see the cathedral, Marisa. It has an unexploded British bomb at the altar. It dropped in 1941 but was defective. It did not explode."

She stopped and stared at him.

He met her eyes and gave an elegant shrug. "It hasn't exploded yet, I should say."

Then he flashed her a wicked grin, and they resumed their trek down the stairs till they reached the front hallway.

A British bomb in Genoa's cathedral? Waiting for what? she wondered. *Benediction?*

The elegant gentleman and the young American girl walked briskly down the street to the edge of the water, where imposing ships lay poised under the admiring gaze of strollers on a sunny day. Ship watching seemed to be a major sport in Genoa.

She smiled to herself as Don Carlo took her arm to cross the crowded square. He was making everything easy for his boy and making it easy for her to fit in as painlessly as possible. She wondered how Peter, impetuous and ardent as he was, would have felt about her presence there. He would have been delighted at the paradox, of course, with all the sparks that sizzled from these pranks of modern history.

She looked around her and wondered what tangle had tricked these good-natured people gifted for enjoying life into marching behind a strutting puppet to take over the world. *Mare Nostrum,* she recalled from her history books. *I wonder how the Spaniards digested that, considering their affinity with this fabled sea—unless, of course, Franco had been a sleeping partner all along.*

She then gazed with interest at the white-clad traffic policeman in the middle of a busy circle of six streets. He was perched in something that looked like a pulpit, directing traffic as though it were the New York Philharmonic. His arms waved frenetically with intense musicality for the span of a green light. She paused to watch him.

"This way," Don Carlo said, pointing her in the right direction so she could get a better view of the house where Christopher Columbus had been born.

Christopher Columbus seemed to have been born in the middle of an Italian traffic jam. It could not have been more appropriate.

"Let us begin at the beginning," Don Carlo said as they reached the first American's door. "Tell me about yourself, but remember, short of finding out you have been secretly voting for Senator McCarthy, I don't think you can change what I feel I know about you already."

She knew then that she was home safe.

She spent the night alone in a guest bedroom on the third floor of the spacious house, a guest room that seemed young and frilly to her. On the second floor, she had counted four bedrooms, though she had not visited any except for a brief glimpse of Riccardo's. It was large and had bookcases lining one wall and a huge bay window overlooking the sea. There was a selection of drawings on one wall, all framed in the same thin black wood Riccardo used in Paris, so as not to distract from the work itself.

On the far wall, catching the light from the window, were two large canvases of street scenes done in his bold swaths of brushwork that made the subject an excuse for the relative value of color. The paintings were both done in a variety of reds. He had a way of rendering the reds so that they appeared totally different one from the other, as though they required different names. His painting seemed to challenge the viewer, she noted once more, not cajole or even seek to please him or her. One day, perhaps he might explain. She had only gotten a raised eyebrow from him when she had suggested as much in Paris. Since she knew next to nothing about theory, she did not dare insist.

She moved to look at a panel with five small drawings of young people. They were not really portraits but clearly inferred something special about each one. Two were of girls, and three were of boys. As she was looking at them, Riccardo called out to her to come along. He said it was getting late. It was her turn to raise an eyebrow. *Late for what?*

She joined him at the staircase, and they went down to the kitchen together. He was frowning and mumbling about whether anyone had thought to buy some cereal "for the quaint foreigner in our midst who otherwise might call for eggs and sausages like the English trade union guests did last year." She tried to tell him she was happy with bread, butter, and English marmalade, a jar of which she'd just caught sight of on the kitchen table, but Severina burst in with a box of cornflakes, so Marisa's first Italian breakfast was not a culture shock. She gave him a sidelong glance.

He looked contrite. "I will tell you about the drawings later on, and we can even discuss why street scenes should be red. Sorry if I barked." He was avoiding her eyes as a child might do, and she melted.

"No," she said. "I was trespassing. I will try to be more discreet from now on, but it comes hard for me. I hardly know the meaning of the word." She kissed his cheek lightly, keeping the interaction brief in case anyone should pass by. Severina came in and beamed at them both.

"I was in New York a few Christmases ago, and Nonno came over to spend it with me," Riccardo said brightly, reminiscing as they settled around the table for an international breakfast with large cups of Italian coffee. There was Earl Grey tea for the mysteriously anglicized Riccardo, who did not like coffee even when Severina made it.

"We had a delicious Christmas dinner at the home of his wonderful Jewish journalist friend and his very hospitable wife and children, and the guests included a *prêtre ouvrier* from Toulon, an Iglesia de la Liberaciòn priest from Colombia, and us. All the others were Jews. It was amazingly Christian, I thought. We drank mostly to the memory of President Roosevelt. And they gave me a book about Sacco and Vanzetti, all wrapped up in pretty paper. How can anyone doubt that Americans have good intentions?" he asked, smiling at her to make up for his earlier abrasiveness.

Wordlessly, she understood his reaction. It was almost as if he had put up his hands to cover his face, to cover the drawings she had been looking at.

He had not invited her to look at the drawings; she had done that on her own.

My space, your space.

He knew that Don Carlo had spoken with her. He knew that she knew. He felt exposed.

"I only hope your friends are not all in jail by now, thanks to Senator McCarthy," Marisa said with a sigh, pretending that her invasion of his privacy had not happened and that the room with the drawings and the red paintings was still behind a closed door. "You can show me the rest of the house when you have time," she said mildly.

He nodded and poured himself another cup of tea.

Opening the curtains on the past was more of an ordeal than he had imagined. He realized how foolish he had been in imagining that she would be anything but understanding or forgiving or would suggest anything beyond discretion. She had sensed from the start his need for an unshared space, which was what had drawn him to her so imperatively—beyond the blue eyes and the way her back looked when she took those long strides, of course. It was a gift, he thought, like her blue eyes—the gift of understanding his need for his own darkness.

He knew she accepted the invisible door between them—because she knew that it was a glass door and that she might see through it if he called out. But that option was his, not hers. She understood that without putting words around it, and that made him sure he had found the miracle he had scarcely hoped for. He had found her reading de Nerval in the Café Flore.

Now he bolted up from his chair, splattering tea leaves all over the table and dropping spoons to the floor with a clang. He pulled her up from her chair. "I love you, Marisa. I love you because you are unique for me." He kissed her hard on the mouth as Severina came running into the kitchen. He let go of Marisa and took the aging woman by the waist and waltzed her around the table, singing like an organ grinder at the top of his voice.

"*Pazzo, pazzo, il ragazzo e pazzo!*" she cried out as he danced her out the door into the kitchen garden, and Marisa watched them laughing and singing as they went down the path.

I have been for a ride on his roller coaster, she thought, *but I am home safe now.* She knew that with him, the roller coaster would probably always lurk around the corner, but with a little bit of luck, they would be able to ride it out to the end together.

Throughout that first visit to Genoa, Marisa saw the growing pleasure in Riccardo's eyes as he watched her gradually become part of the household.

Severina was the one who clinched it. Upon Marisa's arrival, she examined Marisa with sharp eyes. She accepted her kisses on both cheeks but politely held back, in Riccardo's estimation, till she was absolutely convinced. That moment came on Christmas Eve, when they went to midnight Mass like a delegation. The group included Don Carlo, the friends who had had dinner with them, their teenage daughters, and Severina, who was wearing a fine beige camel-hair coat that had been her Christmas present from Paris, looking for all the world like the queen mum. She took Marisa's arm, going down the aisle to a pew apparently reserved for them.

Marisa had been quizzical at going to Mass at all, misinterpreting the role of socialism in personal practices. She learned quickly that Don Carlo might be a critic of the church, but he was a Catholic critic from an old Ligurian family that had included many other such critics of the church over the ages, plus a fair number of bishops as well. All, however, went to Mass at Christmas.

Marisa was being given a crash course in Mediterranean sociology, and she appeared to be fitting in more quickly than anyone had anticipated.

A few days later, they took a shabby little ferry crowded with passengers, poultry, a few noisy goats, and any number of noisy children with their Christmas toys in hand.

They arrived in Santini, some forty minutes away, on a still, mild winter day.

She was entranced by the Genoa coast, by the outlines of the beautiful maritime ports that shone brightly against the blue of the sea.

"I can think of worse places to be banished to," she said to Don Carlo, who nodded. He looked pensive for a second and then confided that during those years, he would at times close his eyes and pretend he was in darkest Poland just to fire up his anger, because it had been hard to think of this blue sea as punishment.

However, those moments had passed quickly when the caribinieri came around.

"So there we were, captives in paradise. Riccardo grew up speaking the dialect of the islands, of course, except on weekends, when I tried to teach him English with the help of the BBC. The radio was kept hidden in an old trunk upstairs. We made a game of learning the language, and in retrospect, he learned it easily because it was a game, and we were winning. None of the police ever heard us, because Severina would warn us if someone was coming. It worked.

"Now his English is better but perhaps less charming than when he recited the weather report for all the coastal regions just as the BBC weatherman did. Ask him one day about Fisher, Dogger, and German Bight, which are some bits of rock up there but nowhere near the Ligurian Sea."

Santini proved to be small. It had a tiny harbor with white houses rising to a mound with an ornate stone church at its top and not much else. Clumps of olive trees hundreds of years old, cypresses, and citrus trees made the place look like a child's drawing. The fishermen's houses were squat and whitewashed, with patchy gardens here and there.

Santini looked like a toy, a theater set, or a fantasy village in a new Italian movie with Sophia Loren. Its small baroque church had a miniature replica of the elaborate Genoa cemetery next to it, standing against the bright blue sky. A sense of timelessness was forgiven in the onlooker's imagination.

"It looks as though it has been here forever, doesn't it? The Greeks, the Romans, the Spanish Armada, the English tourists—they come and go, but our tiny outposts live on quietly forever. I should have thanked the Fascisti; otherwise, I would never have thought to visit," Don Carlo said.

He had been watching Marisa react to her first glimpse of Santini. He smiled slowly. She was as moved as he'd expected her to be. He glanced over at Riccardo, who had been watching them both. Riccardo nodded and murmured to his grandfather, "*Te l'avvevo detto*" (I told you so).

After much juggling with long division, they figured out that Santini was just a smidgen bigger than Manhattan.

It had some 150 houses and an uncountable number of piers for boats of all kinds. Fishermen, sailors, and a surprising number of occasional farmers made up the population.

"And the major job category is, of course, smuggling," said Riccardo with a touch of pride. She'd noticed that as soon as they'd landed and been engulfed by people waiting on the quayside to greet them, Riccardo's Italian had softened, changed keys, and become a little more difficult for her to decipher. If asked, she would explain that she had been learning Italian since early evening on day one. She seemed to have a knack for Romance languages. She had picked up French rapidly despite its *u* and *r*, which defied vocal gymnasts, and she had a better accent than anyone would have expected. The same seemed to be true of Italian. By listening to Riccardo on the phone speaking Italian, a collection of long vowels and frequent pauses, she had managed to pick up enough to figure out the general gist of his conversation without asking. It was a knack that made them both giggle.

Now his Italian had lopped off into Santini's dialect, with even longer vowels. She asked Don Carlo about the difference, and he answered, "Yes," genuinely surprised that she had heard it. "Now, that is really *il destino!*" he said to Riccardo, who was helping Severina negotiate the step up to the pier.

"*La signorina parla proprio bene il Italiano, anque come noi,*" Severina explained triumphantly, as though she had invented the girl herself. Riccardo felt his heart swell as much with relief as with pride. Severina's approval was vital.

He turned to take Marisa's elbow, but he was too late. She was already on the pier, talking to one of the greeters who had reached out a strong arm to help her up. Riccardo spotted Mario and laughed out loud.

"*Piu presto que gle occhi, Il Calabrone Verdi. Come prima!*" he called out, harking back to their childhood games, when the Green Hornet was their hero thanks to a pile of tattered comic books someone's cousin in Jersey City had sent home to the old country. Mario was their Green Hornet because he was faster and smarter than all the others, including Riccardo.

Now Riccardo took him by the shoulders and said to Marisa, "This is my Mario. He was the smartest one on the island when we were six, and he still is." He turned back to Mario. "This is my Marisa," he said to Mario in English, taking him by the arm. "You can kiss her on the cheek with your hands behind your back. I'm timing you."

The handsome Mario did just that and said in good English, "I might be smarter, but he is luckier. And it seems you speak Italian; I just heard you say something to Severina."

"No, I don't know more than a few words. I am just guessing at it. But give me a couple of weeks, and I might. I must have been bewitched by the olive trees," she said, laughing at herself.

"No," said Riccardo sharply, turning his eyes on hers, changing his tone, and looking at her as though they were alone. Mario glanced from one to the other sharply, but his eyes lingered on Riccardo, and he drew back slightly to leave him space.

"It was at the Flore. I know because I was there," Riccardo said. An unexpected urgency flashed into his voice as he went on. "I was there when the bewitching started, and it goes a little bit further every day. Don't you see?"

He had spoken with urgency despite his smile. In that second, Mario slowly put his arm around Riccardo's shoulders, saying confidentially, *"Benvenuto a casa, Riccardo. Benvenuto."*

Earlier, he had watched Riccardo speak to her and caught their closeness. He saw then, with something resembling an electric shock, that what was happening between Riccardo and this charming yet visibly unspoiled girl with the candid eyes was different and new. More than that, it was vital.

The sound of Riccardo's voice and the tension Mario saw in his friend's eyes spoke of something urgent in the close-knit world they shared—a completion of sorts.

Riccardo loves this girl!

Mario took this revelation in with shock. This young American girl, who was totally alien to the world that had created him, was Riccardo's choice.

Within the space of a second, Mario's heart soared. In the seconds that it had taken for him to absorb what had happened, he had run an emotional gamut from mild curiosity about her to a surge of love for her. He loved her because she loved Riccardo.

Mario turned to Don Carlo and gave him a boyish bear hug. Their eyes exchanged silent messages of shared joy.

"A very happy new year!" Don Carlo cried into the din. Then he nodded at Mario with a smile of enduring complicity.

On New Year's Eve, Don Carlo opened the house to the whole village with tables full of food: cheeses, sausages, pâtés, different kinds of bread, salads of a dozen colors, fruit of all the seasons, bowers of grapes, and pastries Marisa had never seen before.

As she nibbled her way through the festive table, Riccardo raised his glass to her, quietly drawing her to a corner where they were almost alone, parted from the crowd.

"This is my first drink of the evening," he said to her. "I am one hundred percent sober. Now that I've made sure you know that, I would like to say—no, to ask—very seriously: Will you marry me, Marisa di Fort Tryon?

"You've seen my island, my family, my friends, my ships of Genoa, my house of Cristoforo Colombo, and my *terra di exilio*. You see everything about me. So, my love of the Café Flore, my princess of Manhattan's tip, will you marry me? Even if I am bad tempered when you interrupt me just when finally the color is right and I only want to work? Or when I want to go down to dinner at midnight instead of eight o'clock or to discuss the world with your American friends and still prefer Sartre to Camus as well as the rigidity of the French Communist unions to the saccharine unions the CIA patched together to compete in postwar industry? All this and more, Marisa, my beautiful angel from the top of New York. Will you marry me?

"In a few months, you will be twenty-one. We could come here with the orange blossoms. Nonno is friends with the US consul, who can help with the legal papers. He would be happy to help. Will you take my grandmother's ring right now and say, '*Grazie mille*'? *Adesso*?"

His voice was low, almost a whisper, creating another island for the two of them. They were alone amid the other voices and holiday laughter. The proposal was a whispered invitation to enter eternity with him.

She was tethered to his voice, his words, and his infinite trust, and she looked down at the sapphire ring he was putting on her finger. It was a bright blue stone in a thin gold setting that was, miraculously, a perfect fit.

She was startled by the ring, this link with his fractured past. He was joining past and present and offering her their future. She was choked. For a minute, she was wordless.

The new tears that had been part of their coming together inched in, tiny and tender, as her words seemed to come by themselves.

"I will spend forever trying not to bother you when you are looking for the perfect straight line or the clearest blue.

Most of all, I will love everyone on this island forever—Don Carlo first of all. But first of all the firsts still means first after you. Because I love you, my Riccardo, and I will love you forever."

Their heads were close together like pirates discussing the price of pearls.

Farther along the table, Don Carlo was deep in conversation with Mario over plates with cheese and sausages. He glanced at Riccardo and Marisa and then edged toward them. "What is he doing, telling you how to make pesto?"

Riccardo turned to him with the look of a cat who had already swallowed the canary and was about to sing.

"I have asked her to marry me when she is twenty-one this spring. And she said yes. Are you happy for me?" he said quietly.

He looks so young here among the figures of his childhood, Don Carlo thought. *Yet so confident.* "He is so like Lucca, so like his young father," Don Carlo told Marisa. Riccardo held up Marisa's hand to see the ring. Their eyes met.

Don Carlo looked at his grandson with all the love of a lifetime. "What do I think? I think I must be the most fortunate man in the world right now. What do you think I think?" He bent down and kissed Marisa on the cheek.

"To the second half of the century, the half that will make up for the first!" Mario called out, raising his glass to the young couple while pirated champagne corks popped in the background.

On the train back to Paris, she looked at Riccardo with an expression he had come to cherish. It was as though she couldn't quite believe he was there. He had never questioned that look, because he feared that putting words to it might make it vanish, but it flattered him and reassured him at the same time.

She met his glance and nodded. "All right, I was thinking that I have walked into your big Italian movie of a life with just a carpet bag of my own. I am Little Orphan Annie with no one from the old country to turn to or to invite to my wedding. It's as if I was born one day at the Café Flore. It is very odd, don't you think? My dearest friend from kindergarten on bolted from New York one dark night, and I have no idea what became of her. I have no equivalent of Mario to hold on to. My school friends and the kids from the park have scattered. I've lost touch with my life." She smiled ruefully. "I really would love to have a Mario to talk with, to reminisce with. You don't know how lucky you are," she said pensively.

He nodded, understanding. "I do know. But I will not lend you my Mario; he is too good looking. Anyway, right now, he is finishing a doctorate in history in Milano and has interesting connections with a Swedish designer who visits Milano frequently for la mode, but he especially has a beautiful doctor, a traumatologist who bandaged his head when he fell off his Vespa and who lives in Milan all the time, very close to him. She watches his bandages as often as she can. Yes. Ah, Mario." He sighed and raised his eyes to heaven. "Where to begin?

"My grandfather sent him to the *liceo* in Genoa when we were able to leave the island. He came with us because he was gifted, and we loved him. He got better marks than I did in school. We have been like brothers all our lives. Except that he has two other brothers of his own and a sister, Anna, Giorgio's wife. His father is a fisherman, and his mother was the baker's daughter, so she helped in the bakery too. They're Santini islanders.

"They are typical of a class that has been changing vitally since the war. Now all kinds of people stop off on the island from big white cruise ships, and the local girls think they are all new Lollobrigidas and will marry Gregory Peck any day now. And to prove that the world has changed, they have Mario to point to in the village—Mario, who will become president of Italy instead of going out smuggling cigarettes on his father's boat. Santini is like a miniature of the new postwar Italy. Nothing is the same."

He turned to look at her seriously yet with a tease in his eyes. "So we must be careful to love each other and not lose each other. If you have no childhood friends, I am sorry for you, and I will lend you mine. I know that one does not replace the other, but who can tell? Anyway, one day you might be walking down the Champs-Élysées and bump into one of those high school faces, and there you are. Paris is one of those places where you run across your past without trying. Just like the Rienzi in the Village."

She giggled at that and wondered once again what had happened to him at the Rienzi, because he talked about it cryptically. As she recalled, it was a place for interesting young men with liquid eyes. She and a classmate had sometimes had espressos there in the early evening, despite the fact that neither really liked the bitter coffee they felt obliged to drink.

Marisa smiled up at him. "Predestination," she murmured.

He let that go, not quite understanding. It was no time for their language barrier, he decided, so instead, he bent over and kissed her hair.

Riccardo's reassurance was nice, but she couldn't help thinking back on Lane, her equivalent of Mario, and she felt once again the chill common to a stranger in a strange land.

***

"Where do we begin?" Marisa said, standing in the middle of the Shoe House's living room, looking around, hesitating. They had returned to Paris early in January after celebrating the new half century at a big party in someone's amazing palazzo in Genoa, followed by observing the beginning of the Holy Year in a mass at the Cathedral of San Lorenzo, with the British bomb still nestled unexploded at the altar. Then Severina had produced glorious dinners in honor of their engagement till it was time to leave.

Now they were back in the real world of Paris's picturesque but underheated Latin Quarter, in the rainy cold of winter. The damp penetrated to the marrow despite their constant feeding of the coal stove in the living room, which heated both floors as long as one did not let it go out—which one did. Marisa, born into central heating and not adept at the feeding of foreign coal stoves, made a vow to get a good job as soon as her college year was over and install central heating, despite the fact that no one seemed to know what it was. It was an exotic invention in the eyes of the Latin Quarter, she was told, to Riccardo's amusement— amusement tinged with a real concern for his fragile, long-stemmed American beauty and her chills.

"A bigger stove," Giorgio suggested sensibly, and he added that he knew a plumber who sold large stoves at a good price.

Riccardo observed that Marisa was discovering the underside of real life beyond the American house, where they'd brought their hot water with them. "But let us go for a bigger stove," he added. "Otherwise, she might run away back to overheated New York."

Giorgio looked at him sideways and muttered, "I doubt that."

The answer to "Where do we start?" would be multiple and manifold. Marisa had been friendly with a young photographer at the American house, Charlie Mitchell, who had moved on to a studio just a few blocks up the rue Monge. One day she ran into him on the rue Mouffetard as he was taking pictures of little old ladies choosing cabbages as if they were hats. He then began eyeing other old ladies negotiating the purchase of butter, still rationed, which was like a highly ritualized ballet because it involved surrendering ration coupons—or not.

She invited him upstairs to meet Riccardo and to see the studio. Charlie was interested in painting and liked to photograph canvases. He had taken her to a few vernissages before she met Riccardo, which had familiarized her first with the rather daunting word *vernissage* and then the milieu, which was thornily inbred in Paris. Charlie freelanced for several agencies and was part of the press scene. When they reached the studio, Riccardo was out, but she made a pot of Earl Grey, and they chatted amiably. Charlie told her that he had thought of her the other day because he had heard that World Wide Network, an independent radio operating out of New York, was looking for a not-too-expensive assistant for the Paris office, but not till after the summer vacation.

WWN was headed by Milo Hines, a veteran Paris reporter of the Hemingway vintage. He was a leftover from the fabled beginnings of radio news reporting in the prewar days. WWN was a small but sharp-edged outfit bred in the

Roosevelt New Deal era, and now, as a result, it was a pet target for the spleen of Senator Joseph McCarthy and his obnoxious acolytes Cohn and Schine.

Milo Hines, now in his sixties, called himself a reporter, not a journalist, thus pricking the ego balloons of the postwar crop of pretentions he collided with at the Crillon or Harry's. Marisa had been to both with Charlie several times, at the same table as Milo Hines. She admired the veteran, and she'd listened to his storytelling with pleasure. A thick-set, round-faced man, he was fluent in French and Spanish. He had learned the latter during the Civil War, which he'd covered from start to finish. His English, however, was still amazingly southern, considering he had left his native Louisiana long ago.

Milo had taken a liking to Marisa almost immediately, possibly because she'd laughed at his stories, he would admit. He'd liked her even more when she'd answered his question as to why she wanted to stay in Europe: she'd replied with candor that she had fallen in love with an Italian painter who lived there. Only then had she added that she had wanted to be a reporter all her life and that Paris was a perfect place to start.

He had liked the way she listened to the others talking around the table, and he'd liked her smile too, which was not only pretty but also quick. He knew that a good reporter needed what he called table manners but also had to have an ear for a story. This kid, he would say, had all that as well as a pleasant voice for radio.

That was why he said he would hire her at the end of the summer. "Finish your year, take a month's vacation, and come here to start on, say, September 1. No matter what the calendar says, that is when the new year begins in Paris, at which point we open with the strikes—first the Paris metro, then the buses, and then the railroads. After that come the crises in parliament. Then everyone holds his breath for a while. When that peters out, the newest in sex scandals come in, which brings us to Christmas, and after that, who knows? You'll tell me."

He stood up and joined her on the other side of his desk, reaching out his hand. "We'll shake on it, Marisa. Oh yes, you will have to decide on whether it's Rinaldi or Short, though I rather fancy Marisa Rinaldi myself. Sounds like one of those new barefoot actresses." He laughed at her slight fluster.

They were standing in his office, a shabby two-room suite with a lived-in look to it. The filing cabinets were made of wood and might have been considered antiques. There were at least a dozen pictures on the walls of icons of their time, such as Lindberg, Mistinguette, many Roosevelts, and Mayor Laguardia, which, in time, she would come to treasure. They lent an air of history as it happened to the shabby premises, just as Milo himself did. The office was on a narrow street off the opera, close by the *New York*

Times bureau and not far from the Paris office of the *Herald Tribune*. It was also within walking distance of the Crillon Bar, the Ritz, and Harry's, three favorite watering places of the trade.

And, she thought, *there's a direct bus from Riccardo's studio.* Then she corrected herself. *A direct bus from home, I mean.*

It seemed like a dream—walking into a job in Paris that would hire her just when it suited her best, with a boss who smiled like a doting grandfather. He clearly looked forward to training her in a profession she had hitherto only dreamed of.

When she got home that afternoon, she burst into the studio and told Riccardo that some Ligurian saint had risen from Santini's rocks and was casting spells on their lives. She stood at the door, glowing. He turned his head, distracted, and smiled vaguely. He was working.

He was a million miles from her. In an absent voice, he said, "*Certo, certo,*" and he went back to the canvas for several hours more.

The perfect straight line was a jealous mistress. Marisa learned that early on.

She moved out of the American house for good in February. Giorgio came and took her suitcases, her bookcase full of the books she had acquired along the Seine, and the painting of one of Riccardo's blue ladies that he had given her at the beginning. "If you like it, I would like you to have it. It is yours," he'd said gently, making her feel like a princess in a fairy tale. Now she carried it out the door and down the steps, leaving the American house behind. She placed it carefully at the rear of Giorgio's big black Citroën, which never failed to make her think he looked like a gangster on the run in a Jean Gabin movie.

"Where do we begin?" she asked, standing in the middle of the cobbler's living room. "Where do we put me?"

"No," said Riccardo, shaking his head. "Where do we put *us?*"

The question was never really answered. They began in dribs and drabs, carefully respectful of the other's turf, notions of intimacy, and body clock. Neither of them was an early riser, but Riccardo pushed it to the limits of society, as Marisa put it. In their first marathon meeting, they missed the closing of the shops not for the midday break but for the entire day, which ended at seven o'clock in the evening. Riccardo's body clock was on Tahiti time, she decided.

Not to worry, she thought. She learned to get up and dress without waking him. He learned to wake her gently around two in the morning but softly soothed her back to sleep after another kind of dream. They were perfectly matched and careful with their bounty.

So they began. They tiptoed around the shadows left by their previous lives, adapting old schedules to new hours. They altered space in the little house, where space seemed to have been missing. Moving the couch and the sling chairs one way allowed for a matching desk and a filing cabinet, which were as out of date as the ones in Milo's office, under the staircase, thus giving her a corner of her own. They bought a clever lamp that lit either all or only part of the space, depending, giving the room a sense of privacy.

Riccardo hung a nude drawing he had done of Marisa climbing the stairs. Her long legs and the sense of lithe movement were unmistakably hers, although her features were not visible. It was an excellent portrait that defied portraiture.

Riccardo was the kind of young artist who was seldom satisfied with what he did. Furthermore, he was not eager to discuss it lightly, though he welcomed serious dialogue on art. He belonged to no group in Paris and was an outsider in what he did as well. He was a loner leaning toward an abstraction that was still in its infancy. He was by no means sure of himself but gave no hint of abandoning his way of searching in favor of easy solutions. On the contrary, he set stringent goals for himself. He despaired easily when he fell short of them.

The New York School was in the air, and abstract expressionism was opening new horizons. His stay in New York in 1948 had been fruitful but not conclusive.

Now his time in Paris was a moment of contemplation and experiment. Abstraction attracted him, but he was still unsure of himself.

He felt awkward, he confessed to Marisa, when well-meaning people asked him when he was going to have a show, because he was nowhere near ready to show, and that in itself seemed a defeat.

"I need time," he told Marisa, who felt her heart go out to him.

She tended to blame herself for distracting him, but Don Carlo assured her that distraction was what he needed. "Patience," he advised her, "and kindness. I am sure you are good at kindness, but patience is the province of saints, and I am not sure you are a saint."

She loved him for that and took to phoning him for guidance at tricky times, such as when Riccardo was up on the roof, scowling at the sun or blowing smoke at the moon. He loved his roof, which she came to realize was his retreat. She did not use it as much as she would have liked, but she reasoned, *This is his house. I am only his resident squatter. On tiptoes at that.*

He was not easy to talk to about his work or about what he called his timetable. Then there was the question of the bed in his studio. When he'd been living alone—or, rather, as alone as a bachelor lived—the bed in the studio had not been a problem. However, with a resident bed warmer, the problem of privacy arose. Riccardo worked alone. Though he liked to turn around and see her fast asleep in his bed, he was less comfortable seeing her going about her business while he was concentrating on his canvas.

She suggested a version of what her brother had devised in New York. They used a two-sided bookcase to divide the room from floor to ceiling. It was considerably less than soundproof, but it would do for the moment, he decided. The illusion of separation was all that he needed for now. Riccardo got along well with illusions, she realized.

Paradoxically, however, it was he who set the date for the wedding, and it was he who insisted on the marriage. He required, she realized, a declaration of their presence together, their status—a proof of their being. Marisa saw once more that though he was handsome and practiced, graceful in society as well as comfortable among others, he was an abandoned child who needed reassurance.

Sometimes they misunderstood each other's words. It would often have less to do with language structure than with their differing notions of time. Punctuality was a cultural divide. She learned to be explicit about appointments, as she came to realize that the phrase "around six o'clock," for example, could be anywhere between five o'clock and eight o'clock for him.

Free time was utterly free for him, either to just lounge upstairs on the roof or to vanish somewhere on his own without telling her afterward where he had been or why he had been there—not that he did anything special, much less forbidden. His alone time had something more intimate about it, something about being his own responsibility. Or he simply liked to be on his own. He had to learn that part of living with and loving Marisa meant sharing what he saw as the bare bones of his life with her. She realized that doing that did not come easily to him, but he was trying, and she loved him for that.

That year, he had been invited to show in a new Paris salon. He was pleased to be included this time. He admired the organizers and was interested in several of the established artists taking part.

A salon as a showplace for the day's art was an intrinsic part of defining one's identity in the Paris scene. Salons were important to him because they gave him a showcase for his work, but they also forced him to choose which way he was heading. The world of abstraction was only then opening, and it offered new areas for experiment and new horizons of discovery. He was on the edge of a serious turning point in his work.

Riccardo was young but not foolhardy. He was cautious in his choices, and though his work was daring and purposeful when he finished a canvas, no one could imagine the agony of decision that had gone into its completion. Each painting was wrenched forth as though, he said, he gave birth to them all. He seldom discussed the workings of his mind with Marisa, because he was not sure she was familiar enough with what he called his vocabulary to understand. He did not want her to see him as something out of a nineteenth-century caricature of a harassed artist bleeding over a study of a cloud. No, he protested, it was nothing like that.

"On the other hand," he might admit with a grin, "it is not far from that either."

In an expansive mood, he would sit up on his roof, smoke a cigarette, and talk to his attentive American beauty about the ways and byways of the creative process. He did that once in a while but not often. His work was a private affair.

He kept the key.

Marisa watched the change that would come over him when he talked about what he was doing, almost afraid of the intensity he showed. She was keenly aware of the fundamental difference between him and everyone else.

His was not a profession; it was a vocation. She came to see that he did nothing in terms of his work that was not well reasoned. What she saw as spontaneity in his strong brushstrokes, a strength that made them attractive as well as intelligently placed on the canvas, was not haphazard. Each stroke was placed purposefully there and nowhere else. It took her time to realize how deliberate each stroke was and how the colors filled a purpose. Accident was nowhere involved. He might have been young and amusing offstage, but he was totally deliberate when it came to his work.

He admitted to his grandfather that since Marisa had come into his life, he felt he was at the edge of a new viability. He smiled a little and said, "Like a new morning—the way the song puts it."

He was almost embarrassed at what he'd said.

Don Carlo did not elaborate on the simile with Riccardo, but later, he confessed to Marisa that he had heaved a mighty sigh of relief when he'd heard the boy tell him that. "The artist's path is impossible to visualize from the outside," he said to her when he was on a long weekend visit to Paris. "One can't imagine the torment that goes on in Riccardo's mind in finding what you call the perfect straight line."

But she could imagine. She knew exactly what he meant.

She had come into Riccardo's life knowing little about the process of creating a painting. She could not define what he was looking for, but she understood clearly his need to find it. His work was the core of his being; all the rest was there to prop up whatever it was that produced that work.

She came to understand that whatever it was that drew an artist to work was as vital to him or her as his or her heart or lungs, only twice as fragile. She looked at his beautiful body occasionally and thought back to the unicorn of her childhood. The princess took care of her special charge. Her smile told viewers precisely how carefully she minded him. It was just as true that Riccardo needed someone soft yet strong to lean on, because his quest put him on a lonely and sometimes even frightening road.

In turn, she came to understand why artists were often seen as difficult to live with. *Only a part of them is with you,* she recognized. *The core is secret; it is his alone. It is the part that is not shared, the door that is left unopened.*

As loving, gentle, and comical as Riccardo could be and as dependent upon her as he seemed to be, there was a line she could not cross. She recognized that quickly and was alarmed at first. However, instead of running away or fighting to crash the gates, she retired. She moved to one side and gave him the space he needed.

She not only was in love with him but also saw him as a charge put into her care.

She never put these sentiments into words, for he would have laughed out loud, but she hinted at her vision of her role to Don Carlo one day, and he nodded wisely and then said something about the angels having sent her to him in his hour of need.

"One day," he murmured confidentially, "I will tell you about the last young lady with blue eyes or, for that matter, the first one, who was probably even worse. Artists lead lonely lives underneath," the wise grandfather warned her. "They go down uncharted roads and often land on their asses, if you'll pardon the expression. As soon as I saw you and as soon as I saw how he looked at you, I realized that I am a very lucky ancestor."

Marisa would observe Riccardo at times as she was pretending to be invisible, darting through the studio when he was working. She would glimpse his serenity or its flagrant absence. In the latter, case she would be quick to leave him to his demons, her heart going out to him silently. She would smile at him almost shyly then, seemingly for no apparent reason, and wait for him to smile back, unaware that she had just come upon the ultimate definition of patience.

Sometimes she felt as if she had taken holy orders.

***

Marisa was seated at her desk, frowning, as though the course of the rest of her life mystified her. She shuffled a mess of loose papers and glared at an open diary in front of her. She would take her final exams for the year-abroad diploma—which was better than nothing, in her mind—in late May. They could have their lovely Italian wedding in June. *Mid-June,* she thought to give herself a reason to buy the summery Parisian wedding gown she dreamed of. The thought of having a Parisian wedding gown tickled her.

What a long way they had come in so short a time, she marveled.

She cast her mind back on that last period in New York, recalling the dark, clouded months adrift in unacceptable deaths and the incomprehensible defection of her mother, followed by the blurred time when she was on her own, never more alone. She must have been numb, she supposed now, to have been able to get through to the day when she'd boarded that ship and left it all behind her. However, much still remained unanswered, she mused, wondering whether the blurred image she was left with would ever clear in her mind.

Occasionally, she would let herself think back on the park with the Cloisters' bells in the distance, to distant voices and the scent of the nearby Hudson. It was her river, she used to say when she was little. That made her father laugh, while Peter snapped, "No, it's mine. I'm older." She thought of the river and the rough ground around it, where the railroad tracks used to carry freight trains and hobos when she was a little girl.

The hobos then were shadowy men in ragged clothes who huddled by the river's edge with bonfires going and the smell of cheap whiskey in the air. John Steinbeck had written of similar men in California, and as an adolescent, she had been fascinated by his tales and the characters he'd drawn with apparent empathy.

She had liked to scare herself with their portent of danger and the end-of-the-road image they evoked in her imagination. She had been fascinated by these people who had extricated themselves from their own lives and hopped trains to put ever-mounting distance between themselves and their realities. The image of that kind of freedom had astounded her when she was young. It had frightened her too. *Freedom, yes, but with no one to share it with?* she thought. *Isn't freedom meaningless if you are alone?* The thought gave her a chill, a shiver that had almost made her sick when she was still a child.

Now, much later and in the safety of Paris, far removed from that darkness, she had a curious half memory of a man, perhaps a hobo, lying still on the ground that night, between the river and the railroad tracks, and she shuddered. The hazy silhouette rose stubbornly, but she banished it to some darker recess along with the many other painful echoes of those uncertain days. She made an effort now to erase them from the mirror of her mind. She wanted to wipe her New York slate clean of them, free of her mother's departure and her father's fading away into a place called death, as though he had opened the door to it himself.

That had been a time of parenthesis for her, parenthesis between Peter's death and her arrival in Paris. Her proper life had resumed only when she'd arrived at the Cité Universitaire and taken her place among a population of her contemporaries, uprooted by choice, who were building their lives on the rubble left by war. *Building* was the operative word. She was now just one among many who made up a new generation of strong-willed individuals determined to wipe out the scars of the 1930s and '40s and construct a new society after the chaos that had all but destroyed half the planet.

Everything was possible in the eyes of her generation, and they went after the future like no one before them had, she liked to think. It was in the air, and she felt it was precisely that which buoyed her on. She'd realized she was not the only one who thought like that when she'd gotten to know others at the American house, which was, possibly because it was well heated, an informal magnet for all sorts of young people in search of a conversation—an audience rendered captive because of the temperature, according to the already world-weary Jeff and François, her first friends.

Conversation came easily to Riccardo, she saw, and she wondered at the differences between young Europeans and Americans their age. There were instantly recognizable differences, she noted, but perhaps that was due to the intrinsic difference between their relationships: she talked to her friends at the Cité; she confided in Riccardo.

Riccardo had asked her about her family, but he had asked gently because it was clear to him that she was reluctant to go into detail about her mother's sudden departure. Without her spelling it out, Riccardo sensed that her coming to Paris had been her way of reaching out for a whole new life for herself, a life in which she might set the rules herself.

When he'd first met her and they'd begun their first conversation without end, he'd become aware of the multiplicity of the meanings of virginity. He cherished her for her tenderness, for what he could bring her, and for how much she needed him, so he did not press her to describe further in detail whatever it was she had clearly fled.

He was tolerant of other people's ghosts.

Little by little, she unfolded to him—but almost apologetically. Her estranged mother was, in any case, beyond his grasp. He could not picture a woman who walked away from a bruised daughter, leaving her in the care of the local bank.

Marisa recognized at once that he could not cope with the mental picture she drew of her mother. She saw him flinch at her words, and then he would instinctively put his arm around her. She tried to describe her father's death or simply the reason she was so orphan-like compared to others who had lost a parent, but her words were windows to what he saw as pain, so together they tacitly let the discussion drift off with as few details as possible, letting it fade into the darkness it deserved.

Marisa blessed him for that, because the light they lived in made everything in the past seem dim in comparison. However, she knew that he was touched by her fragility and only too aware of her limitless trust in him.

Out of the blue, while sitting at her messy desk, she thought of the enigmatic title of a Christopher Fry play she had loved. In a flash of recognition, she understood its meaning. The play was called *The Dark Is Light Enough*.

Of course it is, she thought.

***

The winter months went by with amazing speed and a plethora of bumpy obstacles. There were strikes of all kinds, including some that took Marisa by surprise. It had never occurred to her that the post office could go on strike, and she searched her memory to recall any hint of such a suggestion in her father's conversations. She found none. In France, apparently, no such reservations arose. A week's walkout disrupted airmail particularly, and as a result, half of the documents she needed for a wedding in a foreign country were at least delayed, if not lost.

A variety of transportation strikes ensued, such as the buses but not the metro, the metro but not the buses, or both, with the railroads thrown in for good measure.

Marisa was upset and dismayed at the idea of not being ready with all her documents for a June wedding date. She envisioned herself having to hitchhike through a strike-bound France in her silver ballerinas to get there in time. Riccardo tried to calm her, sometimes succeeding with a litany of wild alternatives. "We could fly to Scotland and marry on that rugged heath they have, where no one cares much what kind of papers you have as long as you wear kilts," he said soothingly.

They rode bicycles during the transport strikes or walked when the sun was out. She strolled home from her exams for her junior year diploma because it was a beautiful day, and Paris seemed to enjoy playing hooky.

She did not pretend to understand the French, and she often wondered how this frequently cranky population had managed to produce a city that was a constant charm to live in.

Since she had barely prepared for her final exams, she was convinced she had failed them. However, mail delivery resumed at the end of May, and she learned she had passed with honors. "Hallelujah!" she cried out upstairs to Riccardo, who was locked up in the studio and could not hear. The neighborhood cat walked over, seeing her in the open doorway, and scanned the premises, looking for something interesting. Finding nothing edible in view, however, he continued on his way to the richer precincts of the crèmerie next door. She watched him go and smiled.

That's life.

She told Milo she would be ready to start work in September if everything was still on schedule. He assured her everything was on his side. "It is all signed, sealed, and delivered. You just go on and have a splendid honeymoon. It doesn't get better than that, you know. And come back in September. I will have real life waiting for you then. That will be my wedding present to you both. Come back in September, all suntanned and happy. I'll save you a metro strike."

He laughed lightheartedly.

✳✳✳

On Thursdays, after five in the afternoon, Riccardo took Marisa to vernissages around Saint-Germain-des-Prés, the French ritual of the opening of new art shows in Paris's endless range of galleries. She thus became familiar with his colorful yet highly compartmentalized world. He went to some galleries, not all. He spoke with a few artists but not many. He did not appear to be particularly close to any of them. Wherever the notion of easygoing camaraderie among artists in Paris came from, it was certainly not visible there.

Marisa noted early on that Riccardo looked good in crowds. His boy-on-a-dolphin grace did not fail to cause a little ruffle among women, though none of that seemed to register with him. If it did, when she was with him, he did not let on. That, in turn, amused her. He talked with people comfortably and occasionally introduced her as his fiancée but invariably included her in conversation and seemed pleased   to have her at his side.

There was, however, a curious touch of reticence she noted in him. He was attentive to the work of others, but he kept a distance. She was curious about this but did not ask him why. Without putting his reasoning into words, he maintained a space of his own when it came to his work. He never discussed it with her. It was his private province. Instinctively, she did not seek to go beyond the doors.

He had few buddies among the gallery goers, but they continued to spend most of their free time together or with her friends from the American house or Charlie, her photographer buddy, and a couple of his cronies. All these friends came by for dinners, or they went out with them to Latin Quarter bistros, such as nearby Giorgio's. However, their most rewarding social life in those early days came through the theater and, close on its heels, the cinema.

The recognition of cinema as a viable art form was a new consideration. Perhaps it was an intrusion into the concept of theater, or perhaps it was an art on its own. The question was on the table. Riccardo held back. He said that his revolutionary instincts, his anarchist genes common to all good Italians, failed him on this issue. He said reluctantly but definitively that entertainment was not art, whereupon an uproar went off in their living room, making him laugh with joy that only in Paris would calling an entertainment by its proper name ignite open social warfare among friends.

However, cinema had arrived, and no one in their circles went to the movies anymore; they went to the cinema dogmatically. Paris, Marisa thought, was a life-changing adventure.

At that time, a new concept of dramatic art exploded into a postwar blaze of creativity on all levels. Riccardo was captivated by it, and he reminded others that in theater, they were talking about concepts of dramatic arts as opposed to technical quality and camera angles. He stood his ground. As a result, they had few friends in film but lots in the theater.

The early postwar period was a moment of great adventure in all the arts in Paris but especially the theater. The war had exploded all the barriers, and Paris's new TNP had injected a different brand of fire, a new and different talent, and wider horizons for experimentation on the stage, some of them even jostling the notion of the stage itself.

At first settling into a breathtaking antique theater in Avignon, the former Palais des Papes in the south of France, and putting on Brecht or Euripides in entirely new concepts, Jean Vilar and his troupe spearheaded the movement in Paris. He called his venture the Théatre National Populaire and rented a vast hall in the middle of the Right Bank, dramatically perched on a hill overlooking the city.

It also accommodated the working class by making curtain hours earlier, thus allowing people to catch a metro home. It lowered the prices of seats and even introduced the season ticket. The masses were invited to partake of their country's cultural heritage at cut-rate prices and in time to catch the last metro home. The concept of availability of culture was a revolution, a battle won in the class war that was visible threading all through the fabric of newly reborn Europe.

The TNP was the first such venture but not the only one.

Jean Vilar had ignited a fire, and others fanned the flames. New theaters with similar agendas sprang up all over Paris and even in the provinces. Riccardo and Marisa took the train to Saint-Étienne, several hours away, to see a highly recommended version of *Mother Courage and Her Children* in a city otherwise known for its pollution. Once they got there, they bumped into a half dozen friends from Paris who had come to see the same play.

Brecht and his followers, or his adversaries, came up with other more-revolution-minded innovations contrived to break the mold of classic staging. Sometimes the choice of texts was merely a byway. Then, picking up the pieces of various prewar adventures, such as surrealism or Dada, the amazing theater of the absurd, with such groundbreakers as Eugene Ionesco, took the movement further and in another direction. The theater had become something like a moon shot for their generation.

Riccardo and Marisa went to the theater as easily as another generation would have gone to the movies. They went to the cinema too. Riccardo, however, continued to call it "the movies," and Marisa took care to keep him out of the way of cinema cult figures, thick on the ground, who got on his nerves. She was amused by the acidity he was capable of in the company of inflated egos. "Paris is a mecca for air balloons," he remarked one evening within earshot of several film personalities. Fortunately, they thought he was talking about critics. Marisa sighed.

They were extremely busy. She would write to the Irons, who were still taking care of her affairs in New York, "What with theaters, galleries, and movies, I barely have time to work."

The Irons, her only link with home, were happy for her, though they were still a little nervous about her marrying an Italian artist, no matter how cute he was. There was always a little silence that fell after any mention Cathy made of the Short family in her Fort Tryon Park circle, as though their sudden disappearance from their usual bench was the result of an unexplained earth tremor.

Riccardo bought season tickets to familiarize Marisa with the TNP. "Gerard Philippe," he told her, "is a miracle of grace, but don't fall in love with him, because he has a charming wife, and I would be very unhappy."

Before meeting Riccardo, Marisa had only been to the Comédie-Française on the assumption that her French was not yet good enough to appreciate a play she did not know by heart. She had seen *Richard III* at France's major national theater, however, and thought it dreadful. Instead of the sparseness the text called for, it had been overly dramatic to the point of ridicule. She had seen *A Midsummer Night's Dream* as well, and that, she'd decided, would be the last time she would endure Shakespeare in France. She told him this with her blue eyes flashing angrily.

"They have no notion of Shakespeare. They are still playing at the Hundred Years' War with the English, and they end up being ludicrous. Imagine a pint-sized humpbacked Richard leaping all over the stage, piping out in a squeaking yelp, '*Mon royaume pour un cheval.*' Come on!"

Riccardo was charmed by the ardor in her eyes and her anger at what she saw as French arrogance in theatrical matters. He had seen that production too but had found nothing particularly arrogant about it. However, cultural wars were private matters, so he kept an Italian neutrality on the subject while delighting in her fiery defense of her Anglo-Saxon realm. Thus, with a few cultural adjustments to accommodate Marisa's private wars, he booked them into most of the year's best plays.

Eventually, they were to take a little trip to Berlin not only to see the divided city and the Brandenburg Gate but also to experience the frisson one sensed in crossing over to East Berlin on the U-Bahn, the city's two-dimensional subway system, to see Brecht's Berliner Ensemble, with his wife, Helen Weigel, doing *The Resistible Rise of Arturo Ui*.

There had been a touch of visiting Lourdes and witnessing a miracle in that.

Riccardo liked actors. He enjoyed the concept of performance. He liked dancers too and made her look at ballet in a new way. He introduced her to modern dance, though she had been reluctant to even try. She saw that he took pleasure in opening her eyes to something she had hitherto not seen. In a way, he taught her how to see. Without sermonizing or talking down, he showed her what to look for. He was presenting her with a new language, as though he were opening a row of windows she had not noticed were there.

He had a few actors and a pair of Italian ballet dancers among his friends but almost no painters. Her friends had an informality about them that his did not. This puzzled her—but much about him puzzled her. She was hesitant to ask why.

Though she knew she could confide in him about everything and felt confident that nothing was beyond his understanding and tolerance, there were areas of silence on his side she dared not enter.

Riccardo was a gregarious loner, she concluded.

However, she did not put this thought into words. He was not one for labels, especially when they described him so adroitly. He was extremely private, she came to understand, despite his frequently comic behavior. He enjoyed casual company, but he enjoyed being left alone even more. He was a conundrum with tender eyes.

Marisa studied him softly and found nothing but knots of new riddles. She was content to spend the rest of her life working them out.

In late March, she discovered the perfect wedding dress on the rue Saint-Honoré, at a small but exquisite new boutique. The dress was made of lacy cotton and looked young and irreverent. The bodice had a boat neck, the waist was tight, and the billowy skirt was ankle length—a perfect New Look combination. It was formally casual, flattering to her small waist, and kind to her round hips and her height. Furthermore, it went perfectly with a pair of silver silk ballerinas she had found at Repetto's on the rue de la Paix. She was enchanted.

When she got back to the studio with her prettily wrapped purchases, Giorgio was sitting at the counter, drinking an espresso, while Riccardo was nursing a mug of Earl Grey tea. They looked like a pair of Mafiosi discussing a heist, and she giggled at the mismatched cups in their hands. *Riccardo is a closet Brit,* she thought with a giggle, *with a teacup never far from his elbow.*

She ran upstairs to hide her dress on the top shelf of the closet, telling them over her shoulder what she was doing and asking Riccardo to please not look at it, because that would be bad luck.

Giorgio let out a yelp and quickly made the sign of the cross. Just the thought of such heresy put him in shock. He got up to leave, but Riccardo stopped him and called out to her, "Hey, what would you say if we hired a bus to drive to Genoa instead of everyone going separately? There is a twelve-seater minibus going cheap. And Giorgio has a license to drive trucks, so he could drive it. Once there, we can put everyone up in one small *albergho* down the street from us. We can rent the third floor, ten rooms in all, at a reasonable price. Now, I don't want Nonno to go bankrupt on this, yet I want it to be the happiest day of his life.

"I can make a deal with Vittorio, the son of the hotel's owner and a buddy of Mario's and mine, for a reasonable price, and even if there are a dozen new strikes or maybe some leftover old ones, no one minds traveling in a bus down to la Côte d'Azur on the beautiful Nationale 7, and everyone's happy. What do you say, Marisa?"

"I say wonderful. Giorgio's Genovese jitney. It sounds like heaven."

Giorgio took his leave, telling Marisa he was doing an osso bucco that night, should they get hungry later on. He winked.

After he left, Riccardo remained standing in the middle of the room, looking unsettled. "What's wrong?" she asked.

"I don't know how to tell you things that are—what's the word?"

"Awkward?" she offered.

"Yes, of course, awkward," he said quickly.

"You look as though you are about to tell me to forget about the wedding and go get a new bikini, and we'll all go swimming instead. Is that it?" she said.

"No. Not at all. I want to take you to London tomorrow to see Laurence Olivier do *Coriolanus* and also so you can see a doctor for ladies, so you can get a diaphragm. Is that awful? God knows it's embarrassing even if it isn't awful."

He laughed self-consciously. He was blushing.

"You are so young, Carina. Do you even know what a diaphragm is?" He looked miserable when he moved over to her and put his arms around her waist, rocking her gently as if she were a child. "Everything is upside down," he said ruefully.

"The world capital of sex has to turn to the chilly Brits?" she murmured, giggling.

"Actually, so must all the other Latin lovers, not to mention every other bit of Europe where the bad-tempered Luther did not triumph. Think of it—a narrow-minded little German monk opening the way to really free love?"

She burst out laughing.

He looked desperately uncomfortable. "Have you ever seen Big Ben?" he asked. "No, silly, the clock!" he exclaimed, breaking into nervous laughter at the face she was making.

Then he toppled with her onto the couch in gales of childish giggles, all traces of embarrassment forgotten.

The next day, they took the Silver Arrow, the svelte cross-Channel train out of the better spy novels, and checked into Brown's Hotel. They saw two plays in two days. They visited one doctor, one pharmacy, and three museums, and they had lunch at a Lyons Corner House as well as dinners at Rules and the Sherlock Holmes Pub on the Strand. Marisa was overwhelmed, enchanted, and hooked on London for the rest of her life.

London had that effect on New Yorkers. Visiting London was oddly like coming home.

Riccardo knew London from visiting it with his grandfather almost as soon as the war ended, he told her. He ignored her question as to how he knew just which hospital to go to for that particular consultation.

She watched him on the steps of the National Gallery as he busily told her what paintings she must not miss. "To begin with, the Goya just by the front entrance."

She felt herself choke up at the way he was guiding her into another dimension.

He cared for her so visibly and confidently that it sometimes overwhelmed her. She listened to his instructions on how to visit the National Gallery for the first time and made a note to pay particular attention to the Goya.

Off they went, with birth control no longer a roller-coaster ride in their young lives. She wondered, however, just how often he had made these little trips to London without his grandfather leading the way.

Before leaving the gallery, she bought a reproduction of the Goya portrait Riccardo had pointed out. It was of a caballero with an amazingly male look in his eye. She wondered how to say *raunchy* in Spanish. When they got home, she put the picture in a frame and placed it on her desk. The caballero kept her company.

They took a different route back to Paris and stopped over in Dieppe to see its museum and the coastal villages that had become familiar to everyone thanks to the impressionists. It was indeed bright and blue and flecked with choppy waves in the distance, just as the painters had proclaimed it to be all those years ago.

"You know what?" Riccardo said jauntily. "I am going to learn to drive. I will ask Giorgio to teach me. And I will ask Nonno for a Topolino so we can tootle around for weekends, and I will paint Dieppe and Le Tréport and dreamy Honfleur, with all the pretty slate house fronts. I will forget about the challenge of abstraction or the essence of blue. Then you can sell my pretty paintings for me, sitting in the port of Honfleur, and we will buy shrimp from the fishing boats that come in. We will forget Paris and aesthetics and the meaning of relative values. We will have a dozen fishy bambini who will all speak Italian, and no one will ever bother us again. How do you feel about my heaven?"

If his eyes did not harbor a pool of contradictions and unanswered questions, she would have said, "Yes, now." As it was, she did say, "Yes, now," but it was only a joke, and they both knew it.

"I can't promise you an easy ride," he said, sounding exhausted.

She shook her head. "An easy ride would bore me. Besides, I knew that from the first time I looked at your aquiline nose. I knew this would be a luxury, but that didn't matter. I deserve luxury. Don't you think?"

"Oh, I do. And I only wish I could show you how much I do right this minute, my Marisa from Manhattan's top. So let us take the next train back to Paris and count our blessings."

✳✳✳

Giorgio rented the minibus for four days. They counted their friends and decided they were all a perfect match for a lunatic wedding party in Italy, while in Genoa, Mario bargained for the top floor of the hotel down the street, including breakfast in bed.

"Mario is wasted in an academic career," Don Carlo pronounced when he heard all this.

"Yes, he should have been a street peddler. He would have made a fortune, and we could have all retired," Riccardo said to the general assent of the Paris contingent. "With a sideline in picking pockets for extras," he added, a touch of sadness for paradise lost in his voice.

Apparently, the hotel owner practically gave the space away for the privilege of taking part in Don Carlo's grandson's wedding, which would surely be in all the glossy magazine pages of Europe, including *Paris Match* and *Hola*. Mario promised him the photographers would include him in the pictures, so the whole of Northern Italy would know which hotel was the region's home to the stars and who *il padrone* was in person.

Marisa had no idea of all these goings-on, but Riccardo did and was delighted. As a result, their Paris friends would go away with a thoroughly inflated notion of Italian hotel owners' sense of hospitality, and on Mario's suggestion, they all dutifully took souvenir snapshots of the hotel, with its proud owner standing by the front door, just to please him.

When Don Carlo got the bill, he was touched that the owner had given him such a generously cut-rate price, to which Mario said, "Amen."

The atmosphere was more than festive; it was like a celebration of everything worth celebrating in life: love, summer, beauty, youth, peace, stars, sun, and the unending joys of being, as well as the concept of forever.

"Marriage is the one sacrament that celebrates the notion of forever. Does it not?" Mario said. They all agreed with him. His doctor friend, Monica, seemed to wear a meaningful smile. The others looked on while a little flash of sparklers flitted through the air.

Mario? Monica? *Magari.*

The wedding took place on June 24 in the cathedral of San Lorenzo in Genoa. The beautiful altar was decorated with white roses and blue irises whose perfume mixed with the incense that lingered in most churches and prepared the senses for the miracles to come.

No one seemed to remember the British bomb that had failed to explode when it was dropped in 1941, which lay quietly embedded in the altar. As the vicar spoke about fidelity, the bride wondered whether a special Hail Mary might be included in the wedding service. She smiled at Don Carlo and would have bet he was following her thoughts.

Marisa looked like a princess even younger than her twenty-one years in her organza Parisian wedding gown. An imperious organ sounded the opening chords of

Mendelssohn's "Wedding March." Marisa, holding her breath as she caught sight of Riccardo at the altar, walked down the aisle on Don Carlo's arm till she at last reached the tall young groom.

She met his eyes with a smile he thought he recognized from his earliest dreams. Standing guard next to her, Don Carlo was proud to be giving the bride away.

Mario stood next to Riccardo at the altar. His thatch of black hair was combed just like Riccardo's. The boyish gesture of wearing their hair in the same cut went back to their earliest school days and was especially precious to them that day.

Riccardo stood straight and solemn with a serenity that was both touching and tender. His happiness was written all over his face.

Willowy Ann Wallace, in a smart, full-skirted designer Parisian gown in pale blue, made the bridal picture complete.

It was to be a wedding everyone would remember with warm pleasure for the rest of his or her life.

The reception was held in the Rinaldi house with Severina watching over logistics like an empress. She was dressed in a long burgundy velvet gown with a single string of pearls and matching earrings. She resembled one of Genoa's matriarchs, a far cry from the peasant girl from Santini that she was.

She had made Marisa welcome from the moment of her arrival, as though she had been given some secret guarantee. She prompted Marisa to think back on the colorful history of Genoa, including its aristocratic cavaliers, naval battles and military conquests, and sharp rivalry with Venice. Severina had been born and raised on a tiny, impoverished spur of land no one paid much attention to, yet as the regent of Don Carlo's household, she reigned over her charges with grace and authority as though to the manner born.

Even the genuinely aristocratic Don Carlo showed her deference on the wedding day. When he caught Marisa watching Severina preside, he said to her, almost in her ear, "Riccardo is like her own. She has been with us since he arrived in Santini in a basket. Then, when his grandmother died, she took the whole household in hand. She has been our point of sanity in a very insane world since then. And I can tell you now that she welcomed you from the first day. Really. And you can't believe how both Mario and I were relieved when we saw it."

He laughed confidentially. Marisa looked around at Don Carlo's guests and the special affection they showed for the whole Rinaldi household, which had been cruelly battered by the century's first half yet was elegantly astride in this second chapter. She could not help thinking back on her own parents, who had few friends, no relatives, and no one to share the Thanksgiving pumpkin pie with. Just as quickly, she banished the image.

Not now, she said to herself. *Not today.* Instead, she moved closer to Riccardo, who was deep in conversation with Mario about train schedules, and she said a silent prayer to whomever it was in heaven who was in charge of brides, to give thanks for this precious young man who had stepped out of the sea like the boy on the dolphin and brought her home.

There was a touch of magic in the warm June air.

Peter would have been happy for her, for them, and for himself. He would have liked Genoa and its swashbuckling Mediterranean history, which was visible in the Rinaldi house.

Riccardo turned to her, looking like a corsair under a portrait of one of his ancestors, who probably had been a corsair.

He took her arm and said, "We have to go. We are taking a plane for Greece at seven this evening. We will have dinner looking at the Acropolis, Signora Rinaldi. And tomorrow I will show you that boy and his dolphin you seem so bewitched by. Are you happy?"

"Happy? Happy?" She gasped. "But Greece? You said we were going on a cruise to Egypt," she managed to blurt. "But Greece! That is fabulous!"

"You are the one who brought fables to us. We will go and see just what this boy looks like. Perhaps I look more like the dolphin, my Marisa? Will you exchange me at the door?"

An hour later, Giorgio drove the little bus with the wedding party to the airport. The bride and groom were now elegantly turned out in brand-new summer clothes. As they pulled up to the gate, Riccardo obtained a solemn promise that no one would throw rice, confetti, or even gold coins after them. However, such promises were not necessary; they looked exactly as a bridal couple should in their smart new summer finery. Marisa glowed.

***

In Greece, they combed the beaches, visited the museums, and counted the sculptures. Marisa glowed even more when he finally had to admit that he did, in a way, have a vague resemblance to the boy on the dolphin perhaps.

She learned that the boy was called Arion.

Marisa gazed at Riccardo as they lay on a sandy beach on one of the extravagantly named little islands. He was so tan that he shimmered like a glossy ad featuring a boy lying on a Greek beach. *Perhaps even riding on a dolphin, if one was so persuaded,* she thought.

She could not believe the way he tanned.

Arion indeed.

Toward the end of July, they trickled back to Paris. They had lost count of the islands they had visited, and they'd collected a vast array of museum catalogues and photos of Penelope, Melpomene, and other Calliopes to keep their Apollos company in the studio drawers and to remind them of the uniqueness of their honeymoon in the culture of the Mediterranean.

Greece was welcoming to tourists, it was affordable, and it was beautiful in a way that made you wish you could write an ode, Riccardo observed. Or wish you were living in an age when one still wrote odes. Then they both admitted that they did not quite remember what an ode was. "Except when it is on a nightingale," Marisa said.

They both decided it was time to go home.

That took them another week, as they also decided that since they still had a little money left from Nonno's extravagant wedding present, their honeymoon, and since they were in the neighborhood, they might visit Istanbul and then take the Orient Express home to Paris. "How's that for a final curtain?" he asked, and she melted at the suggestion.

She was a serious Graham Greene fan, he remembered, recalling the time they'd browsed London bookstores, where she'd bought a half dozen paperbacks.

He gazed at the pleasure in her face when they boarded the train and entered their little sleeping compartment, ushered in by a smartly uniformed attendant. Her eyes danced as they dined elegantly in the fabled dining car, and the food was excellent.

They failed to hear any murders in the night, but they were not really listening.

It was a honeymoon worthy of Don Carlo's dearest wishes. "What better way to face the rigors of holy wedded matrimony than dolphin hunting on the Greek islands?" Don Carlo had written on the card that accompanied his check.

How right he was.

***

"Welcome to forever," Riccardo said as they went through the door to the living room on the rue Mouffetard.

It was the first week of August 1950. The Korean War had begun the day after their wedding, on June 25. Marisa did her best to pretend she had not seen the headlines in the *Herald Tribune* on all the newsstands in Greece.

Though the radio job she had waiting for her in Paris would not be overly affected by this particular horror story, there might be a tremor or two in European politics as a result of it, she imagined. However, when she phoned Milo Hynes on June 26, he told her to concentrate on her honeymoon and come back rested and ready. "On our turf, no one is going to get excited till autumn. Not till September," he reminded her. "Enjoy yourselves, and take pictures to show me," he added.

Six weeks of hostilities in Korea demonstrated that the conflict was not going to be just a skirmish. On the contrary, a giant step had been taken, and the ripples were felt on a worldwide scale. The Cold War was all over the board now, and there wasn't a rule book in sight.

"Welcome to forever," Riccardo said as they entered the house in Paris. He drew the line at carrying her over the threshold, though. She went into the living room and saw with surprise that Giorgio and Anna had not only kept an eye on it in their absence but also left fresh flowers waiting for them. Upstairs near their bed, they found a bouquet of red and white carnations, while on the roof, all the plants had been freshly watered. The terrace looked like a corner of Genoa, she thought, with a bottle of white wine in a cooler and a tray of glasses waiting for them.

Riccardo looked around with a touch of wonder at how much loving care Giorgio and his wife had lavished on them.

It was Giorgio who had suggested buying the shoe repair shop to turn it into a studio for him, and it was he who'd negotiated the sale, price setting included.

"And I can keep an eye on him," he had said to Don Carlo when he suggested the house as a place for Riccardo after his return from New York.

It was clear that the boy should go farther than Genoa to work and live without his grandfather's shadow. He needed to be on his own, to find his way in the arduous scene he had chosen. Don Carlo knew that Riccardo, above all orphans, had to find his own path, but he also feared the burden his gifts meant for him. Riccardo was fragile. Living in Paris would strengthen him. If he lived a few hundred yards away from Giorgio, that would be a giant step forward. *Non e vero?* Don Carlo thought. *And who would find anything wrong with that?*

A few months after Riccardo returned from New York a little bit thinner and even nervier than before, Giorgio brought up the subject of a house in the Latin Quarter that would make a great studio. His suggestion worked.

"Paris is only a night's train ride away from our doorstep," Don Carlo pointed out to everyone's satisfaction. Furthermore, the price was reasonable. Riccardo assumed he was being set up, but he could not find any reasonable objection, so he sat back and let himself be disposed of. He thanked his grandfather silently; a small smile said it all. Giorgio and Anna had seldom been happier.

That had been three years ago. The plumber next door had gotten older. When Giorgio had prodded him about selling, he'd grumbled a little but answered with a gruff no.

"Maybe next year," he had muttered to Giorgio sometime before the wedding, "but what's the rush? Your artist is still young, and so is the pretty new model. *On verra.*"

Then he'd beamed his toothless grin at Giorgio, enjoying the situation. Giorgio had offered him dinner on the house for two before leaving for Genoa and the wedding, but the old man had said he would come alone and eat twice instead, if Giorgio didn't mind. Giorgio had agreed, thinking it would take all the ruse of Genoa to beat a wily Auvergnat who had come from a cluster of volcanoes in the middle of France and had known how to bargain before he could walk. Giorgio had nodded, giving in.

All in good time. We are just beginning after all, he'd thought.

***

Riccardo watched Marisa as she was unpacking. There seemed to be no order in what she was doing; she just took things out of her suitcase and shoved them into little piles. Bras, panties, mismatched two-piece bathing suits, and socks were piled next to heaps of postcards, maps, rolled-up posters of boys on dolphins she'd collected, and one splendid panoramic view of Istanbul. He shook his head at the traces of the teenager she must have been not all that long ago.

Her age, though not that different from his own, still seemed to him vitally important in knowing who Marisa was. She was young, trusting, and vulnerable. He loved her with all his being, perhaps because of the charge she was to him. Her vulnerability was his responsibility. He saw that, and he also saw that she did not see it. She would have been indignant if he told her so. He did not tell her. He enjoyed the responsibility, and he assumed it.

"You know how I knew which hospital to go to in London?" he asked out of the blue. She looked at him sharply.

"It was for Anna," he said. "She has not been able to have a baby. There was a specialist there who was supposed to work miracles. Nonno arranged for them to have an appointment, and I went with them for my English. Unfortunately, the doctor could not make their particular miracle."

He looked over at her and said, "I want you to know that. Also, about something else. You have come from no family at all straight into a big Italian family in one jump. You know? You jumped into a whole bunch of curious people who lived on a little island no one ever heard of till Nonno was exiled there. And then, around him, the islanders became my family. Otherwise, I would have none, except for some faraway Milanese Rinaldis or the Corsos no one likes in Florence. However, I do have Mario and his tribe. They are my family, and they will be there for you too now. Now and forever. Can you understand that kind of feeling, Marisa of Fort Tryon Park? Especially now that you know how I've come to have such interesting addresses in London?"

She felt abashed about Anna and the London address yet couldn't see why he had not told her right away. She just shook her head and murmured that she was learning. "I am also learning how to accept that you had a life before the Flore, and that is hard to get into my head, because I didn't. I had no life before you, my handsome Arion, so I have no guidelines. I don't know who to be jealous of, so

I am jealous of everyone, and I mean everyone—everyone you say hello to. So it is hard for me to channel things." She moved toward him and put her hand on his hair as though to comb it. "I know you think that fidelity is relative, but I don't. Not relative at all. So I am world-scale jealous in several languages and tenses—past, present, and future."

He had removed her hand but held it as he bent forward laughing.

She suddenly lurched at him, hissing, "Like a pussycat with tiger's claws."

He ducked in time, and she flopped onto the bed, still laughing as she lost his hand in her fall. Suddenly, the front doorbell sounded shrilly, and Riccardo stopped midcatch. The doorbell was piercing. Reluctantly, he went downstairs to find Anna standing there with a tray of goodies in case they were too hungry to wait for dinner. "Welcome home, *amore mio*," she said with a huge, guileless smile. "We missed you."

***

The first Paris transport strikes of the season came just two weeks after Marisa started her job at WWR. She settled in smoothly thanks to Milo's good-natured patience in showing her how to go about things. She wrote her first story, for example, as though it were for a newspaper. However, WWR was a radio, not a newspaper. It demanded another rhythm and cadence. Milo showed her how to catch that cadence, and she learned quickly. She had a good ear and an attractive voice that hit the microphone softly with a cadence made to be listened to. It was a knack. She had it.

Milo was delighted, for he had caught a trace of it when they'd first chatted at the Crillon Bar. "Radio people make up a sort of private fraternity among the press, and it pleases a veteran to discover a rookie," Milo told her later on. "Then comes the test of time," he added ominously. She only understood what he'd meant when the transport strike season opened. They then had to do everything but sprout wings to get to the microphone on time.

A few minutes here or there meant nothing to the world of print. A few seconds meant everything to the world of radio, however. She caught on to this fact instantly. From then on, she was always early.

Milo breathed freely. He could trust her. That was all he needed.

Milo lived with his French wife in Montmartre, north of the opera, where the office was located, and he could, if pushed, walk to the office. He had a car and did not mind driving. What he minded was parking in a corner of Paris that had no parking for miles around. Coverage of his garage bills had been written into his contract.

He claimed that Paris metro strikes were enacted for the sole purpose of keeping his weight down, because he walked back and forth to the office during strikes. Mademoiselle Boileau, the ageless secretary who had been there since the mid-1930s with only a slight leave of absence during the German occupation and who showed no sign of retiring now, lived within walking distance down the Boulevard des Italiens. The radio engineer, improbably named Casimir, lived in the suburbs but came in and out of the city on a Vespa, so he did not suffer anything more than traffic jams, which were bad enough for a radio technician.

Marisa did not drive—not yet at least. Learning to drive was on her agenda, but for the time being, Giorgio drove her to the office at the opera during strikes. However, his schedule in the restaurant wouldn't permit him to fetch her in the evenings, so she scrambled for cabs. One day she happened on someone she knew at AFP, the French news agency, located not far off at la Bourse, who lived near her and who could drop her at the Luxembourg Gardens. Her acquaintance was pleased to help.

"Strikes are handy for making friends," Penny, the young AFP reporter, told her, amused. "I have a friend who met her husband when a flight from London got held up, and they started grumbling together on a bus that took them back into the city. They ended up taking the train and ferry the next day, and the rest is history. She claims strikes are social lubricants, which is one way of looking at it."

As Penny was talking, Marisa had a curious sense of déjà vu, a faint recollection of that phrase, "social lubricant," used in the same or a similar way. However, the traffic snarls broke into her hazy recollections, and she was soon concentrating on Penny's skills in skimming through traffic against a background of frenetic Parisian car horns.

Marisa had been talking about taking driving lessons, but no one around the Shoe House paid much attention. She ran into an unexpected case of Italian prejudice in Riccardo's quaint notions about female drivers—and Giorgio's too. "*Ma, non e vero,*" they would protest while generations of Genovese elders in their genes danced at the same time.

"You know that is not so," Riccardo said.

She laughed to herself. *The hell I do.* She made a mental note to look into driving schools.

Then she thought that the experience of a young American woman learning to drive in Paris might make a good feature story, with a couple of side swipes at male domination of the steering wheel—or the throttle, more aptly.

Meanwhile, the usual strikes and a few juicy sex scandals seemed to hit several Parisian social strata at once. That, plus the government's game of cabinet ministers' musical chairs, kept her busy. All were part of the season—*la rentrée,* as it was called in France.

The whole country had gone away on vacation in August, especially the revolving doorkeepers of the cabinet.

That September, Marisa wondered how the cast of politicians managed to absorb the intricacies of each ministry they took over and ran expertly, though perhaps only for a short sprint, with such versatility.

They didn't.

It was the ironclad coded class of French civil servants, products of highly competitive universities called les Grandes Écoles, who did. The graduates of these specialized, selective schools provided the mind-set of French government architects. The ministers who played musical chairs just signed along dotted lines. The others were the caste that made France run, except possibly the present minister of the interior, a supercop with a nervous trigger finger and springs under his shoes who bounced back smartly as governments came and went while he stayed on.

The incumbent was a rigid, unsmiling man who looked as though he might enjoy setting his dogs on strikers or students demanding this or that as the country painfully righted itself after the war's end not long ago.

Marisa disliked him. Milo had given her three questions to ask him at a press conference he was giving on student protest marches that the police had quelled brutally. There had been several.

Marisa's friends François and Jeff had been involved in a scuffle just in front of the Café Flore. Out of nowhere, three Algerian youths had come running up the boulevard with a half dozen uniformed cops at their tails. A bloody though brief skirmish had taken place, upsetting the tables in front of the café. François's eyeglasses had been knocked off his face by a uniformed cop who promptly crushed them with his heel.

François, who was tall, thin, and the image of the frail intellectual, had been rescued from disaster by a hefty stranger who stepped in, towering over the cop. The stranger had pulled a much-shaken François into the café, where Jeff had gone to pay the bill only minutes before. Together they'd gotten him upstairs to the men's room to clean up his face. The café would not be a friendly site, so the police had just given a cursory look inside before moving on. It had been an ugly moment, but it could have been worse.

That was the sort of incident the incumbent minister of the interior let happen on his watch. Marisa found him detestable not only for what he let his cops get away with but also for what he encouraged. Raids on Algerian neighborhoods, called *ratonades*, or rat chasing, were becoming commonplace.

There was a racial divide she found unacceptable growing increasingly visible all over France. The long and vicious Algerian War was already a reality.

These incidents had become a minor scandal, but once the dust settled, everyone but Marisa forgot them. The tension remained in Marisa's mind, centering on that particular politician, who was to remain in varying cabinets for the ensuing decade. He recognized her in press briefings from then on and made it a point to never reply to any questions she might put forth. On the other hand, Marisa could show off to the other journalists that she had just begun and already had her own personal enemy—a permanent musical chairs player at that.

At Harry's Bar afterward, Milo raised his glass to her and called out into the crowd, "A star is born!"

Politicians had waterproof egos, she learned in her first season. However, radio reporting had an extra little satisfaction wherein the reporter could pop an unexpected query, a destabilizer. No public figure liked to appear to be stuttering over an answer to a trick question, of course. In radio, there had to be some sort of answer, because silence was a main enemy, and the answer had to come quickly. Radio was one moment of truth.

Politicians hated to be maneuvered into a corner, while reporters tried to become experts at such maneuvering. Milo noted that Marisa picked up on the technique from day one. Indeed, on their first day out, she directed an impromptu question to the newly appointed minister of the interior, the one she did not like, outside Parliament. She darted a look at her boss and caught his approving eye. She then shot out a request to the minister to define his position on Algerian independence: "Decolonization—yes or no?"

The minister, who had been expecting to talk about Indochina, was too slow to field her question. He turned his head to block her from his field of vision, but Marisa moved sideways, knowing she was still in the TV cameras' ranges.

"One or the other, *M. le Ministre*," she insisted in a polite voice. He continued to ignore her, and she added, "*Pour la radio, M. le Ministre*, a few words for World Wide Radio."

Shooting her a look of surprised outrage, he turned his back on her and addressed another reporter instead.

"The minister is leaving the question open, it seems. He is now on his way into Paris's strike-bound traffic jam that is paralyzing the city's center. This is Marisa Rinaldi for WWR."

She looked calm but was trembling inside. She had flustered a government minister. She knew he would remember this run-in, but so would everyone else on the sidewalk. So would her peers.

When it was over, she wondered where she had found the nerve to do it. Marisa looked at Miles apprehensively. He was beaming at her as though he had invented her himself.

"That was what I might call an exercise in artful dodging," Milo proclaimed, beaming.

"Using the mike is an art," he told her later. "You either know how or you don't. You do. I am a happy man." He sighed. "Now I can go fishing on Mondays instead of having to come home in the traffic on Sunday night."

Milo had a thatched cottage in Normandy. He did not want to retire; he just wanted to stretch the weekends a little and to be able to take off a week or two here and there when the fancy took him. He just wanted a change of pace.

General MacArthur had recently made history with his "Old soldiers never die; they just fade away" quotable conclusion to his career. Milo appropriated it, adding the proviso of a trout at the end of the week, on Saturdays, in a secret little river near Honfleur.

Marisa was the answer to his old age, he told others while at the Crillon Bar, making them see the pretty young novice with warm affection.

A few of them were a tad disappointed to hear that she had just married an Italian painter with connections.

Marisa took to her job with enthusiasm and a touch of trepidation. Her French was passable, though she constantly mixed up the feminine and masculine. "Most English speakers have problems with the sex of words," Don Carlo had said to console her in Genoa when she tripped over a half dozen wrong genders in one attempt at a conversation in Italian. She was resigned to corrections.

After her three-month trial period at WWR, she signed a contract for a permanent job. The only rabbit Milo could not pull out of his hat was her salary. She was hired abroad; therefore, she received a European salary, not the American equivalent, which was at least its double.

She had known that at the beginning, and she also knew there was not much she could do about it for the moment. She was certain that eventually, Milo would get the bookkeepers in the New York office to change their minds. In the meantime, he never let her pay for a drink and put her on a flexible expense account. He knew all about money and the lack of it, and he thought that these kids, as he thought of Marisa and Riccardo, needed a break.

Milo should have had a brood of children. Instead, he had found Marisa, and he had every intention of keeping her.

"Not to worry," she said to Riccardo after her first month's paycheck came into her account at Morgan's Bank on the Place Vendôme. "I'll make it up with all these amazing French health insurance benefits—free medical care, the dreaded dentist, and maternity leave. It even covers you," she said. They were sitting in the living room, where she was reading the small print that came with her contract.

He raised an eyebrow and said pensively, "Would I have a cesarean, do you suppose?"

He had come down from the studio and exchanged his working shirt for a warm turtleneck sweater. He looked edgy and distracted. "Come on. Let's go for a walk first," he said, stretching out his hand to yank her up from the couch. "And you know what? We haven't had a drink at the Contrescarpe in ages."

He fetched their coats. Oddly, almost uncomfortably, for the first time, he actually felt married. It was an uncommon sensation, he realized, and it was a little disquieting. Nothing had changed, yet everything had changed.

But it was not only delayed reaction today. There was a reason for it—like steps on a ladder.

He locked the front door absentmindedly.

"Watch out," she cautioned, pointing to a puddle.

"It's too late," he said with a sigh, and he took her elbow to cross the street. Then he rectified his remark and said, "Or maybe too soon."

At the café, seated on the heated terrace, he ordered a half bottle of champagne. Marisa turned to stare at him, as he had anticipated she would.

"I have a secret," he said, letting his eyes play over her concerned face.

Once again, she marveled at the mobility of his features. He was distracted by the scene going on in the middle of the square opposite them, where three clochards were making themselves comfortable for the winter night under the leafless trees, close by a fountain in the middle of the square.

It was a nightly ritual he had observed with interest and a touch of horror since his arrival in Paris almost four years ago.

The landscape of survival, he thought with a shudder. At length, he turned to Marisa and took a deep breath. "What would you say if I told you I am going to have a show?"

She opened her eyes wide, astonished. She stared at him, noticing that he seemed relaxed, even at peace. He waited quietly for her to answer. A smile was slowly coming into his eyes as he tasted her surprise.

"I would say that's wonderful. Absolutely wonderful. But where? Here or Genoa?" she said, searching his smile for clues.

"Oh, here. Right here even. Rue de Seine. At the Galérie des Deux Mondes. Remember?"

Of course she remembered. It was a new gallery owned by an art dealer whose father had had galleries in Berlin and London before the war. Helmut Mundt, the father, had worked with the surrealists in the 1920s in Paris and shown their work in Berlin, thus making a name for himself as an international figure. He'd immigrated to New York in the mid-1930s, in time to salvage his collection and his good name, for he was one of the first non-Jewish German art dealers who chose to leave. With his young son, Robert, he'd established himself in New York in 1936, his collection of contemporary European art as well as his reputation intact.

As an early anti-Fascist, he had met Don Carlo in European intellectual circles. As a matter of routine, he'd put Riccardo on their first mailing list in Paris. The son had just opened a new gallery on the Left Bank, showing their stable of well-established artists on new and handsome premises.

"It looks more like an investment than a gamble," Riccardo said tartly as they came up to its windows, which were open to a crowded social scene, on the night of the vernissage.

As soon as they walked in, Marisa noted that Riccardo was wearing his best icy frown. She half expected him to turn around and leave, but he just muttered.

"All big, old names. No one under the age of a hundred. *Andiamo*," he muttered, turning toward the door.

She said, "No, let's see the paintings first—so we can be sure we don't like absolutely everyone." She pulled him toward a delightful bunch of squiggles done by one of her favorite painters, Joan Miro, a Catalan semisurrealist who lived in Barcelona.

Riccardo continued to mutter about the social register mailing lists. "These are the wind-up social register people, who might be more at home in the Deauville Casino than in art galleries showing Miro or Arp," he growled, still scowling. She wondered what he knew of the Deauville Casino as she watched him sulk through the cleverly lit space and graze mink as he tried to get close to a painting by Otto Dix.

She put out an arm to avoid a collision. Then, to his surprise, a man who turned out to be Robert Mundt recognized him and held out his hand in greeting. Riccardo was taken aback, but Mundt was saying amiably that they had met at a show in London when he was with his grandfather a few years ago.

Riccardo tried to squirm out of his embarrassment but not before realizing that he had missed whole sentences of what Mundt had said. He had been cordially telling

Riccardo that he had seen two of his paintings at a show of contemporary Italian artists in Milan not long after their meeting and had admired them. "I am glad to see that you received the invitation for tonight," Mundt added.

Riccardo tried to not melt into a puddle of shame. He had completely forgotten the two canvases he had sent to Milan. *They must be there still with the gallery,* he realized. He had forgotten the whole episode. He had meant to ask Mario to go pick them up for him.

Riccardo closed his eyes, blinking in embarrassment. *How could I have forgotten that?* he thought, astonished at such irresponsibility. The gallery in Milan was reputable, and he had been pleased at their inclusion of him in what he thought was a prestigious show at the time.

At the time. That would have been just when he'd met Marisa. *Of course!* He had forgotten everything beyond the color of her hair and what had happened to him with her. He stood there feeling like an ass, half contrite at having seemed surly to the amiable Mundt, who was still talking— and he was still not listening. To fill the gap, he mumbled something polite about the quality of Mundt's choice of artists in this show.

"But we are looking for new postwar painters too. And I would like to see more of your work," Mundt said. Riccardo, still climbing back to the surface, took his words in quietly. He nodded and gave what he hoped was a sensible show of interest.

"We are launching our gallery in Paris with this show on purpose," Mundt said. "The next show will be with today's young artists, not yesterday's. I am interested in where those two canvases of yours I saw in Milan might be taking you, and I would like to come visit your studio to see the rest of your work. Perhaps we can talk?"

Riccardo nodded and mumbled something polite, albeit clumsily. He even managed to thank him for his interest.

Riccardo and Marisa then moved on, leaving the dapper dealer to fade back into the mink lining of a fashionable opening night in Paris.

Once they were outside, Marisa assured him he had not shown confusion. *Nor did he show signs of soaring spirits either,* she thought to herself. He seemed politely pleased, albeit at a distance.

"I don't know how you manage that aloofness," she said.

Marisa had been watching wordlessly and marveling at him.

Later, he would tell her that he had learned that behavior when he left the island and arrived at a real school in Genoa for the first time—a proper school in proper Italian, not the island dialect that was his native tongue. He'd learned to stand silently and breathe evenly, giving nothing away. He'd learned how not to apologize.

"It's my secret weapon," he whispered confidentially into her ear, brushing away her hair. She realized then that he had just confided in her, telling her something precious. He had given her his only key.

They were walking through the gallery, when he stopped in front of a painting and, next to it, three small lithographs by Max Bill, a painter Riccardo prized. Max Bill had a strong reputation throughout the art world, with the possible exception of Paris. He was the antithesis of a surrealist. His work was spare, bereft of frills, distractions, and, especially, messages. Riccardo felt at home in Max Bill's work, at home in its naked strength. It spoke to his own search to pare down all but the essentials in a painting, concentrating on color and form as substance—what Marisa called the perfect straight line.

Later, on the café terrace, Marisa looked at Riccardo's face, waiting for an explanation. She remembered his reaction to the show, but she had no idea that Mundt had come to the studio afterward to see his work. With an effort, she refrained from asking him why he had said nothing about how he felt about showing his work to a man who could change their lives, his life especially.

She respected his reticence but only up to a point.

Riccardo's reluctance to have a show was complex. It brought into play the many sides that made up the whole Riccardo—sides that he did not share with her or, for that matter, anyone else, not even his grandfather, she guessed.

She glanced up at him, half adoringly and half appraisingly. What had changed? What had convinced him to show the work he had accumulated over the past years in Paris, work that she knew he often questioned? Why did he feel sure of it now?

She scanned his face in the soft café light; it was relaxed and almost boyish. Then, in a quick reversal, she decided not to ask him.

At least she would not ask him outright. She was stirring the question around in her mind, looking for a way to phrase it, when he said, "Are you wondering what made me decide?" Astonished, she nodded, not trusting her voice. She almost felt like laughing.

"Well, I just looked around and thought, *Perque non a la primavera? Per mi, per te, per noi.* I could have the kind of show I would like to have in that gallery, the kind of show that I should be able to have—on my own. Does that make sense to you?"

Then he frowned and looked at her seriously. "What I am doing is one step in a long road. But it is a serious step in itself. It can stand on its own. I am sure of what I am doing now. So?"

In the slight pause that followed, he began to tease her, to reach out for her to make sure she was still there. "So? Will you come to the opening?"

He was suddenly relaxed again, playing on his own personal roller coaster, refreshed, young, and sure of what he saw ahead. He picked up her glass, gave it to her, and then took his own.

"Champagne?" he said, clinking glasses. "Mrs. Rinaldi of the tip of Manhattan? Tell Milo you will need the day off."

They drank the champagne. "*A domani*. To tomorrow and to you," he said. Then he sat back in his chair heavily, as though he had gotten rid of a huge burden and was suddenly tired, as if the words had exhausted him.

In the silence, he appeared to be searching out the clochards across the street. He found them beyond the circle of light from the lamppost in the middle of the square. They were curled up on beds of cardboard and layers of newspapers, covered in rags for blankets, already deep into their own night.

Marisa noticed how he looked at the clochards, Paris's coddled dropout class, figures of affection for the most part. She saw no affection in his eyes, only disgust.

"Why do you look at them like that? Everyone loves the picturesque clochards," she said.

"No, not picturesque. They make life look disgusting. Like there would be no room for trying? Or for working? They make living into not having a meaning. Worthless," he said almost angrily.

He started to rise as though to leave, but then he noticed she had not finished her champagne. She tried to hold his glance, but he turned his head and sat down again, his shoulders still taut.

He was waiting for her because he was polite, not because he wanted to stay. She finished the wine and made moves to leave, gathering her cigarettes, scarf, and gloves, and then she rose, making noise with the chair.

He rose too but did so silently, stiff under his navy jacket, his hands shoved into the pockets and his expression closed. They walked up the market street briskly. Marisa watched his closed face.

He seemed to view the street as a cemetery for dead appetites, with its cabbage leaves, celery stalks, and crusts of baguette that would be the morning's banquet for the pigeons. The streets looked derelict perhaps, but all city streets might look derelict under dim streetlamps on a moonless winter night.

"You are not fair," she said to him, her voice stern. He kept walking for a bit, but she soon saw the anger begin to drain slowly from his shoulders.

By the time they reached the top of the hill, he was calm again, and his strides relaxed. She turned to look at him under the corner lamppost. Shaking her head, she said gently, "I will never understand you, you know."

He laughed lightly and shook his head. "Thank God," he said with a sigh.

The local alley cat sauntered down in front of their open door, casting a passing glance inside. He looked around and sniffed, as he usually did, but seconds later, he moved on. Riccardo gave a deep bow and doffed an invisible hat to him. Then he said out loud, "Never mind, Commendatore. Come back when you have more time."

***

By mid-November, a year from their first meeting at the Flore, which they celebrated lovingly like a pair of truants, she was happily snuggled into her routine at work. Her time at the office left Riccardo undisturbed for the entire day, which was vital to him, she realized.

She knew he loved her, but she also knew that his own tenuous peace of mind depended as much on his work as it did on her. *In that order,* she would tell herself with a funny half smile. She arranged her office hours to be from nine to five with a relatively short lunch break.

French lunches would eventually pare themselves down to a more European standard, but the early 1950s was still a period of tradition, and most Frenchmen still took two hours for lunch as a matter of divine right.

Offices still closed down at noon and did not reopen till two o'clock. That included most shops and even pharmacies. *Have a headache at noon, and pass out by two, unless you are near a major crossroads,* she thought. She discovered that early on. Paris had its social codes for everything. Rigidity, she learned, was a many-layered concept.

Along with her life at the radio and her new ease with the sound of her own voice, she kept close to her pre-Riccardo life. Her buddies from the Cité Universitaire were comforting mainstays. She enjoyed their company, their warmth to her, and their affection for Riccardo.

Jeff offered to take pictures of Riccardo's paintings, saying he wanted to learn how to render a painting visible as such in a photo. That might well have been his intention, but Riccardo thought he might have another motive aside from doing him a favor, because it was an expensive proposition, having good pictures done of paintings.

Jeff spent months coming by for an afternoon; setting up lights and sheets for shading; and adjusting cumbersome apparatuses to catch the grain, texture, and essence of the painting. Riccardo was amazed at how well the pictures came out and how alive the paintings looked.

They talked about doing a book. "A slim volume," Jeff said enthusiastically, and he kept his eye out for a publisher.

After their photo shoots, they would go to Giorgio's for dinner, and Marisa was in heaven. Jeff and François had been her first friends in Paris, and she treasured them. She could talk to Jeff about the ambiguity she felt in living abroad and the shadings of reluctance in losing New York, because he had the same nagging reservations she did. Losing one's roots was not a painless process, and the individual was always a foreigner abroad.

They also laughed at themselves, admitting that brats more pampered than they were would be hard to find. François would be getting his degree from la rue d'Ulm next year and was unsure what would follow. He would have to choose between teaching in the provinces and finding a job in publishing, perhaps as an editor. He was twenty-five and knew he was the luckiest lad in town with choices like that, yet he was terrified of making the wrong one.

Marisa leaned on both young men for their warmth in taking care of her. Jeff and François were her surrogate brothers, she claimed.

Ann Wallace agreed, for it was she who had introduced them to Marisa at the Cité Universitaire to begin with. She was only sorry Jeff preferred François to her.

"We are one happy disjointed family," she said, "and the Café Flore is our chapel."

François and Jeff had also left the American house at the Cité Universitaire and had found an apartment in the Marais, a huge floor-through that had once been an atelier for a theatrical costume designer.

Floor-to-ceiling mirrors dotted the space. They kept them there, which gave the apartment a touch of infinity, as if it defied measurements. They often found pins and needles in between the floorboards, plus an assortment of tiny beads and sequins in the window frames and behind the radiators. They kept a huge antique hooded sewing machine as their hall table, with a vintage telephone on it.

Le Marais was soon to become one of Paris's most fashionable corners, for which they took credit.

Marisa felt ready for new friends, however, in her not-quite-assimilated persona of a young married woman. She reached out to Penny Horak, the friend who offered her rides to and from midtown Paris during the sporadic transport strikes. She was another American married to a European and living in a third country.

"Yet another perfect stranger," as she put it. Penny was on the English desk at Agence France Presse. She came from Fort Lee, New Jersey, and had gone to NYU a few years before Marisa. She was also warm and had a quick sense of humor.

Marisa did not know much about her except that she was married to an architect, and from what she'd said of him on their rides through traffic-snarled Paris on strike-bound days, he sounded amusing and intriguing.

He was Czech but had been in Paris since before the Communist takeover. He had come to Paris in 1946 on a scholarship to study architecture, and he was a French citizen by now.

He was a little older than Penny, Marisa gathered, and attractive to women, because one of Penny's favorite topics of conversation was the conundrum of the other woman when one was a working wife. They had a five-year-old little boy and an au pair girl who spoke Czech to him.

"Vladek says he might have lost his passport but not his country, and his son might live in Paris, but he is Czech, and that is a reality not to be tampered with."

Marisa was impressed by that and amused at the way Penny approached the whole question of marriage in Paris's café-sitting classes. She was cool about it all, almost as though she were merely an onlooker.

She was the opposite of Marisa, who was worried about dual allegiances or no allegiances at all in the case of these international children, who would grow up speaking three languages and have a novel notion of identity.

Penny's answer to that was a cool glance at her and advice not to anticipate pitfalls that might not be there.

Marisa admired her cool just as she admired the way she drove through Paris in a mad general strike, when even the traffic cops were known to run for cover.

They arranged a dinner for the following week at the Rinaldi Shoe House.

Riccardo promptly forgot all about it and kept working according to his own body clock. Since he was working seriously, she did not want to push him.

However, a night's table conversation with new faces could only be good for him, she decided with Giorgio, who would be bringing the dinner over around seven thirty. She would only have to heat it gently in the oven before serving it.

It would be their first real dinner party since their marriage. She phoned Riccardo as she was leaving the office and reminded him, in case he had forgotten. "Of course not. You reminded me this morning. And Giorgio has already set the table and brought over enough antipasti for a peace conference. Who is coming—Marlene Dietrich?"

Riccardo teased her, but he was touched by Marisa's concern, and he realized that however casual she might try to make it, this evening was a rite of passage. She was giving their first dinner party. He found her excitement touching.

As soon as he saw Penny, however, he recognized her as a face from the crowded corners of somewhere else. He hesitated as they were shaking hands in the doorway, but there seemed to be no recognition in her eyes, so he said nothing.

In any case, her husband took over the conversation once he had seen the paintings on the living room wall, and he maneuvered Riccardo into showing him the studio before sitting down to dinner.

Riccardo hesitated but agreed as long as it did nothing to disturb the food arrangements, because, he explained, Anna's cooking came first.

They made a short tour of the paintings that were visible in the studio without pushing canvases aside. Vladek was clearly interested and asked just the right questions.

Penny and Marisa remained downstairs to look around the charming ex-shoemaker's shop. Penny gave a delighted giggle over the sling chairs, and Marisa told her that Riccardo had lived in New York before Paris. "On Bleeker Street, oddly enough."

"He did?" Penny murmured. "And he read his issues of the *New Yorker* at the Rienzi, I'd bet?" Penny said, now smiling in a different key.

Something had clicked. Marisa saw it in Penny's eyes. *A flash of recognition?* She let it go. *Let's see what happens,*

Marisa told herself. However, she instantly set herself a limit as to how far she would push curiosity.

She promised silently not to embarrass Riccardo.

The Rienzi was now a long way away after all.

The two men came down from the studio. Vladek saying that he was already looking forward to the upcoming show because he liked what he had seen upstairs.

He was a tallish man, squarely built; was about forty-five; was dressed smartly in a blazer and slacks; and had the kind of blue eyes that twinkled in different lights. Marisa saw what had attracted Penny, and she could also see that Vladek was a born flirt. He couldn't help it, she thought. His eyes did it for him.

Yet when he looked at his younger American wife, those same eyes seemed to reflect a tenderness that probably made up for the rest.

She was tempted to tell Penny to relax, as her husband was a prince. *A Danube prince no doubt, but who can quibble, especially if you come from darkest New Jersey yourself?*

Marisa turned to Penny, who was standing by the bookcase, talking to both men comfortably. She was saying something about New York painters, when she stopped short and took another look at Riccardo. She hesitated and then said, "We've met before. It's Rick, isn't it?"

Vladek raised an eyebrow. There was a silence that seemingly turned a single second into an hour. "No, it is

Riccardo, if you don't mind. And yes, I believe we have met before. Some time ago. In New York."

No one breathed for another eternity till Marisa said, "And now that we know each other's names, shall we have dinner? It is not my cooking, you will be happy to hear. The food was made by Riccardo's guardian angels, who have a restaurant down the block and feed us royally."

Riccardo had known before Penny arrived that Marisa's new friend was from New York and had gone to NYU, but he had not thought much more about it. The entire student body of NYU had not hung around the Rienzi during the one year he had, of course, and not all of them would have noticed him or Marla. It was a busy café, and he recalled that the lights were generously low.

He had thought no more about it till he saw Penny come in the door. Then his heart had dropped. She was one of a handful of pretty girls he had not talked to but with whom he'd exchanged flirty little silent smiles across the tables during the time he'd lived around the corner.

It had been nothing more, but she would have known about Marla. She would have seen them together and would have guessed. He and Marla had made a couple one noticed—he knew that, of course. Marla was older but beautiful and had presence. And he was younger, among other things.

Now he was half angry and half embarrassed at the triteness of the situation. He was also pained for Marisa.

He knew that Marisa had found a special friend in Penny, because she knew the same New York that Marisa clearly missed. Penny knew the right movie houses, where to buy smart clothes at slashed prices in Brooklyn, and where to eat in Chinatown.

This was awkward.

Riccardo leaned back and said casually, addressing all of them, "I think Penny and I must have brushed tables in the Village some time ago. And perhaps even knew the same interesting person, Marla Hitchens."

He said it lightly, but Marisa caught the weight of every word. She froze.

Penny joined in adroitly, invoking other Village landmarks, such as the Cedars Bar, which was by then a cult center for the likes of Jackson Pollack and Mark Rothko.

"And everyone else on the first floor of the Museum of Modern Art," Vladek said, cleverly dismissing the entire subject and helping himself to cucumbers and artichoke hearts.

Gotcha! Marisa thought, darting a look at Riccardo. He was nibbling grissini, looking as unreadable as her favorite Greek dolphin boy. *At last, I have a name for one of your slinky ghosts,* she said to him silently.

Up till then, she had taken the situation playfully, but when she looked at him now, she suddenly sensed that it had been a little more than what he'd said.

In a flash, she regretted the whole episode, for he did not look as though he could handle a massive upset.

Finally, Riccardo looked over at her from a vast distance and made himself smile. Voices echoed across the table while the pickled mushrooms performed miracles of social arbitration. Anna's superb cooking calmed the seas. He sought out Marisa's gaze softly. She smiled back at him, offering a touch of balm. She took a grissino from the plate next to his hand. She grazed his finger—in forgiveness perhaps.

It was that kind of evening. Absolution for the past was in the sauce.

Vladek silently opened his heart to both Rinaldis. He was just old enough to treasure their youth and silently wish them joy. He was perhaps a tad jealous of Riccardo, he admitted to himself, not only for his gift in painting and for his delightful wife but also for whoever the woman in New York might have been, because her absence alone made her sound devastating. Vladek admired women of substance, particularly in their absence. He also felt sorry for the young couple and directed the conversation toward milder regions—the Cold War, for instance.

The conversation stayed on other topics for the rest of the evening.

After a pleasant few hours of discussing theater, atomic-age morality, the end of colonialism, and the definition of the word *socialism*, all in good spirits and amid considerable laughter, their guests left.

Marisa finally got the chance to corner him, a chance she had been waiting for all evening, with a glint of rampant joy in her eyes.

He watched her enjoy herself much as he would a child, and he blessed the heavens for having allowed him to find her and take her home to his life forever.

"Come up to the terrace," he said, shaking his head.

When she did not move, he took her by the arm and brought her to the stairs. "No, it's raining," she protested, digging her heels into the fluffy Greek rug.

"I won't tell you anything if you don't come upstairs," he said, retrieving her hand. "Anyway, it's stopped." He pulled her forward and propelled her up the steps into the studio and then to the terrace stairs. "Come on, or I will turn you back into a virgin," he threatened. She followed meekly.

Once they were upstairs, he opened the beach umbrella that lay forgotten by the round garden table and then sat her down on what turned out to be a wet chair. He perched on the edge of the table, eyeing her like a district attorney.

"Her name was Marla, yes. And she looked like someone called Marla—unusual. She did something dangerous in a brokerage firm that I did not understand, and she made mountains of money. She bought my paintings and thought I was from Mars because I would not let her pay for them. And she was totally scandalized that I showed no curiosity about her stocks or her options and even less for what she called her futures.

"But she was also beautiful and charming and, in the long run, very wise. She was cultured and had traveled and was older than me. And no, I was not really in love with her, but yes, she thought she was in love with me. Because it was more romantic that way—the young Italian painter in the little studio upstairs."

He made a face and then turned to look at the night sky. "She knew she was pretending, because she was also a very intelligent financial genius. So in the end, she let me go back to Italy with all my hesitations and doubts and my serious lack of what she called ambition. Which was not what I call ambition. She wanted me to be someone else. She couldn't see why I did not want to be someone else."

He let his voice edge off into a cold distance. "She was not interested in my need for the perfect straight line. She said that was self-indulgent. Once that became clear, she said good-bye. She told me, 'Come back when you decide to see a shrink,' which she did not really think I would do but which I'm sure she did instead of me.

"She was, underneath, a very nice financial genius. Since she was also my neighbor on Bleeker Street, I decided *basta cosi con* New York, and I came running home to Genoa— until Giorgio told me about this shoemaker's shop in Paris, a building in which no one else lived.

"And I found my own orphan, my lovely orphan who thinks I am a boy on a dolphin and who understands what it is to be whatever it is I am."

He looked at her with something so precious in his eyes that she had no name for it.

"*Alora*? Now you know. Are you ready to forgive me for having lived on Bleeker Street without looking for you in the unicorn's nest?"

He let his smile grow warm. "So how many more sad stories do I have to tell you about my *mille amori* while you were growing up? I am older than you—have you forgotten? And I come from a country of Latin lovers," he added, taking her arm and putting it around his neck.

Then, raising her from the chair, he moved her over to the steps leading down to the bed.

"Do I have to do this every time you learn about my Casanova past? You would die to know what Mario and I did when we were fourteen years old in the woods with the daughters of the caribinieri, but I won't tell you. I am a gentleman. I was even at fourteen," he said, puffing.

He put her upright at the stairs, took her chin in his hand, and said to her only half in jest, "What must I do to convince you that making love to you is the only other thing I want to do for the rest of my life?"

He laid her gently down on the bed, looking carefully into her eyes for the tears he expected to follow.

But there were none. She was smiling instead.

He frowned at that. "I've spoiled you," he said.

***

Penny and Vladek became their "Let's go out tonight" friends. They went to the theater together often because both couples had subscriptions to the TNP, the magical troupe that was changing the world's definition of the concept of stagecraft.

Though Vladek was an exile from the Communist regime in Czechoslovakia, he was not a rabid anti-Communist. He still had faith in a middle way. He looked upon Yugoslavia with more interest than most Soviet bloc watchers, seeing in Tito a third way, as he put it.

Riccardo nodded as Vladek spoke about such pleasant horizons, but he also warned him that he sounded like the Left Bank's last optimist.

Vladek enjoyed talking art with Riccardo, and they found common ground in what they both meant when they used the word *art*.

Vladek was encouraging about the work Riccardo was doing for the show, which was scheduled for June. He said also that perhaps he might be able to come up with a commission for a fresco to go on a public-housing estate that was to be built in a working-class suburb next year. His firm had the contract, but no one had shown much interest in his idea of a fresco yet.

Riccardo's eyes lit up at the thought of doing a fresco. He had taken an extra course at the university in Florence in fresco work but had never done anything bigger than the patch the university had allotted him.

He had enjoyed the medium and often thought he might find happiness in doing billboards along the autostrada, for want of a proper wall. Vladek said that if he did not get the contract for the suburb proposal, they could always take the idea to East Berlin, which was seriously into walls these days.

Riccardo slipped into a relaxed kind of friendship with Vladek, comfortable yet undemanding.

He was not given to socializing and had even apologized to Marisa early on for being something of a bear. She joked about it, but he knew it was one of his many paradoxes she worried about.

It was a pleasure for her to see that he had found in Vladek and Penny something that was coherent with himself.

"How many people do you run into who talk about frescoes for the masses in need of your sense of beauty?" she murmured.

"*Grazie*, Signorina," Riccardo whispered in her ear before biting the lobe.

A commission for a fresco was a remote possibility, but he kept it at the back of his mind and thought about it when he was in search of what he called a break in the weather of his mind.

Riccardo was grateful to Vladek on several levels, and now, having found him, he admitted to Marisa how solitary he had sometimes felt in Paris in ways that counted most— ways that had touched what he called his Mario nerve.

Mario, the constant friend, was now just as constantly absent. However, he laughed at himself for being dependent.

"Like a junkie," he said. "Be pragmatic; get more friends. That's all it takes. Go out and mingle, as they say in the *New Yorker.*"

He had become an adept of the magazine while he was in New York and had had a subscription to it since then. Marisa had been startled to see copies lying around the house when she first arrived. "An Italian in Paris reading the 'Talk of the Town'?" she had said, enchanted.

"Not surprising. I kept the best of what I found there with me. It travels well," he'd assured her.

The ghost of Marla Hitchens had been just about banished by then, he realized. For a second, he wondered what had become of that remarkable woman with the stainless steel mind, who was gifted not only in finance but also in determination of the aggregate number of orgasms a single night might yield in the proper hands.

He would be eternally indebted to her. Marisa would have been too, for that matter, if she had known.

They went to Genoa for Christmas, but Marisa could not stay for New Year's because Milo was going on home leave, and she would be almost on her own in the office.

They returned on December 27, which seemed like being short-changed. Don Carlo came back with them, and on the thirtieth, Mario joined them, bringing Monica, the Milanese doctor, with him, thus establishing a new status in the family, all of whom welcomed her joyously. Monica was beautiful, blue-eyed, and fair and had a sharp sense of humor and infinite curiosity about their bizarre family, which she clearly wanted nothing more than to join.

The way she looked at Mario rang a familiar bell in Don Carlo's heart, for it was precisely the way Marisa looked at Riccardo. "What more could an ancestor ask for?" he said to Giorgio, standing off to one side and watching the four young people at a table in the restaurant, deep in conversation. "What more indeed?"

Giorgio's restaurant closed for New Year's Eve upon the ancestor's order so that Anna could enjoy the holiday at Le Train Bleu, the magical restaurant at the Gare de Lyon, where they all went to see the new year in, greeting it with open arms.

Mario and Anna looked alike, Marisa noticed as she once more marveled at the sense of family Italians carried with them in their genes, like brown eyes or elegant noses.

Monica fit in perfectly, as though they all had been waiting for her to drop Milan and adopt Genoa and Santini along with Mario—with Paris thrown in as a bonus. Monica seemed to have settled in without hesitation, Marisa noticed, pleased at her company.

"Happy New Year, children of Santini," Don Carlo sang out, raising a glass of champagne.

At this joyful table on a day made for love among friends and family, Marisa shot a silent prayer to Peter, begging him to cast a gentle eye at her Italians, who were making up for the shattered ruins the war had left them. *Ruins upon which we are rebuilding as best as we can,* she thought.

"Peace on earth," she said aloud, raising a glass to New Year's Eve.

Riccardo caught her eye, knowing precisely what she was thinking of, and he reached over and gave her his glass to drink from.

Peace on earth indeed.

***

There were many ways to celebrate the advent of a new year.

Milo, for example, liked New Year's Eve in New Orleans. His long-ago hometown, he claimed, was the only sensible place to be on New Year's Eve if one had a choice.

He took a two-week break every year instead of a month-long home leave every two years, which was mandatory in most overseas contracts.

Milo was different. He liked working. He was an anarchist, and she'd realized early on that he was a one-off. There were other veterans of the colorful prewar press still around the various bars—the Crillon, the Ritz, Harry's, and, lately, L'Ambassade de Champagne on the rue de la Paix—and all of them had a certain charm, but Milo was special.

Not tall and handsome, as Hemingway made the whole breed out to be, he was potbellied and moonfaced, but he had melting brown eyes if he liked a person or dark bullets if he didn't.

He detected a lie before it was out of the liar's mouth; he sniffed, hedging, and caught a compromise before the sentence was finished in the offender's mouth.

His round smile, special for such occasions, was the delight of cartoonists, and he had a selection of such drawings over his desk, framed and signed—his diplomas, so to speak. He doted on Marisa but was a hard taskmaster, and he taught her the differences between yeses and nos that meant a variety of maybes. She was the only cub reporter to last the full year under his tutelage, she soon learned.

At last, Milo's successor had been found, his buddies declared, and she had soft manners and big blue eyes to boot.

She felt indebted to him, beholden, and, paradoxically, warmly comfortable with him, because what he was looking for was simply the nature she came equipped with. She knew she was no more gifted than the others before her who had not lasted. Perhaps they had not learned how to listen as children the way she had.

"At last," she told Riccardo, "I have found something I can be grateful to my mother for. 'Look me in the eye, and tell the truth,' she would say."

Marisa shuddered a little and then peered at him, showing him how her mother had looked at her. He flinched and put his arm up in self-defense.

"Did she really?" he said.

She nodded. "You learn the many colors of truth if you start out like that. You learn to sift it out of a pile of sand, if it is there at all. Otherwise, you recognize absence for what it is."

She seldom mentioned her mother to Riccardo, because he seemed uncomfortable hearing about her. He seemed to be repelled by what he knew of her, and he could not understand her defection.

There were few reasons for contact with her now anyway. The rental checks came into Marisa's account at the bank regularly. She heard intermittent news from the Irons, her friends who took care of things with the tenants for her, on the rare occasion when there was something to take care of. The tenants in the apartment seemed to be there for the foreseeable future.

The apartment was a worry that caused no worry, she claimed, crossing her fingers. It was as though the spiky episode that had made up the first twenty years of her life had been filed away somewhere in the dark.

Marisa now had mixed feelings about returning to New York, even for a visit. She had no contact with her mother at all. She had sent her an announcement of her wedding, using the address that she had in Northern California. It had come back while they were in Greece.

She didn't tell Riccardo. She could not bear to look at the outrage in his eyes at any reference to her mother.

There was little she could do, but Marisa was uneasy about it. She was able to deal with her mother's rejection of her, but she was not sure she was capable of rejecting her mother.

Occasionally, she had nightmares in which her mother's steely arms reached out for her, pleading for rescue from drowning, being consumed by a fire, or falling off the edge of the earth. There were horrific tidal waves, rampant fires, or mighty cliffs falling away under her grip, and her mother was trying to pull herself back from certain death but not succeeding.

These nightmares were infrequent and unpredictable, but she would wake in a state of hideous disarray, with indistinct images of havoc lingering on for long minutes after.

She tried to minimize their importance, for she recognized that they only proved that no one was free from the past, even if the boy with the dolphin breathing peacefully next to her had taken up her entire present.

Fortunately, Riccardo was a sound sleeper.

***

The winter flew by with lashing cold rains, leaks in the ceiling, and a nasty sore throat that went from one to the other and then to Anna and Giorgio and back again till March winds blew the germs over the Alps, and Riccardo grew increasingly nervous as June approached.

He had finished ten large canvases in time for his birthday in May, as well as four smaller ones that were complementary. Working for a show, she learned, was not the same as just working. She understood that, and she was sensitive to the ordeal of deadlines. In all, she was proving to be a supportive roommate he told her one day as an expression of utmost praise.

It made her feel like a saint.

"The process of creating a painting seems like something in the order of alchemy of the five senses," she confided to Penny, who was a good listener. "And the process of judging what is right or what is redundant in a painting where structure is the object seems so arbitrary as to appear like voodoo."

"How does he know what is right? How does he know that the form or the color or the shadow will fit, will hold meaning? How does he know when to stop?" Penny asked. She was drawn to the logistics, she said.

"Ah," Marisa said, nodding. That was something she did not ask him. She avoided spell-breaking questions, as she called them. "No, now I stay quiet and unobtrusive and avoid the studio because I know he doesn't like to work with me in the room. I see the process play itself out, with a few mishaps at the beginning—false starts. They are good in theory but discordant when you open your eyes, as he put it."

Marisa smiled a little, almost shy now. "It is a privilege. I think of it as watching someone else find life. And now we change the subject," she said firmly, though still smiling.

That had been the night before last. He had been painting over one canvas with harsh brushstrokes while he talked, as though he were striking it dead. "If canvases were cheaper," he told her, "I would burn them alive up on the terrace."

As she watched him slapping the canvas hard first one way and then another, flailing with his brush, she believed him.

Her friend Ann Wallace had been in Trieste all winter, digging around among the traces of James Joyce; his wife, Nora; and their children, who all spoke Italian, which they would do for the rest of their lives.

Ann seemed to be as taken with the odd city on the edge of Europe as the Joyce family had been, a city perched like a leftover crossroads of unclear identities, at home in all or none of them.

Ann wrote glowing letters about the odd little city, which was Serbian and Italian and often German speaking, its identity like a romantic cracked mirror of European contradictions.

Marisa would have loved to hop on a train and spend a few days with Ann, doing what she was doing, which was walking in the master's footsteps to listen to the words he'd heard on the streets and rendered so roundly.

Through Ann, she had discovered Joyce; his worlds, both real and ephemeral; and the places he'd cherished. With Riccardo, she would go on Joyce walks in Paris, the two of them reading bits of prose here and there. They sat at the Closérie des Lilas and pretended they were waiting for him to join them.

"When you make a lot of money, we can take a train and go to Trieste," she said to him one evening when he was reading a translation of one of Don Carlo's articles in the prestigious *Les Temps Modernes*, which was Sartre's fief.

The subject was subjection, the root of colonialism, the twentieth-century cauldron that was in the process of boiling over in Asia and Africa, searing across Europe's guilty thin skin, involving Indochina, North Africa, Asia, and, more imperative, black Africa.

"Trieste?" he echoed, as though it were a suburb of Patagonia. "You haven't seen Firenze or Venezia *sense parlare di* Roma, *ma che* Trieste? But of course, I will be happy to take you there. On our way back from sub-Carpathian Ruthenia."

He got up, stretched, looked over at the staircase, and moved toward the painting slowly and reluctantly. Then he swiveled around to look at her.

She was staring after him, smiling slowly, when he turned. "Let's go out for a drink. Before it rains again. Let's go to the Flore. *Perche no?*" he said.

She burst out laughing. "Sweetheart, it's almost midnight! But I will meet you there tomorrow after work. We can have dinner, and we can forget about everything except Gérard de Nerval. Is that a date?"

"Mhmm," he agreed, feeling silly for not knowing what time it was and then feeling comforted because he was now sure that he was nearly finished with climbing walls, his term for anxiety. There were enough paintings ready for the show, so he could climb down now and try to just live again.

He turned his gaze to the painting on the wall, which he had just finished yesterday. *It works,* he thought. He breathed slowly and soothingly but with his eyes still riveted to the curious dark reds he had settled on at the end of a long search.

"I rest my case," he said, quoting some movie he had seen years ago. The authority in the words had remained in his heart ever since. He looked hard at the painting and nodded. *I do,* he told himself. *I rest my case.*

He went happily to bed.

A half hour later, she joined him only to find him stretched out on the bed, lying on his stomach with his head facing the window and his eyes closed, breathing like a child. He was still dressed in his soft painting clothes. She took off his shoes carefully, negotiated the bedding to cover them both, and then slid into bed beside him and turned off the light. He looked more than ever like her Arion, the boy now without his dolphin, wholly in her care.

***

Spring inched its way into the weather while the weeks of preparation for the opening of Riccardo's first Paris show of his paintings filed by.

He was nervy, edgy, distracted, and easily cross yet able to laugh at himself. "I am sure having a baby is easier," he said one day when he was taking a break on the terrace.

He was watering the plants with rainwater he'd collected in a bedraggled tin container he kept for that purpose. When she suggested finding a receptacle that looked less like a war-zone relic, he refused.

"It belongs here," he snapped, "and I love it. One day I will clean it up and make a seascape on it, but I won't throw it away."

He looked amazed that a mere new bride would take such liberties, so she held in the laughter and apologized softly.

"Riccardo has his own scale of values, and brides are meant to knock before entering," she said when she told Penny the story some months later.

They were talking over a couple of pricey sandwiches on the terrace of the Café de la Paix, where they sometimes met for lunch.

Penny was giving her a list of people to invite to the vernissage, which was now a fortnight away.

"Actors are worse," Penny said. "They die every day with matinées on Sunday. I know. Before Vladek, I had a live-in affair with a guy who was delightful when he was poor and out of work, but as soon as he got a part and was working, he proved to be homicidal. I had a hard time explaining that to my mother, who found him glamorous, and I suppose he was sort of, but he went manic when he finally made it. A paradox, I know. But the artistic temperament is deeply mysterious. Anyway, I will take pleasure in inviting all my intellectual friends, including a few native New Yorkers, though nothing like Marla Hitchens." They both giggled.

"He is anxious to sell, I know, but he is more anxious about the reviews, the reception he will have," Marisa said. "And he is nervous about people wanting to be nice to his grandfather by being nice to him. He is very touchy about being Riccardo Rinaldi, not Carlo Rinaldi's grandson."

Marisa sat back, smoking a Benson and Hedges reflectively. "He is very—what's the word?—intent on being himself and no one else, not the son of the martyred lovers or the grandson of the Pink Eminence. Someone called Don Carlo that recently, and the Italian press picked up on it. Don Carlo thinks it is funny, but Riccardo apparently socked a guy who used the term in his hearing. It was when he went to Genoa last month while I stayed here. Mario was with them, and he told me about it. I was horrified. He actually socked him."

She sat back in her chair and watched the passersby on the busy boulevard. She was about to say something about sitting there at that corner and running into everyone you've ever known, when she noticed a fair-haired young woman standing stock still, staring at her as though she had seen a ghost. A second later, a burst of recognition nearly choked her. Penny looked at her and then followed her gaze. "Oh, there's Laney. Hi, sweetie," Penny said pleasantly.

Marisa gasped, whirling from one to the other. "Laney? Lane? I can't believe this," she said hoarsely. She stood up slowly while they stared at each other, and then they rushed into each other's arms while the whole terrace of the Café de la Paix looked on, ready to applaud.

The coffee waiter, a tall African dressed like an Arabian prince come in from the desert, with his steaming ornate coffeepot ready to pour in one hand, was watching her with a slow smile warming his face. He said in French, shaking his head slowly, "*Seulement au* Café de la Paix. Only here," and his silvery *Arabian Nights* slippers seemed to glide him over to Marisa's table to refill their cups.

"*Bienvenue*. Welcome, my ladies. Welcome to Paris."

Questions, answers, and laughter mixed with tears flooded Marisa and Lane while Penny sat back, amazed. She looked from one to the other and said, "But I could have given you each other's phone number if anyone had asked." She gazed at them benevolently. "I wish I had a long-lost friend who would bring out such affection," she said, and then she excused herself because she had to get back to work.

So did Marisa, but it would wait, she decided.

Lane was still looking at her with an expression of disbelief. Words seemed to fail her. She reached out and touched Marisa's hand as though fearful it might vanish again.

"So what happened?" Marisa said.

Lane threw her head back. "What happened? McCarthy happened. Senator Joe McCarthy—that's what happened. Oh my Lord, where do we begin? Let me get my breath."

They bustled with the chairs, putting them as close as possible to each other so they could hear each other over the traffic without raising their voices, like conspirators getting ready with the secret of the age.

Lane moved toward her, smiled, and then began. "To describe it: it was the middle of the morning. Two hunky guys came to the door. Sissy opened it—my sister.

"They walked straight in like cops in a movie. Mama came out from her bedroom and fluttered, waving her hand like ZaSu Pitts, telling them they should first sit down since they were in her house. They should first sit down while she phoned her lawyer as well as the American Civil Liberties people and their lawyers too. Oh yes, there would be lots of lawyers.

"The two men looked surprised. No, they looked amazed. But they still did not sit down. The bigger one raised his voice and told her they were there to serve a summons for her to appear in court downtown. Mama stepped back and said, 'Over my dead body,' or something operatic like that, whereupon my father came in the front door with his suitcase. He had been in Florida, working. Remember? He was a traveling salesman.

"He sees Mama in a long pink dressing gown and a snood. Remember her snoods? She loved them. And she raised her voice and said, 'Seymour, they want to arrest me.' The cops shrugged and tried to hand her the summons, but it just dropped onto the floor, and she started walking slowly toward them as though she might hit them.

"But Daddy suddenly turned on them, demanding they leave his home that minute. He said it calmly. He was very low voiced—angry but white angry. He was a World War l veteran. He knew his rights. And unlike everyone else in their crowd, he liked guns. He kept several.

"I can see them all standing there, looking astounded. They looked so unprepared. They hadn't been expecting resistance. No one had ever resisted them. I almost felt sorry for them.

"Oh, Marisa, only my mother could get into a mess like that. She literally chopped our lives in two."

As Lane talked, Marisa felt that by a stroke of magic, the years between had been lifted, and Lane's voice had come back into her universe as clear and colorful as it always had been, as though she had turned on the radio of her life and found the right station. Marisa stopped listening despite herself, not able to put the developments all into place at once, not daring to believe in the magic life had brought to her.

Then she shook her head and pulled reason back into view. Of course there was magic but only the magic of accident.

"It is so hard to believe that we could just run into each other like this. Penny seems to attract coincidences," Marisa said.

Penny, holding her gloves and bag in her hand and still poised to leave them, made a face but admitted she had a point. "I knew her husband by sight in the Rienzi," Penny said lamely. "When you see him, you will understand why I remembered him," she added with a little grin.

"You're married?" Lane said gently, sitting back as though to catch her breath. "To someone gorgeous? But what are you doing here in Paris? How did you get here? Why did you leave Fort Tryon Park? Why did you leave New York?

You would be the last person I would have expected to run into in Paris," she said, laughing.

Penny, who was clearly having trouble tearing herself away, said, "Let me introduce you. This is Marisa Rinaldi, wife of painter Riccardo Rinaldi of Genoa and the Latin Quarter. And this is Lane, who is married to another architect, a friend of Vladek's, and they have a little girl called Anouk, who is a dream. And now I really do have to get back to work. You arrange the next chapter. Call me soon—very soon." She got up and reluctantly left them to the next chapter.

Marisa realized she would be seriously late to the office, but she could not walk off now. Instead, she sat down and tried to stop her hands from shaking.

"My head is spinning with visions of how else we might have met, like on the twenty-one bus or—"

Lane stopped her. "No, wait. I owe you at least an explanation. I know that; I have always known it. But by now, I have learned to live with what happened then, and I never really expected to have the chance to explain."

After a long moment in which Marisa looked at her features, noting that her skin was still fair and smooth, with her light hair growing out of a fine line along her forehead, Marisa felt awkward and clumsy. "You must have had urgent reasons if your mother had a summons," she said. Then she felt her mind draw a blank. What was so threatening about a summons? She waited for Lane to begin.

"It was from the House Un-American Activities Committee, for her to appear." Lane shook her head, her features mobile, mirroring disgust and incredulity. "Imagine my mama, with her fund-raising for all those causes—the poor in the Bahamas, a Jewish free state. And some damn fool gave her name to the McCarthy witch hunters, and she was summoned because they had a warrant out for her arrest for spying. Can you imagine—my mother and her hats, her snoods, and her pink Bonwit Teller suit?

"They were out for blood, those first McCarthy guys, though, and saw nothing wrong with putting her in jail for raising money for the victims of Stalingrad. It was serious— serious enough for my father to decide to get her out of the country right then and there. To run out on the summons. So he got us on the first ship leaving New York for Europe the next day. We sailed for Lisbon at noon, the four of us, leaving everything behind. It was as though we were all born again on that Portuguese ship. And his orders were utterly uncompromising—no traces left."

She sat back and looked at Marisa, her pretty eyes clear yet concerned. "Everything had to be totally left behind for us to create new lives abroad."

Marisa nodded and said, "I can see that." Then sat she back, smiling in a tired way. "I had invented all kinds of scenarios about what could have happened to you, but not this. Not McCarthy. And certainly not Lisbon—which is the capital of a dictatorship, as it happens. But not Europe at all. In my mind, you were all gone but still in the States—somewhere where your dad could keep selling his Band-Aids or powder puffs." She laughed, remembering all the nice-smelling things they'd had in their bathroom—sweet-smelling things, such as salts and crystals.

"No, it was surgical supplies. Bandages of all kinds," Lane said, still smiling wanly, making it ever more remote.

"The Portuguese authorities have been kind to us. My parents live in a pretty house in Estoril, in a circle of other foreigners who drop names of deposed kings and queens who are now their neighbors. And they play canasta and look out over the Atlantic and think of Brighton Beach, just on the other side, which was where they started, if you scratch a little. They came a long way. And Mama no longer badgers people over civil rights or how brave they were at Stalingrad. She talks about gardening and her grandchildren. Sissy has two boys who live in Brazil but who come to visit every summer, and I have a little French girl called Anouk. We go to see them whenever we feel like it, because I now have a French passport. For a while, I had no passport at all. Then I married Jean-Claude, and he made me legal again.

"And here we are, like there has been scarcely a break in the conversation, Marisa. I am so happy to have found you. I hope you will forgive me for the pain my disappearance must have caused you at first, but I had no choice."

They sat quietly, as though they were learning how to believe this reunion was real.

"I have to get back to the office," Marisa said. "I'm late as it is, but we will meet whenever you want."

Lane broke in. "Come to dinner tonight. Not a minute later." She rummaged in her bag for a notebook and wrote down an address. "Please say yes."

Marisa laughed gently at her rush. She nodded. "Riccardo is having a show in June and is working all sorts of hours because of it. This is his first Paris one-man show, so he is as nervy as a cat, but he will be so moved by my finding you that he will drop everything to meet you. He is very Italian in everything but especially when it comes to ties— family, you know, and special friends. My losing my best friend touched him. When we first met, I told him, um, well ..." She felt she had said too much too soon. She was not sure what she should be saying. "He has been a major earthquake in my life. You'll see." She ended up smiling a little shyly.

Awkwardly, they kissed good-bye for now, while the *Arabian Nights* coffee waiter nodded at them with a big, benign smile, as though he had arranged it all himself.

Marisa gazed at Lane's still-pretty figure walking toward the Boulevard des Italiens through the busy Paris street scene, sensing once more the haunting image that, in her mind, followed her flight from Lane's locked apartment door: the persistent disjointed image of the night of her father's death. She thought back to scrambling around on the craggy edges of the river alone. *Without my brother, my sad little father, or my strong-willed friend. I was on my own.*

She banished the memories angrily and chided herself for never having learned to accept those losses for what they were, as an adult should.

Marisa went back to the office, oddly numbed by the amazing encounter.

How is it that you yearn for something for years at a time, and then when it happens, you are left numb and almost unbelieving or, worse still, niggling at the gaps?

She did not tell me everything, Marisa cautiously admitted to herself. *Not about running after the cop with the summons or her father running after them out on the street.* The neighbor had told her those details, and the conversation remained vivid to her now.

Lane had not drawn that picture, just the flight and the pleasant reception in Portugal. Marisa sat back and thought about it.

The disgrace, no matter how unjustified, of having to run away from your own country like a band of thieves—how do you live with that? Just like common thieves. And then settling into a mild dictatorship unaccountably welcoming to American left-wingers fleeing the anti-Communist bullies now holding sway in Washington.

The Salazar government—giving peace and protection to American dissidents? Really? Why would they do that?

Perhaps the Portuguese authorities did not know that's what they were doing. Perhaps the Bergers just looked like eccentric Americans who liked mild climates.

That could pass, she thought, and then she felt contrite about doubting Lane.

She looked into the file on the House Un-American Activities Committee. It was bulging. The witch hunt had gone well beyond the Potomac. It now included so-called subversives ferout of the reach of the State Department, beyond the arena of government employees. The zealots had descended upon the staffs of international organizations, such as the UN in Geneva and UNESCO in Paris.

Americans working for international organizations were held to the same line of questioning as those at home in the United States. The witch hunt had indeed gone global. It was now in the process of running rampant.

The architects of those august international bodies had not foreseen the attack by Senator McCarthy and his team of vicious sleuths, who were out to decimate their staffs, wreaking havoc on their American personnel, disturbing their operational programs, and destroying honorable lives in the process.

It would take years for the international organizations to repair the damage.

Decades later, the bitterness over this episode would still be a factor damaging the United States' reputation and credibility in the international community. This was just the beginning.

Marisa's mind wandered back to the silliness of Mrs. Berger's hats and her lopsided concern with labor and the valor of the Soviet army in Stalingrad, all mixed in with her daughters' clothes and their Fifth Avenue labels.

Lane looked like her mother—fair haired, with a pert face that had remained pretty even when she'd had braces on her teeth. Lane had unusual velvety gray eyes that went violet when she wore the right colors.

Her crooked front teeth had distracted from her prettiness when she was young. Once the braces had done their work, however, she'd emerged as a beautiful version of her mother, especially when she wore blue.

All the Bergers laughed easily, Marisa remembered, even the frequently absent Seymour. She shook her head in wonder at the image of all four of them fleeing the country on the first ship out of New York harbor and ending up in Salazar's Portugal.

Because of a summons? Land there perhaps, she thought to herself, *but settle down to live there? No.*

So what happened? she wondered. *What happened next? And what am I in all this? An accidental victim?* She bridled at the term.

Marisa had never thought of herself as a victim of anything. She was a fighter, and her fists clenched now as she ran the word through her mind. She sat stiffly at her desk, stroking her hands as though to assure herself of their strength, scowling.

Milo happened to walk by and saw her through the open door. "Hey, you look ready to take aim and fire." He laughed, walking on.

After catching up on her desk work, Marisa looked through the files on the Un-American Activities Committee stories in Europe and found no mention of Portugal at all. There was ample information on Americans accused of Communist sympathies in Europe while working in international organizations, but none bore a connection with Portugal. As dictatorships went, Salazar's regime was a quiet enterprise. It concentrated on its own subjects and its rich little corners of Africa. It seemed to be off the map for progressives. The only foreigners of interest were the former royals waiting out their exiles on their Atlantic seashore while drinking a sparkling pink wine that came in a pretty bottle.

On the spur of the moment, she put in a call to a number in Lisbon to the only person she knew there, Jim Snow, a freelance reporter who sometimes worked for Milo, whom she knew only slightly.

After introducing herself and making sure she was not interrupting anything important, she gave him a résumé of the facts. He was caught up in the situation instantly because political asylum sounded unlike most reasons for foreigners to choose Portugal as a landing place, aside from their resident royals. "We are more in the line of colorful anti-Communists," he said with a laugh. "I can't imagine anyone of the card-carrying persuasion digging in here. No, really? On the same beachfront as the house of Savoy or the Bourbons of Spain?"

They both laughed, but he went back to her question. "On the other hand, there are lots of foreigners on the Algarve as well as Estoril, and Lisbon has a well-established English resident community, so nothing is impossible, as long as they behave.

"It could be a pleasant place to get forgotten in, I guess. It is not rife with activity, you know. You should come visit, because it is very pretty and comfortable to sit and watch the rest of the world go to hell while you listen to fados. I love it." They chatted for a while longer, and he took down the Bergers' names—those she knew at least, because she couldn't remember Sissy's real name and had never known the mother's.

She felt foolish, but they were that sort of people, she explained. Everyone called Mrs. Berger Toussy, wherever that name had come from. He chuckled a little and said, "I've changed my mind. They sound like they would fit in here perfectly. I know two princesses called Poussy and a duchess known all over the Med by the name of Beujy, and I will stop there. What did you say the papa did?" He was clearly enjoying himself.

"He was a traveling salesman in medical things—surgical stuff. They used to have a lot of nice-smelling powders along with the bandages, as far as I recall. He was a traveling salesman around Florida, I think, and maybe Cuba too." Her voice faded.

Then, as though they had been sharing a thunderbolt but only now noticed it, he asked slowly, "Just nice talcum powder? You sure of that? It couldn't be other kinds of powders you might run into off the Florida coast, could it? Could it?"

She was stunned. It took her time to say, "That is insane. It's hard enough to think of this overdressed middle-class Jewish family from Upper Manhattan running away from anything worse than a traffic fine, let alone the Communist Internationale, but drugs? With a capital *D*? I will faint. I can hardly imagine anything more out of character."

"Okay, okay, I am probably wrong about your people if you say so. Still, it is not beyond the realm of the real world these days. Drugs are a new postwar ball game, you know. A whole new playground. Another thing—not all gangsters look like George Raft flipping a coin these days. And international heavies look more like Dr. Kildare, because by now, they are second or third generation and went to college. But never mind. I will ask around, and if I hear of anything, I will get back to you. If they are here, someone will know them. Give my best to Milo." He hung up, leaving her with her mind in turmoil and her heart in tatters.

Riccardo was sizing a canvas when she came in, his hands and arms streaked white with the stuff he used to make a canvas a paintable surface. She did not like the smell and made a face. "From this merde comes a beautiful art treasure," he said mildly, watching her flash by.

She ran upstairs to the terrace, saying, "Come up. I have the most unbelievable news you have ever heard. Come up, but wash your hands first."

He was going to say that he would finish sizing the canvas, but he changed his mind and did what she asked. A bottle of Perrier and some glasses sat on a tray in the middle of the studio. He brought them upstairs with him and poured out a half a glass each, emptying the bottle.

She looked radiant, he thought. "*Dunque, alora?* Are you going to tell me? Have the Germans come back?" he asked.

"I found Lane," she said quietly.

He stared at her. He waited for the rest, holding his breath.

"I found Lane at the Café de la Paix. She lives here. She has been living here for years. She is a friend of Penny's, and her husband is a French architect. She has a little girl called Anouk, and they live near the Invalides. We are going to have dinner with them tonight. So this is what happened. Sit down."

He was sitting down but squirmed a little in his chair, rapt, watching her as a doctor might. Her eyes were bright, like little pieces of sky in her face.

"They ran away to Portugal because the McCarthy witch hunters served her mother with a warrant." She broke off and let her reporter's voice drop. "Oh, Riccardo, I have found Lane after all this time, and all I can do is nitpick her story. And then I think back on that night." She stopped and frowned, for there were still parts of it unexplained— not only unexplained but also unmentioned.

He waited for her to tell the story her way. He watched her carefully, seeing the tautness in her face, where there should have been joy.

"Anyway, I said I would bring you over tonight to have dinner and meet her husband and see her baby," she said.

He got up and took her in his arms. Then he kissed the top of her head, murmuring about how deep a shock it must be and telling her that it was normal to question anything that deep and that she should not worry about little things she didn't understand. "Don't cry, my love. Laugh at the nitpicks, whatever they are."

He rocked her gently and tried to imagine her joy in finding a piece of the puzzle of the terrible rupture in her young life. He hurt for Marisa, his scrappy bride, with her severed past.

"Finding Lane, no matter the circumstances, is something to celebrate," he said reassuringly, but then he stopped and peered at her. "Portugal? Not Portugal. Portugal is as bad as Spain."

"Yes, I know." She laughed softly. "But it is just the sort of thing her parents might not have thought of. They live in Estoril with a bunch of demobilized royal families, and the climate is mild. Looking out to sea on a sunny day, they can think they see Brighton Beach, which is where they came from to begin with. All this time, I could have bumped into Lane in the ladies' room of the Galeries Lafayette and died of a heart attack. Oh, why am I quibbling? I have my friend back. The circle is closed."

He thought that was an odd thing to say but did not question it. He was overcome with tenderness that one of the open wounds of her patchwork past had been healed in a haze of comic confusion.

However, Portugal tempered his flight of fancy.

"My chopped-up Marisa," he murmured, kissing her hair. "No time. We are going there to have dinner tonight and to meet Anouk." He kissed her hair even more, kicking off his paint-splashed sneakers. "I will help open your appetite," he told her—and he did.

***

Marisa was expecting a French version of Vladek, but Jean-Claude turned out to be different. He was just a bit taller than Lane, half a head shorter than Riccardo, and he looked like a pirate. His salt-and-pepper black hair was thick and longish, and he had a short black beard, bright dark eyes, and a smile that lit the room. He had that indefinable thing called charm. Riccardo called it personal electricity, Marisa told Lane later.

"Yes," Lane agreed, "he is special. Jean-Claude answered De Gaulle's appeal for free Frenchmen to join him, mostly because he was in North Africa anyway. He was in Algiers. He had just finished l'École de l'Architecture in Paris when war broke out. He had gone to work on a model school project somewhere out in the bled. So he stayed till the war came to him, as he puts it. He was in Libya in one of the units that mined the desert and thus got Rommel out. Have him tell you his stories about what he calls his couscous period; he makes it sound like a prank. Only eight guys survived out of his original unit, but he never tells you that.

"When he got home, he found out why his parents hadn't answered his letters: they had been deported in 1944. They ran a quiet little network that smuggled Jewish children to Spain. His father was a retired schoolteacher. No one knew what he was really up to. They died in the camps."

They were pensive for a moment, standing together at the window of the living room, looking out on the Seine. The ornate bridge was lit up, and the river below reflected a hundred little lights from a passing Bateaux Mouches.

Lane had told her about Jean-Claude with a special kind of admiration in her voice, as though he were of a breed hitherto unknown to her and doubly precious for his rarity.

"His parents were practicing Protestants. They went to what he calls temple. When I told him that my parents went to temple too, he looked a little confused. Semantics." She laughed. "He is not much of a churchgoer, but he asked me even before we were married if I would mind bringing up the children as Protestants. Considering what happened to my relatives in Europe—my father's cousins in Belgium were decimated—I didn't know whether to say please or thank you. So Anouk is Anouk Marie-France Clément."

Her now-familiar voice was warm, tender, and confiding. Marisa answered with what she hoped was the pleasure she felt in the simple act of exchanging addresses. She said, "I never got beyond what happened then in New York. You know? My father stopped living after Peter. He just let himself drift away. When I went to tell you he had died on the living room couch, you were not there. They said you all ran away.

"That stays so clear in my mind—my running through the scrubby grounds near the river, not wanting to go home, wanting to find a reason for all this punishment on my head, and then seeing a body in the brush and being frightened and then running up the slope to the house. My mother was sitting with neighbors in the kitchen for the first time ever, and my dad was lying dead on the couch. And what I thought of most was that from now on, I had no one to help me. I had lost my brother and my father and, at the last moment, even my friend."

Marisa pulled herself up from slouching on a pillow-filled couch, looked at Lane, and felt like a fool, regretting having poured that story out.

"I wasn't going to tell you all that," she said sheepishly. "I'm sorry." She looked over at Lane and found her pale and wide-eyed. "Oh dear, I've upset you. I'm sorry. I should have kept all that in its bottle, where it belongs. Forgive me."

"No, I am the one who should ask for forgiveness. I had no idea how you might have taken our whole predicament to heart. Of course, your brother's dying like that—being killed to free Rome—was so cruel, so symbolic. You were Catholics after all."

Marisa blinked. She had never thought that being Catholic had anything to do with the Allies' battle for Rome. She almost smiled. However, she did not smile; she sobered suddenly. There was a silence.

Then Lane said flatly, "We could not get in touch with anyone. For their own good. It would have implicated them. We did that for their own good. We just sort of melted into the background in Estoril. With only our hand luggage at that," she murmured, now in control of her face and voice.

"All those nice-smelling powders and creams I remember," Marisa said lightly, "and Band-Aids. I remember them from scratched knees after roller-skating falls. You lived on the ground floor—easy to get to for first aid."

Lane listened to that and smiled, but her posture showed she was back in charge again and contrite for the harm that had been done to Marisa, the innocent bystander, the postman's little girl.

"What was the reference to scrambling around the rocks down by the railroad tracks you mentioned? When was that?" Lane's voice showed nothing but curiosity about a stray detail, one among many others.

Marisa hesitated. She was afraid to pursue this vein, afraid of finding the unbearable, the intolerable. She shook her head. "It is more a shading. There was a body half hidden under the scrub, there by the tracks, where the hobos used to make their bonfires at night. There. But I think it was my imagination. It was a hideous experience, one nightmare on top of another. Don't think of it. I try not to. It was a long time ago and in another country," she said, smiling wanly, as though she had turned over all the new pages in the book.

Lane seemed to breathe freely, and her face relaxed into a smile.

"Out, damned spot," Marisa said. Her clownish recitation of *Macbeth* made Lane laugh.

"You always were good at quoting," Lane said, making Marisa laugh, remembering.

That's true, she thought vaguely, only now realizing how far she had come from her beginnings. *Why should I pretend to know what this finished young woman here is like now, when all I have to go on are the scratched knees and first kisses of our childhood?*

Would that vision of the half-hidden body now go away? she wondered. Or had it never been there at all?

The sense of severed ties was tangible to Marisa, though she tried to pretend otherwise. It was the result of the immense changes in their lives, and it should not have been unexpected. The whole context of their losing each other had been too dramatic; it had been too much and too long ago.

It was the past. Lane had simply let go and moved away from it. *Now I have to let go too,* Marisa thought. *I have to drop the burden of the past.* Then she laughed to herself at such dramatic language.

I have to reshuffle my cards, she thought instead. *I have to make columns of what I keep in front of my eyes and then stick all the rest into a drawer marked* D. *My dead file. I have to tell Riccardo about that.* She rattled on silently to herself instead of listening to Lane tell her something trivial about the baby.

Then, oddly, as though it were a physical exercise one did for cleaning out the inner man, she breathed out audibly a gust of used air. She pursed her lips and exhaled once more right there in the pretty room overlooking the city at one of its most attractive angles.

She was putting an old fiction to rest—her fiction of a true friendship. It was gone like used breath.

She realized all this in silence. She smiled at Lane a little foolishly. *She probably thinks I am burping.*

Looking up at Lane, Marisa saw an interesting ghost from her young years, a period she no longer had much contact with, spent in a city she had once loved but no longer lived in.

Whatever Lane had told her of her reasons for leaving, as well as however many details she was omitting, was of no relevance to her today. She thought of an interesting English military man who had said, oddly, "Broken ties can seldom be repaired." The quote had struck her as unduly harsh when she'd first heard it. Now she tipped her absent hat to him, for he was right.

This was a broken tie. It was no longer there. When she drew her mind back to listening to what Lane was saying about life in Portugal, Marisa knew there had to be a great deal more to her story than the vignettes she was offering. Yet Marisa did not seek to clarify what was not in Lane's intention to reveal.

Stop it! she thought, cautioning herself. *I am presuming upon her, presuming on a girlhood friendship that was clearly more vital to me than to her. It's a cruel truth to learn but not punishable by law,* she thought icily. Part of their past would remain a foreign country. *And her present is none of my business,* she thought flatly.

Not all questions had printable answers.

"I remember you had a crush on a very good-looking Jewish boy who lived on Fort Washington Avenue. But he pales next to Riccardo. He is really something, like an ad for a Roman holiday. He is also interesting to talk to," she added, giggling like a teenager.

"You probably never expected me to turn up in Paris, did you?" Marisa said. "Now that I think of it, what more unlikely end for the postman's daughter, the kid with the growling mother and the nice brother who was killed in the war? Who would have laid odds on her turning up in the Latin Quarter, married to a pinup painter with a prominent grandfather and an international address book? Not me. Of course not me. But crazy things happen, and certainties prove to be made of plastic, not gold. And"—she shook her head—"I think we had better leave it at that."

She was surprised she had been able to say all that without raising her voice. "What do you say to that?" she asked mildly.

Lane had tears in her voice. "It was too long ago, and nothing I might say would make much difference now. My parents are old, and who am I to blame them? Believing in a Socialist future isn't much of a sin."

"Bullshit, Lane. I don't think for a moment that socialism ever had much to do with anything. But don't worry. What I think is of no importance. I am not making it a topic of conversation. And we will leave it there. I won't take it further. I promise."

Lane looked astonished. "What do you mean? What won't you take any further? Don't dramatize, Marisa. There is nothing to dramatize about. It's bad enough like this.

Please. Just for a second, think of how it must have been for me to drop my life and start a new one. I was nineteen. I'm a little older than you, remember? And I had to vanish from everyone's board. I had to become someone new in another language with a whole other set of rules. Sissy and I were like appendages—excess baggage hanging on to outlandish parents who stuck out like sore thumbs in Estoril at first. Jewish Americans? But they faded into the bridge players after a while, and Sissy fell into the arms of a coffee merchant and moved to Brazil. There was only me, and I found a French war hero who gave me a French passport and a Paris address. So I am home safe."

She had been moving around the room as she spoke in a calm, still recognizably New York voice, but when she said those last words, her tone changed and grew as cold as steel. "I am home safe."

There was a silence that Marisa was not going to sever.

"I can feel like a whole person now. I am me, with a mind and a husband and a child and a future as well as a present. We can be friends again if you let us. I would like that, but it is up to you. Please know that I am sorry. I was always sorry."

In the silence that followed, Marisa saw that terrible day when her father had died. She recalled careening down that rocky path toward the river, where a half-covered body lay near the water's edge. "I went to your house for help," she said, but then she changed keys. "I was a child still and untutored in the social graces. No one had told me to knock first. Now I know." She shook her head as though to blow off the cobwebs of a persistent intruder. "That was so long ago, the day my father died. Let us try to put it behind us." She surprised herself when those words came out. Lane guessed as much. After a minute, they hugged as though they still believed in happy endings.

Riccardo and Jean-Claude came back into the living room from a visit to Jean-Claude's office, where they had been looking at pictures of workers' housing he had done in Algeria as well as in the rural foothills of the Pyrenees. Marisa saw that Riccardo had met someone he enjoyed talking to, and she said a child's prayer in thanks for that.

Suddenly, little Anouk let out a lusty yell that sent them all rushing down the hall to cuddle her. She was standing up in her crib, turning her bright brown eyes on the newcomers with her parents, and her pretty little mouth switched in midyell from a cry to a smile. Riccardo reached out a finger and tickled her under the ear. She stopped crying and babbled something to him, smiling broadly. Marisa thought she looked like Mr. Berger, but she stopped herself from saying so. "And your dad?" she asked instead, out of nowhere.

Lane turned around, holding the giggling tot, who was wide awake and ready for playtime. "Oh, you see it too. She looks like my dad. I say that, but no one agrees with me.

You saw it; she made you think of him. Well, he is alive but not too well in Estoril. His mind is going." Her voice sounded sad.

Jean-Claude took the baby and said, "Not going. It has gone. He is like a child, and it is pitiful, and no one wants to admit it. But he is otherwise strong, and the climate is gentle, so he talks to people no one else sees and plants and replants carnations all over the place. He is obsessed with them and invents new colors from cross-breeding. He has a bizarre garden and many window boxes, and he is happy. There is a lot to say about senility in a warm climate. I am taking notes." They all laughed, even Anouk, who was now in her father's arms.

At the front door, they embraced, saying things they did not mean about a lost friendship newly found. Oddly, a distant vision came to Marisa of the time she'd confided to Lane that Frankie Lopez had kissed her, and Lane had astounded her by asking if he had put his tongue in her mouth. Lane had, in that single question, destroyed the romance of the kiss, and Marisa had barely spoken to poor Frankie Lopez afterward.

Spoil? The word surprised her as she stood on the doorstep. *Spoil?*

Around her, everyone was making arrangements to come see Riccardo's studio. It was as though they were looking beyond her at a whole new landscape, one that stretched out for the rest of their lives. But how could it?

She felt the pleasant night air cajole her skin and help her make sense of what was threatening to break her heart.

As Marisa and Riccardo walked down to the Quai d'Orsay, where they would find a bus to take them home, Riccardo put his arm around her, as though he were her cape. The weather was clement, and the starry sky looked like an ad for Paris in the spring. A cape was not called for. She looked up at him, smiling a little. "*Che bello Parigi,*" Riccardo said, echoing the tourists admiring the postcardlike landscape around them. "*Ma che?* You found your lost friend, and she has a nice life and a nice husband and a pretty baby who stops crying when you tickle her. What is wrong? Something is missing. Tell me what."

"No, no, what makes you say that?" She shook her head vigorously, but he was not convinced. She stopped in her tracks and looked at him, her face pained. "Give me time. I have to iron out the wrinkles."

They walked on a bit. Then he said, "He wants to come over to see the paintings before the show. With Vladek. They're friends. I didn't realize that. Maybe both of them will have lots of frescoes to commission. I will be rich, you will be famous, and all of us will live on the Quai d'Orsay, my American radio wife.

"Giorgio and Anna will move their restaurant to a *péniche* just here on the Seine, and he will feed the parliament on pesto and risotto, so they will be better tempered. Mario will write a book on the mistakes of the parliamentary system, the parliamentarians will then correct their ways, and Nonno will hold seminars on the deck of Giorgio's péniche about the fair distribution of *la fortuna* in the world while stroking the heads of our ten bambini playing at his feet, speaking Santini Italian. And someone in the background will be playing 'L'Internationale' on a harmonica. How is that for ambition? Now tell me what is wrong."

She shook her head again, but after a second, she relented. "Okay. I can't put a name on it; it was just that she was not telling me anything. It did not happen the way I thought. She never saw me as I saw her. I was not important to her the way she was important to me," Marisa said reluctantly.

He was silent for a bit as they reached the bus stop. "If she really knew you that well or if she remembers you that well, she will have realized how you feel. I did."

He looked down at her face, which had grown deeply sad. He put his arms around her and carefully examined her eyes, making her relent.

"Don't ask too much of her. Not this quickly. You have lost a great deal more than she did. She was never alone the way you were. She was always in the center of her own family, in her own cocoon—an exciting cocoon even. A ship sailing away to glamorous Europe? With all her colorful family? You were on a ship too but with only an address book. You don't realize how far you have traveled all alone with no one telling you to be careful of the traffic. Till I took you to my Shoe House roof and taught you Italian. *Non e vero?*"

They were silent for a bit. He waited for her to react to the picture he had finally put into words, for her to look back on it squarely.

"She lost her playmate, whereas you were dispossessed of everything and everyone you ever loved. Marisa, admit the crown of martyrdom. Otherwise, I have no purpose in life. I am here to protect you, to save you from these foreign devils who come from far away from Santini. Don't make it harder for me, *amore del punto di* Manhattan, *mi Americana del unicornio estrangeri.*"

As though from a great distance, she heard the wisdom of his nonsense. It was graphic, the picture he'd drawn of her leaving New York, pulling away from her life on a ship's deck, and going to a romantic notion of a continent that left her forever a foreigner, an onlooker for the rest of her life—a point of view she had never imagined for herself but into which she had slid comfortably. He, of all people, would be sensitive to that. He instinctively gave it a name, a weight.

He had been there to catch her as she fell.

Now she reached up to kiss him, to thank him for seizing upon the prickly kernel of her truth and helping her to build around it.

She thought of the unlikelihood of her ever meeting this gifted young man who sensed her kind of loss and sought to make up for it. The miracle of their meeting rolled over her like an ocean wave.

"My gorgeous, randy lover, you are so—"

He put his fingers over her mouth, saying, "I know what this word *randy* means, and you are my matching sleeping volcano."

Their bus swung around to a noisy stop almost at their heels and all but knocked them into the gates of the French Parliament, which was just behind them. Their unexpected shuffling made a brace of uniformed police guards snap nervously alert to see what was going on.

"That's just what we need now, an international shootout with nervous French cops," Riccardo muttered, and he yanked her up into the bus. He looked out the window and nodded formally at the scowling faces guarding the gates of democracy.

No one shot him.

***

The remaining two weeks leading up to the show were warm and sunny, for which Marisa thanked the heavens, because had it rained gloomily during the tense days of matting and framing the paintings before hanging them in the gallery, nerves would have snapped like chopsticks.

She had not heard much from Jim Snow in Lisbon, who had called and told her he'd had to put his investigation on hold because he had an assignment in Portuguese Africa.

However, he was still intrigued by the story and would be in touch. She felt it was a bit of a reprieve and breathed out again. Trick breathing was becoming a habit, she thought to herself.

Most artists were fussy about how to present their works. They lost patience with the gallery owners, with whom they had, at best, only tenuous relations, accusing them secretly of all manner of arcane double dealings, sometimes justifiably—but only sometimes.

Gallery owners were used to this and were usually immune. Some of them were even good at hanging a show intelligently. Robert Mundt was one such, but that did not change Riccardo's instinctive mistrust.

Marisa stayed out of the gallery before the opening. She stepped aside also to have space in which to reassess her reunion with Lane after that momentous day. They had spoken on the phone a few times but had not met again. The Cléments were going to London for a short visit, but Lane promised to phone as soon as they returned. Jean-Claude's troublesome daughter from a previous marriage was in London and acting up. The story sounded authentic, Marisa thought, but she was not totally convinced. On the contrary, she was numbed by the situation left hanging in the air and deliberately put it on hold till after Riccardo's show.

That was at the heart of her life: the show. He was the heart of her heart, she reminded herself gratefully. She leaned on him, and at the same time, she knew she propped him up in turn.

His well-being at this juncture was the only thing that counted. She pampered him, cosseted him, and let him keep all the crazy hours he seemed to fall into on his own. He confessed to her that the day they had met at the Flore, he'd been there to have breakfast, having gotten up at two in the afternoon. Now she made no noise and let him sleep.

Meanwhile, the Shoe House and its annex at Giorgio's were filling up. Don Carlo was staying downstairs, and Mario was at Giorgio's, thus allowing his sister, Anna, to feed him properly once she had prettied up their extra bedroom for Monica. Mario watched the preparations, smiling happily. He loved his sister, who, childless, had coddled him all his life, just as she had Riccardo. They had turned to Anna when they were little and needed help in navigating the Santini world of Don Carlo, who had become Mario's tutor as well as Riccardo's.

Mario was tallish and slender and looked more like a crooner than a contentious historian of the twentieth century, which was what he was becoming. He was aiming now for a stint at the Italian Institute in Paris, doing research into the advent of Fascism and the unrest that had followed the end of the First World War. Mario had romantic dark eyes, a strong chin with a dimple, and well-chiseled features. His older sister, Anna, loved scolding him about his late hours but delighted in his ways, his brilliance, and his place in the Rinaldi household.

She had mothered both boys from their earliest years on Santini, and she took up a special place in their tribal hierarchy, which was what Don Carlo had created around himself in his exile on their island.

Don Carlo reigned over this happy tribe as a patriarch might, with joy, pride, and a touch of wonder at what his exile had brought him unexpectedly.

Marisa, coming on this odd scene, could only have been touched by the aging man's affection and pride in their company.

Marisa worked the day before the opening, interviewing actors and directors on their way to or from the Cannes Film Festival. Listening to the flapping of their egos, something that normally irritated her, was more relaxing than fording the electricity Riccardo generated in the company of Don Carlo, who had come up from Genoa with Mario to cope with the entire carnival.

The Genovese delegation was well used to Riccardo in orbit. She was still a beginner.

Mario started by packing the canvases for transport to the gallery in such a way that they would not be damaged before anyone got to see them. That had been Riccardo's first worry.

Then came the unpacking at the gallery, where Riccardo claimed everyone was clumsy, careless, and in a rush.

Mario gently but firmly sent him out for a sandwich with his grandfather, assuring him that he would unpack them all one by one, exactly as he had been doing from the beginning, from the time they had taken a painting of his downstairs to the living room in the Genoa house on their first Christmas away from the island.

It had been Mario who had chosen the spot to hang it, chosen the strong nail to hold it, and hung it straight in the center of the panel facing the two windows on the street. It was the perfect place in terms of light and interest. If the windows were open, the painting could even be seen from the street. Without putting it into words, both boys acknowledged the unusual bond that linked them completely.

They did not have to put it into words; it was obvious to everyone who knew them. They also knew it was rare. They did not push their luck, however. They were careful of each other and suspicious of outsiders, or so Don Carlo held. He also claimed that the boys' friendship benefited him more than anyone else, because he'd acquired another grandson in the process, one who was exceptionally gifted and just as exceptionally careful of Don Carlo's welfare in all respects. Furthermore, he lived a short train ride from Genoa, not in New York or Paris. His two boys had filled his life when it might easily have slipped into despairing age.

On the day of the hanging of the paintings in the gallery, Riccardo stayed with Giorgio till it was all over. Then he took them all out to dinner at a Russian restaurant in the Latin Quarter, just to confirm their faith in the merits of the Mediterranean and the flavor of basil on their pasta.

Riccardo was calm. The paintings had been hung gracefully, elegantly, and safely, and the perilous chore had gone off without incident. He looked across the table at his incomparable friend and raised a glass almost sheepishly. Everyone knew what he was going to say and said it with him: "*Viva Il Green Hornet, il mellio di tutti. Il Calabrone Verde!*"

They were island children again. Watching them, Marisa felt that tear come back into her eye. Riccardo saw it with infinite pleasure.

✳✳✳

The weather was mild the Thursday of the opening. "It forgot to rain," she said, getting out of bed carefully. She stood at the window and smiled at the sky. Riccardo was coming out of the bathroom and about to mount the steps to the terrace. She gawked at him for a second and then called out, "Darling, if I were you, I would put on a towel— at least a towel." She giggled.

He looked blank and then realized what she meant and began to laugh. He swiveled back to the bathroom and grabbed his robe but then changed his mind and went back inside the bathroom, where she soon heard him running the water again and singing "Bewitched, Bothered, and Bewildered" in Italian. He was shaving.

She decided that the day was off to an auspicious start—except, perhaps, for the ladies on the upper floors of the buildings to the rear, who would have to wait for warmer days to see Riccardo take sunbaths in his bathing trunks while listening to the BBC news roundup and, of course, its weather forecasts for the coastal regions and the western isles, Fisher, Dogger, and German Bight, the Shangri-la of his childhood.

An auspicious afternoon followed the morning, but with increasing nerves. Marisa made Riccardo eat some pasta with Anna's special pesto complete with the cheese Severina had sent them via Mario, a pecorino.

The cheese had come from a certain Pipo, who kept goats in Santini. He calmed down after that and suggested walking to the gallery rather than taking a bus. Fortunately, he remembered in time that his grandfather, Mario, and Anna were picking them up at four, and Giorgio would drive them there in the minibus.

"Of course, and we make an entry like a Mafia raid, all of us with hands in the pockets," he murmured. "I hope the critic from Le Figaro is watching."

She had bought a stunningly understated suit at a timely sale chez Dior: a full skirt in a smoky blue flannel and a short jacket with flared lapels that framed her face becomingly. She'd found a pair of navy ballerinas to go with it. She knew the outfit flattered her, and she needed that kind of propping up that day.

Marisa was unsure of herself in Rinaldi public arenas. She feared not being up to the arcane reaches of Don Carlo's stature. He attracted snobs of the kind that jostled her. She managed easily among the true greats of the world, whom she met as a reporter. They were no problem. However, she was unsure of herself among Paris's in crowd, the chatting classes, the ones who traveled like schools of flat-eyed fish. Their inflated egos drifted above their heads like vintage zeppelins. She referred to them as the Hindenburg Crew, their women particularly. She hated their ease with expensive clothes, and she envied their intimacy with shoes and gloves.

"I will live here a hundred years," she'd once told Milo as they were walking down the Faubourg Saint-Honoré, "and I will still choose the wrong scarf, as though by instinct."

Milo had laughed and reluctantly agreed that there was something in la Parisienne that was *sui generis* and could not be learned.

"On the other hand, they could try to walk like you for a million years and still come up with those tight-assed mincing steps they do. So don't complain. You're fine," he'd said, which, in Milo-speak, was enormous praise.

Riccardo would endorse that, she thought, though she often noticed how he looked like a purring tomcat when one of those elegant ladies given to gallery openings would engage him in conversation on his interest in color or form or both. She had learned to wait just long enough before gently intruding at the perfect moment. It had become a little game between them, a teasing little tilt in mixed company.

She was determined to keep the interactions light, for she hated the jealousy she felt, because of its corrosiveness.

Sometimes, however, she indulged herself with daydreams of some secret poisoned hat pins she might palm as she followed behind him at a respectful distance through the world of art galleries, theater lobbies, movie queues, the Luxembourg Gardens at sunset, and, most of all, the terrace of the Café Flore, all of which these ladies considered their terrain, their happy hunting grounds.

That way, she was able to laugh at herself till peace of mind returned with the look she saw in his eyes as he told her to behave.

"How pretty you are," he called out, coming up into the bedroom. "What an interesting blue gray. Look—it makes your eyes a different kind of blue. Maybe if they don't buy the paintings, they will buy you and give me excellent critiques for good taste.

"No, I think I prefer to retire to Santini and raise goats— with you next to me, asking, 'How do you say it in Italian?'"

She would have loved to push him back onto the bed and reassure him that everything would be fine, that the world would love his paintings and see what he wanted them to see. They would even ask him for more.

Instead, she took his hand firmly and pulled him upright.

The bell sounded downstairs, right on cue.

Giorgio's Praetorian Guard was at the door in the minibus, happily and confidently surrounding Riccardo, who had gone to open it. Mario saluted smartly. "*Il Calabrone Verde-Mobile*," he said smartly. "*Presente*."

And, she thought, *they are fourteen years old again, off to conquer the world.*

"If it is boring, we can always go to a movie," Mario said. "Today is the day they change the programs."

***

Robert Mundt was standing at the door of the gallery, talking to a smallish couple of a certain age. The man looked familiar, but before Riccardo recognized him, they turned and began heading for the Seine, the woman following hard on the small old man's heels.

They looked familiar, but another painter, whom Riccardo had known in Genoa when they were both at art school, came over, and he lost sight of the elderly couple. It was not till much later that he realized they were Max and Madame Ernst. He wondered if his not recognizing them had been a good omen or a cautionary detail. He asked Marisa, but she was nervy enough without riddles. She decided to drop the matter till tomorrow. Omens were things she left to the Mediterranean islanders. The ones on the Hudson were too pragmatic for second-guessing unfamiliar household gods.

The gallery filled up early, and Robert Mundt was an excellent host. Jean Levrand, Mundt's young assistant, was a personable young French art historian doing his thesis on the origins of modern art in France and the influence of foreigners in its growth, Modigliani and Mary Cassatt in particular.

When Marisa and he had first met, they'd gotten along instantly when she hadn't bothered to hide her ignorance of Mary Cassatt, an American impressionist painter. Mary Cassatt was better known in Paris than in New York, Marisa had learned, to her relief. Jean had put his arms around her and hugged her when she had said, "Who?" inopportunely, and she looked forward to seeing him tonight as a potential pillar during the opening on which her whole life depended, or so it seemed.

Riccardo, who did not need pillars and who had viewed the hugging moment with a cold eye, had just nodded. Mario had picked up on the chill and glanced over at Marisa, who'd given a delicious little grin in return.

Riccardo was now talking to someone to whom his grandfather had introduced him, in a little group that was growing bigger by the minute. The gallery soon looked like an international peace conference, with Italians here, French speakers there, and in-betweeners all over the place.

The light was flattering, and the paintings looked commanding under the cleverly placed ceiling lamps.

The gallery evoked sober elegance that went well with the rigor of Riccardo's work and the restraint of his use of color.

Marisa wondered about the curious artistry involved in hanging a show, in choosing the proper dimensions of space between the paintings to put them to their advantage. It wasn't by chance that the works blended with their environment. It was by clever positioning. Robert Mundt was indeed a professional, Marisa thought admiringly. The show looked elegant, sober, and arresting.

A tall young woman wearing large sunglasses came over to Marisa and introduced herself in English, mentioning a magazine Marisa had never heard of. She startled Marisa, who had been pondering how one hung a show well or poorly, so Marisa only heard half of what the woman had said. The evening was full of art magazines she had never heard of, and they all seemed to be attached to attractive young women.

She could barely hear what the pretty face behind the glasses was saying to her in an odd voice, but she found her vaguely familiar.

Suddenly, voices on her left raised in an unfamiliar language made her turn, and she saw Vladek in deep discussion with an unknown man. At the same time, Penny came over, almost colliding with the pretty stranger in the sunglasses. *Why dark shades in this skillfully lit gallery, where every megawatt was measured by an expert? Maybe she is looking for the piano and thinks she is in the film* The Blue Angel. Marisa was tempted to ask, but the pressure of the crowd was tugging at her nerves, startling her almost. *Have I just developed a case of agoraphobia?* she wondered giddily.

Penny gave her a peck on her cheek and then hastily pulled back and frowned. "You've got a fever!" she said in a loud whisper.

The other woman, who had pursed her lips at the latest interruption, moved an inch closer, as though to scrutinize Marisa. Marisa did feel oddly warm but not feverish. Worse, she suddenly felt a stab of dizziness and feared she might be losing control.

What is going on? she thought wildly, doing her best to ride out the awkward moment. She grasped Penny's arm and then said to the stranger, "Excuse me a second," pushing Penny into a glide over toward the front door, which was open for fresh air. Out on the sidewalk, where the gallery's overflow had repaired to chat or smoke cigarettes, she leaned against a parked car.

The June night had grown warm with the crowd. Through the window, she saw Mario and Don Carlo in serious discussion with two gentlemen who looked like members of the Académie Française posing for posterity.

"If you feel off color, you can go ahead to the restaurant and wait for the others there, you know. It would be better than fainting inside," Penny said.

Marisa declined, saying she felt better. She'd just been overcome by the crowd, the heat, and the relief that there was a crowd and a show of interest. "Not to worry. Imagine if no one had come." She made a stagy shudder.

After a bit, they went back inside, and Marisa made her way to Riccardo's side. He was talking to Vladek and an older woman. He turned to Marisa and reached out his arm to hold her, and once more, she felt dizzy.

He was smiling so happily that she decided not to mention it. But then he looked at her, gave her a sweet frown, and ran his fingers under her chin by her left ear.

He whispered, "You do have a fever. You do. No, please, my love, don't get measles tonight. Or double pneumonia or pestilence. We are going out to celebrate after."

She shook her head vigorously. "I'm fine. Don't worry. And I never get fevers. It is just nerves, my love."

However, as she said that, her heart flipped. Her grip on his arm tightened because it suddenly occurred to her what might possibly be askew with her.

Oh my Lord.

Then, just as suddenly, the dizziness vanished, and she breathed deeply and freely but with cold alarm. Shouldn't she wait till they were at home in the Shoe House? On the roof? Somewhere with just room for the two of them?

"You know what it might be? Tell me then," he said, his eyes bright. "But first, listen. Two paintings have been sold to Rene Gerhardy. You know who he is? He wrote a huge book on the rise of totalitarianism thanks to the Treaty of Versailles chopping up colonial empires without looking where the pieces fell. And he was very unpopular with the left till Nonno wrote an article praising his way of understanding the dynamics of freedom—something easy to read like that. So the left stopped being mad at him. They became friends, and now Nonno is so pleased. Look at him.

"Gerhardy also has a Henry Moore sculpture in his garden. He has two Picassos of the 1930s and one small sculpture of Arp. He lives in Nizza—Nice—speaking of colonies. And as I recall, he has a pretty granddaughter called Adela, who dances very well, I remember. A blonde," he said offhandedly, teasing her. Then, looking deeper into her eyes, he asked, "So now do you feel better? Is your fever gone? And you will enjoy the rest of the night, wherever we go for dinner? Even without your newfound best friend, who seems to have a travel bug that strikes whenever you come into sight?" he said, trying to make light of Lane's strange departure, as though on cue.

A small man with a cane broke into their little coven, speaking in rapid Italian. Riccardo listened politely and eventually introduced his wife. "Professore Podesta is a friend of Nonno's from Milan, and he is Mario's professor of Italian history." Riccardo peered around over the little man's head for Mario to rescue them.

It is that kind of vernissage, she realized, banishing the fever. *Lots of people. Lots of talk. Lots of name dropping, superlatives, pretty clothes, and pretty women. And, for the artist's pleasure, a number of sales.* Two of the large, ambitious canvases went to collectors the Mundt gallery had worked with for many years. Their making a place for Riccardo's works in their collections was a giant step for him. At twenty-seven, he was, after all, still a young artist.

He looked at her with his eyes showing pleasure and, more importantly, relief. She thought for a minute as she watched him listening to Robert Mundt and saw that he was feeling all the right things: relief in the reception his work was receiving and a measure of comfort in having what he was trying to do accepted by others.

His painting required attention. It required further thought. It was not easily accepted or, for that matter, decorative in the accepted sense of the word. It made no compromises to prettiness. However, it captured the viewer's attention and made him or her think.

She felt like shouting out in joy. Instead, she put her hand in his and whispered, "I love you for your locked doors. And apparently so do several other people who collect paintings."

He pressed her hand but then frowned, for it was all true. She did have a fever, and he did deal in locked doors.

Then, out of the blue, something snapped in his memory, and he turned to her slowly, his eyes grazing over her pretty young face. He waited a second before asking her with a movement of his head, his eyes still searching hers, "Could it be? Could you be? No."

They looked at each other like a pair of truants. Could it be? Could it?

They often took chances. Or they just couldn't wait or simply forgot where she had put the diaphragm. She hated the diaphragm, though she was grateful for the freedom it afforded—when she could find it.

As their months together had gone by, they had simply grown careless, too sure of themselves and their luck and, especially, the amazing hunger of their youth. They behaved as though they had invented the miracle of making love. It was their private secret—no one else's.

Now she looked beyond him, beyond the heads bobbing in the gallery space, beyond the conversations that echoed in her ears.

"I think perhaps I might have skipped June up till now. I think the last time was April. Oh my God, what happened to May?"

He stood staring at her, transfixed. He could find no words adequate; he knew no language well enough to say what he felt in that precious moment, a unique moment in which he was alone with himself in total stillness. *My child.*

Finally, she whispered, "I think you won't object. If it's true, I mean?" she added clumsily. He let his glance stray over her anxious eyes, seeing what he loved in her most: her tenderness and her total trust in him.

"Object? My sweet Marisa, you should know that I must be the happiest *bacciagalupe* in Paris. But only till I tell Nonno and Mario, that is."

"What's a bacciagalupe?" she said urgently.

"A dumb Italian, of course. Like me." He leaned over to kiss her, but remembering where they were, he only kissed her forehead. Then he walked her over to where his grandfather was talking to a critic who worked for one of Paris's best new magazines with a left-of-center leaning. Bowing slightly, Riccardo interrupted in Italian, starting with an apologetic "*Momento, ti prego, scusi.*"

He took his grandfather by the elbow and moved toward the door that led to the gallery's storeroom and office. Amid racks of canvases and pedestals bearing sculptures shrouded in white dust sheets in the spooky alcove, he said, "Marisa thinks she is pregnant. I think so too. What do you think?"

Don Carlo stared at him, speechless. "Think? Think?" he echoed. Then he broke into a surge of tears. Riccardo held him in his arms, noting with odd pleasure that his grandfather was still slightly taller than he, just as he had been throughout his childhood memories. He'd always been taller, stronger, and ready to comfort him, even when Riccardo had been a bad boy.

Now, he thought gratefully, *I can repay him in the most precious way possible, with the gift of another child to love.* The love of a child was the most unencumbered, least selfish, and most generous of loves.

Don Carlo groped for a handkerchief, but neither had one, so Riccardo snatched the smallest of the cloths protecting what turned out to be a bronze Picasso sculpture, *Portrait of Paolo.* It was a tender portrait of a young boy with a beautifully shaped head and a fine nose. Paolo was Picasso's son.

"How's that for serendipity?" Don Carlo murmured as they went back inside to join the others. Riccardo kept his arm around his grandfather's broad shoulders, feeling the still-strong older man's muscles under his touch.

"I assume you know that word, *serendipity,* by now. Especially you. It is all over New York, like a new toy," Don Carlo said.

Riccardo assured him, in an absentminded way, that he did. Actually, he did not.

Marisa told him what it meant later that night, when he thought to ask her.

Both marveled at the Rinaldi family's appetite for foreign languages no matter the moment's circumstances.

✷✷✷

Riccardo's first one-man show in Paris ran for more than one month, which brought it up to the end of July. August was an odd month in Paris, since many of the city's shops were closed for the sacrosanct August holiday. The art galleries, however, were not. They had a robust reprieve. Robert Mundt did what many galleries did: he put on a collective show of all his artists. Thus, two of Riccardo's paintings remained on display till September. For a first show in Paris, Riccardo's had done remarkably well. It also gave him the illusion that he had a future and had found at least a crack in the door.

That comforted him immeasurably.

His hope for the future went well with the promise of a baby. It indicated a giant step of change in their lives, a giant step forward.

The day after the vernissage, Marisa took a bus to the American Hospital in Neuilly to see a doctor and talk about her pregnancy in English. She wanted the comfort of her own language at that moment, as silly as that might have seemed to some. In any case, she had no doctor of her own, for she hadn't been sick since she had been in Paris.

"We are permanent transients here, you know," she murmured to Riccardo as she left the house. He liked the notion, though he realized it had its drawbacks and limits, such as now, when they did not have a family doctor.

Riccardo handled illness more simply. Whenever he felt out of sorts, he took the night train and the next day saw Dr.

Rossi, who had looked after them all since they'd arrived in Genoa. He was tempted to do that now, but he remembered that Dr. Rossi did not handle babies. He knew that through Anna.

He sat down on the barstool in the living room, feeling almost light-headed at the realization that he would be a father, that the bambino he'd often joked about would be a reality—a son or a daughter, a child of his own flesh, a completion of an interrupted line.

He thought of Marisa, her youth, and her scarred life. The reality of her lack of family had troubled him from the start and increased his impulse to protect her and shield her from harm. Now to see her carry his child tore at his heart.

They had created their own universe together.

This was her house, her husband, and her child. She had entered his universe there with him. It was he who had brought her into his world, and the responsibility that move now conjured up in his mind prompted him suddenly to make the sign of the cross, something he hadn't done since childhood.

He caught a glimpse of his reflection in the mirror and laughed out loud.

After a bit, he went over to a white canvas that he had prepared the week before, and he took it upstairs to the studio. He installed it on an easel, gave it a coat of an almost-white paint, and then tried the curious new blue he had recently come upon almost by accident. It was made gentle by adding a luminous gray. He'd created a color that startled. He let it sit for a bit and went up to the terrace to see how the sun was doing, giving the painted canvas breathing space while he watered a few plants.

He returned to the canvas and then drew a single line in a downward stroke. It was too thick the first time, so he painted the canvas over and waited again. On the third try, he found it. The line was not in the middle; it was perhaps one-third over to the right of the canvas, and it went from top to bottom. It was about half an inch thick, perhaps a little less. It was a deep blue. It was precisely what Marisa had guessed was the goal he had been aiming at all along.

Now he could tell her he had found what he had spent all this time looking for: the perfect straight line.

He called the painting *For Paolo*.

***

Despite their confusion, everything fell into place. The doctor at the American Hospital confirmed that she was more than two months pregnant and that the fever had nothing to do with it. "Pregnancy does a great many things," he observed wryly, "but it doesn't give you a fever."

He then suggested she might be interested in painless childbirth, a method that had originated in France with the celebrated Dr. Lamaze and caught on all over with remarkable results. The Russians were pushing a similar procedure, but unless she was planning to visit Moscow, he suggested a doctor near her on the Left Bank who did the French version. The baby would be born at the American Hospital, which did not fail to sound reassuring to her American ears.

"You can yell in English then," he said, and she smiled. "Don't knock it. You'll tell me after." He proved to be right after all. It was a serious comfort to be free inside one's own language.

There was a direct bus from the Luxembourg Gardens to the hospital. Oddly, this detail comforted Marisa too. She traveled the city by bus because she did not like undergrounds. She had become an expert on changes, shuttles, and squiggles around the city, just as she had done in New York, where her dislike of subways had begun. Paris was round and compact. Getting around was easier. She tried not to be in a rush, though, for while buses were pleasant, they were not rapid. She liked that, as it gave her time to find out where she was going and where she had been.

When she told Riccardo about painless childbirth and what it was, he felt faint. "Without anesthetics?" he echoed hollowly. Riccardo could scarcely face the reality of his tender bride enduring the gory torture that awaited her. He had a problem with pain. When she described what the process involved, he paled, but fortunately, Marisa wasn't watching him. She was too busy being enchanted. He felt ashamed of himself. He felt he was a coward, while she was looking forward to what she viewed as the crowning moment of her life. He felt even fainter at that.

He put his hand under her chin and apologized silently. She looked up and saw that he was as white as a sheet.

"Poor darling," she said. "Don't worry; it will be all right. People have been doing it for years, and Painless Pierre will make it all an easy dream." He stared at her.

"Oh, Riccardo, we are going to have our own beautiful little baby, a new generation of Rinaldis. I have him right here inside me. My love." She fell back onto the pillow, warmly wrapped up in a dream.

Before she slipped off to sleep, she decided not to tell him the odds of her losing all sexual desire during pregnancy, as the doctor had warned her might happen. Anyway, since there was no sign of that so far, she seemed to have slipped through the gates. *First-time lucky,* she whispered, closing her eyes contentedly.

He watched her sink into sleep. Her features were still so young and disarming, and a sweet little smile lingered along her lips.

A little later, he looked at the calendar and figured out that the baby would be born around Christmas. He went up to the terrace and had a last cigarette on his own, listening to the music of the city, feeling humbled and a little fearful. There would be a real child, his child and hers and a great-grandchild for Nonno.

***

Early the next day, Marisa took the bus to the office. It was a slow day, so she asked Milo if he had a minute, as there was something she needed to talk to him about.

Milo told her afterward that he had guessed even before she sat down in the chair in front of his desk. He'd decided he would not tell her, though, because he had no explanation himself as to why he was sure and why he was so happy for her and for Riccardo too.

In reality, Milo was unhappier about not having children than he had ever shown. Anne-Marie, his wife, had been shattered when they'd learned after two miscarriages that a third would prove fatal. In the prewar years of their early marriage, it had been difficult for them to adopt a child, being of two nationalities and two religions. Then the war had started, and by the time it was over, they'd been well beyond the age. There was a time for everything. They had missed the deadline.

The possibility of pregnancy was one of the first things that had come to mind when he'd hired Marisa. "She and Riccardo will want children. They should have children, for that matter, if only to continue the beauty of their eyes," he had told his wife. He had foreseen the inevitable, even though he could see that Marisa had not. He had also figured out how to manage the bureau with a three-month replacement to everyone's satisfaction. Now, in his office, he was dying to tell her as much.

She sat down in the old leather chair, nervously casting glances at his pack of cigarettes on the desk. He sat down opposite her and removed them from her sight casually.

"Milo, I don't know how to begin," she said, and he couldn't help laughing.

He raised his hand to stop her and said, "Don't apologize. I'm delighted. When is it due?"

She looked at him as though he were a magician. He laughed.

"If you hadn't thought of this, I did. And Billy Logan will be free anytime we need him."

She sat google-eyed, mesmerized by his generosity. Then she jumped up and reached over the messy desk to plant a happy kiss on his cheek. "Around Christmas," she said. She relaxed at hearing him tell her about the seasoned reporter who did pinch hitting whenever needed and who had worked around Paris for years, writing film scripts and criticism, translating books and films, and writing cops-and-robber fiction set in Paris with a sexy girl detective who somehow never caught on. Billy was happy to come in for a three-month maternity leave, which would be on full pay for Marisa thanks to the superior health insurance system General DeGaulle's first postwar government had installed in France.

Milo always took great pleasure in describing French health insurance to visiting Republican politicians, who talked about creeping socialism and tried his patience. It did not take much to try Milo's patience, however.

After a cup of tea brought in by the aging secretary who had been there forever, they all agreed that Marisa would go on leave on November 1 and return on February 1, and she and Riccardo would not have to call the baby Milo or even Kilometro in return. Mademoiselle would begin knitting instantly.

Marisa was so grateful to them that she nearly forgot she was due to go to a press conference Coco Chanel was giving to launch a rebuttal to still more tattletale allegations about what she had been doing during the war with the German High Command—to stay alive, as the lenient would have it, or perhaps only to stay in practice, countered the unkind.

Marisa had learned to curb judgment on how public figures had behaved during the war, especially women.

There was a viciousness toward women, such as Coco Chanel, that disturbed her sense of fair play. Arrant jealousy of women who had made careers as brilliant as Chanel's was colored by envy and lacked any trace of compassion. It was a particularly French attitude and was unbecomingly judgmental.

She suddenly had a vision of the unforgiving, cruel Madame Defarge character in *A Tale of Two Cities* and the role of the narrator she had played in her senior-year production in high school. She thought of Dickens's opening lines: "It was the best of times, it was the worst of times ..."

There are lots of great-granddaughters of Madame Defarge still hanging around today, she thought.

Then, like a jarring flash, as she was crossing the Boulevard des Capucines to reach the Chanel press conference, she felt a bolt of recognition. *That's who she was! The woman at the gallery in the sunglasses!*

Marisa suddenly remembered who the stranger whose voice had been muffled by the crowded vernissage, the pursuing outsider who had tried to talk to her, was. She was Patricia Conway, the girl who had wanted to play the part of narrator and whom Marisa had replaced at the last moment because the teacher had thought Marisa could do with a helping hand—and also because she had found Patricia's nasally voice unworkable. Marisa's voice was low and mellow, and she seemed to know how to use it. Her teacher had told them that, explaining the last-minute change. Patricia Conway had sulked.

I'll be damned. In the middle of the boulevard, she felt herself shuddering. Marisa's memory was a constant surprise to everyone, including Marisa. It was a warehouse full of bits and pieces. She stored up trivia like no one else she knew. Who else but she would remember that grazing encounter from years ago in high school?

Now? Who else? Patricia Conway herself would, she thought with a creepy little chill.

But why? And if the woman was the thwarted narrator of *A Tale of Two Cities*, why hadn't she just introduced herself? And why had she come to the vernissage, for that matter? Had she grown up to be an avant-garde art collector on the sly?

Her mind racing, she tried to remember what she knew about the bad-loser blonde, but she couldn't think of much. She'd lived some blocks south of the park, she recalled vaguely, close to the Drive. *Wasn't she the daughter of a cop?* Faint snippets of memory skimmed by her now, with no real consistency.

She let her mind dawdle over the street scenes of her adolescence: the reaches of Upper Broadway and the big, ornate movie houses that had been such cathedrals in her growing up, such as Loew's 175th Street or the Coliseum a little farther up on Broadway. She recalled ice-skating on winter ponds during the cold months and playing by the river in the heat. She remembered her fondness for the lighthouse where she'd sat and daydreamed for hours at a time, pretending to be doing her homework.

She had wanted to be a lighthouse keeper all through her childhood till Peter had finally convinced her it was not feasible, but they'd learned one could buy lighthouses in off-beat coastal regions, and they'd decided to keep the possibility in mind for after the war.

Oh, Peter. After the war.

There on the Boulevard des Capucines, on her way to listen to Coco Chanel justify surviving, she allowed herself the luxury of seeing Peter come alive again, hearing his voice talk of lighthouses and love, and she tried to tell him that there would be a new life for him in her baby. His life would be rekindled there with her in reborn postwar Paris, alongside a giant dreamer who'd survived the chaos that had claimed him.

A new life, Peter, who will grow to enjoy lighthouses on the rocky coast that nurtured Riccardo. Another chance.

She walked down the street to the House of Chanel, her heart thumping happily, having swept away the riddles that had intruded into her mind about Patricia Conway's second coming.

When she got home that evening, she found Mario upstairs on the terrace, deep in conversation with Riccardo over a pitcher of Anna's lemonade. "You look like a pair of Tennessee Williams's colonels being spoiled by their mammy," she said, kissing their cheeks in greeting. They looked blankly at her. *The cultural divide has struck again,* she thought, suddenly tired.

Coco Chanel had been a huge exercise in the art of suspending judgment and exercising tolerance in times of emotional overdrive.

"I have been telling Riccardo what we think might be the solution to your housing problem," Mario said. Riccardo squirmed and muttered that he did not have a housing problem, to which Mario answered, "No, you think you can just put the baby in a basket and keep him here on the roof till he goes to Harvard."

Marisa suppressed a giggle.

"So," Mario said, "we have been thinking about doing something about the *vecchio* next door to get him to leave his leaking taps and go to his volcano in Auvergne.

"Giorgio says he phoned the *casa dei vecchios* near there, where they could take him for a modest sum, which would be paid for by the Securité Sociale and the veterans because he was in the First World War. We could afford to buy his rapidly disintegrating plumbery, and you could expand on this house, including this roof, and make the whole thing big enough for the bambini, for the paintings, and maybe even for a bedroom for you, not just a corner of the studio.

"It makes sense to everyone but him. He goes into his Hamlet position and drives me *pazzo*. Marisa, forgive me. I should have talked to you first."

Riccardo looked up and said, "*E perque?*" so spontaneously that they all laughed, even Riccardo.

"Will the old man give up his plumber's counter and leave?" she asked. "Did you ever see him there, staring out the door at what was going on in the street? His street? I'd be surprised if he remembered living anywhere else; he's been here that long," she said.

The old man puzzled her. He was polite to her when forced to speak to her, though he avoided that as much as possible. He addressed her as something that sounded like Mamzelle la Modèle, but she wasn't quite sure of that either, since he usually mumbled without his teeth.

He put them in when he went to eat at Giorgio's, though. He liked eating at Giorgio's because the food was soft and full of sauce he sopped up happily with his bread. Giorgio charged him next to nothing, and he came early before the place got full. He'd come by only during lunchtime recently, which made them all surmise that he went to bed early now and was feeling whatever age he might be.

He knew that Riccardo wanted to buy his house, and he had no reason to refuse him, except he was not sure he wanted to return to an Auvergne he had all but forgotten.

"Why can't he go to a home here, where he can see what few friends he has left? He hasn't been to his Auvergne in years, he told me. He might be more pleased with the idea if the metro were handy, or he could take a bus to the Luxembourg Gardens, where he likes the benches in the sun. I've seen him there a number of times." Marisa said this calmly, noting their surprise that she knew anything about the man at all.

Riccardo suddenly got up, and before they realized what he was doing, he was down the stairs on his way out. They looked at each other and burst out laughing.

So it was that they were able to buy the narrow little building adjacent to the Shoe House for a reasonable price with the help of an even more reasonable mortgage.

Riccardo looked at them all as though they had performed black magic for his benefit, turning his beloved Shoe House into a stately home for the new bambino.

Much later that night, he put his arms around Marisa and said confidentially, "We will keep a bed in the studio just for us, apart from our new official *matrimonio* in the enlarged version. We will keep the old bed where it is, where we began. My love, my love. We will go into this big new future that everyone is talking about, but we will keep our own corner. Our own today. You want that too, *non e vero, amore? Non e vero?*"

Thus, the Shoe House changed silhouettes, and their lives changed accordingly. When the builders finished with it, Marisa had acquired a book-lined study with a bathroom on the ground floor, and upstairs they had three bedrooms and a family bathroom with a huge old bathtub on ornate golden feet.

Riccardo's Shoe House had become a stately home. His studio reverted back to being just his studio, still with a bed against the far wall—in case he wanted to see the easel from a different angle, he said. They moved into the real bedroom like thieves, sometimes giggling at the change. The two smaller rooms were reserved for the future dolphins.

The real touch of magic was Riccardo's precious terrace, which had more than doubled in size thanks to a piece of magic Vladek had pulled out of a hat. He'd gotten them permission to extend their roof to match the plumber's and to make it one large garden with sturdy walls around it, rendering it child-proof by design. Riccardo took to dreaming of a heated pool. He looked at garden furniture with a new eye.

Everyone knew that having major house repairs going on when one lived in the house was a horror story, but even in that, the good fairies were with them. It was noisy but amiable.

Their three builders were young Italians from an island just up the coast from Santini, and though driven by Vladek, they were under Giorgio's vigilant eye. He stood over them like a gorgon. They grew to love Marisa through her morning sickness and her wobbly rush to go to work every morning, when she tried to speak to them in her lopsided Italian. She brought them cups of coffee and cakes whenever she could. They also watched her tummy grow with the gentle concern of people who put love and family above all else.

Aldo, Beppo, and Bruno spent what they thought of as a vacation in Parigi. *Una casa cosi simpatica*, they said. *Un artista giovine e la sua esposa Americana cosi spetando un bébé.*

They completed the considerable job well on schedule. Before they left to return to Italy, they helped Riccardo bring potted winter jasmines, orange trees, and a pair of unlikely olive trees up to the roof, after having paved it with Spanish Moorish-style tiles that Riccardo had ordered from specialized ceramists in Valencia.

They laid the tiles expertly, and Riccardo gave them each a framed drawing in thanks.

The three young men felt the job had been an adventure. When the baby was born, they would be the first to receive announcements.

Enlarging the Shoe House had been an adventure, not a trial. Riccardo, who had dreaded the prospect, claimed that Marisa had come into his life on a chariot of errant angels. She held the secret of the unicorn for the happiness she conjured up around her—around them.

Perhaps that made up for the other confusions that had arisen during the same crowded period.

Tricks of memory had jumbled the sequence and made muddles of time where time counted for so much.

The day Marisa had left the Coco Chanel press conference with a head full of value judgments etched out by damaged souls had marked a turning point.

Heiresses of Dickens's unforgettable character Madame Defarge, knitting while the crowned heads fell into baskets under the guillotine at the Place de la Concorde, rose to the surface of her imagination. The image made her shiver even now. Patricia Conway entered, a ghost in flashy sunglasses at Riccardo's opening—a ghost whom she had not recognized and whom Lane had not seen.

Lane, the elusive, had not been there when Marisa's father had died on the living room couch, when she had needed her most. Lane had vanished with her dotty mother, a jump ahead of the voracious Senator McCarthy and his hoods who came with warrants and left ruins in their wake.

During Marisa's flight through the scrubby edges of the park, the little red lighthouse had been out of reach, unable to offer shelter. It was only a token now of her childhood's remembered sense of safety.

Where had Lane been then, and why had they packed their bags and fled at that specific turn?

Once again, Lane had been called away on the night of Riccardo's opening. There seemed to be a pattern to her absence. But why?

That day, after the press conference on the rue Cambon, with the nasty taste of cruelty to others in her mind, she went back to her office and wrote a piece for a broadcast she would do at the end of the week on the remnants of collaboration in France in the present time—remnants that would take decades to fade. In addition to Coco Chanel, many actors, writers, and politicians were fighting off the ghosts of their wartime yesterdays.

These were ghosts who would not fade; she knew that. However, she had been slow in realizing how firmly they were encrusted in the seesaw politics of the present.

And tomorrow too, in all likelihood, she thought. The impact of the war would remain a French cancer and could only be cured by a French remedy.

She did not envy the French conscience; it bore a jagged edge.

She put in a call to a colleague in WWR's New York office, to someone she had worked with regularly from the beginning but whom she had never met. His name was Aaron Kaminsky, and she liked his voice, with its uptown New York accent that was so familiar to her. They had become buddies of a sort, probably because of that. She felt a pinprick of homesickness when she came upon a New York accent like his. There in her exile, she admitted it readily.

She asked him if he had a minute to talk, for she wanted to ask him to do a bit of snooping for her. "Not for any story now up on the file. At least not for now, that is," she said.

She told him about the flight of a whole family on a certain date and inquired about the death or disappearance of an FBI agent, special service man of some sort, or precinct cop on that same day. She described the neglected area beyond the George Washington Bridge; the little red lighthouse; and the railroad tracks, rocks, and high grass before the manicured reaches of Manhattan's northern tip.

Aaron listened carefully, scarcely interrupting her for questions. Not really much to her surprise, he told her he had grown up on 173rd Street and had gone to George Washington High, though ten years earlier than her crowd. He had been in the army in Germany when all this was taking place, he said regretfully. However, he agreed he would look into it, and he had a friend from school who was a sergeant at the Washington Heights Precinct and could give him a hand. He asked her why she was looking into such an incident, and she stumbled there.

"It is personal, as you can guess. It is to close an open question after a long time. Look, I know I am presuming upon you, but without my telling you why, please know that this is vital. No, that's too strong. It's an open sore that might go septic. It is important to me now. Oh, please. I'm so embarrassed, but ..."

He let her wait a second and then said, "Okay, I understand. When I come to Paris, you will invite us to dinner, and while my wife is looking at your husband's paintings, you will tell me your story of the haunted house by the Cloisters."

She felt immense relief in the warmth of his answer and absolute confidence in what he could unearth. Then she wondered how he knew about her husband's paintings.

"Milo talks about you like he invented you. He told me that Riccardo Rinaldi had a great show on and that you'll be taking maternity leave at the end of the year. Mazel tov for that, by the way. Maybe you don't know how much you are Milo's favorite topic of conversation. Ah, well, don't tell him I let it slip. And don't worry either—if there is something in all this to find out, I'll find it. Just give me time."

They chatted a bit more and left it at that. She was moved to have heard him refer to Milo's fondness for her, which was something she seldom spoke of, never took advantage of, and always treasured. Milo, the childless, aging, tough newsman right out of Ernest Hemingway's fictional universe, doted on her. She was the child he might have had, though if asked, he would mutter that most of his buddies' children had grown up to be dentists, so he was happy with his Irish setter and his Saturday trout.

When the phone rang again, she was not surprised to find it was Patricia Conway.

Her name hadn't changed, Marisa learned, because she had married a third cousin. Patricia added, "We kept all the good genes in the family that way," making Marisa wince.

"I could come over to see you, if that would be easier. I won't take up too much of your time. I'm just doing some research into New Yorkers abroad and how they feel about the changing face of their city. I tried to tell you at the opening, but of course ..."

Marisa felt a warning light go on. "But who for?" she asked curtly.

"For myself, of course," said a surprised Patricia.

"But for what? Are you writing a book or a magazine piece? I mean, why are you asking?"

"Oh, it is for a Senate subcommittee on how stipendiaries live abroad. How they represent their homeland while abroad—that sort of thing."

She let her voice go vague, but Marisa was the wrong mark for vagueness. "You'll have to be more specific than that. Look, Patricia, it has been a long time. I'm busy, and I'm sure you will find others more typical than me. I am not a stipendiary either. And I'm married to an Italian, remember." She toyed with the idea of hanging up, but there was something that almost frightened her in the other woman's clumsiness.

Patricia broke in. "Yes, I know that, but suppose I came over to see you for an hour, or we could meet at a café or your husband's gallery. Or your office. I won't take up your whole day."

Suddenly feeling an unpleasant sense of being cornered, Marisa said simply that she had no time free that day.

"Okay," Patricia said, "what about at the Closérie des Lilas tomorrow? It's Saturday. Say three in the afternoon? It's near where you live, so it should be easy," she added, leaving Marisa cornered.

One up for Patricia, she thought.

"Say about three on the terrace of the Closérie. Thanks so much," Patricia said, and she hung up.

Her voice still grates, Marisa thought, realizing that Patricia had walked all over her. *Tough girl. Stipendiaries? Homeland?*

Homeland was a concept that did not sit well in an American context. Germans had a homeland; Americans had a country. There was a fine line there.

Marisa wished she knew how to say *pushed around* in Italian; she would have called Riccardo and told him. She remembered the term *bacciagalupe* and wondered if that worked in the feminine as well. She felt like a dumbbell. She had acted like one as well, and she had been pushed around.

She sat back and tried to think calmly about Patricia Conway, recognizing now that there was something unsavory in her request—something the French called "eel under rocks," *anguille sous roche.* She had burst out laughing at that amazing metaphor when she'd first heard it, but now it seemed to be uncomfortably apt: an eel slithering around under her rock.

If Milo hadn't been up in his Normandy hideaway, she would have talked to him about the curious reappearance of a minor figure from her high school past, with an investigating husband in tow. *A senate subcommittee investigator? Maybe.*

She thought of the usually well-informed staff of the press attaché's office at the embassy and wondered how late they worked on a hot Friday afternoon—and how ready they were to talk about the unlovable House subcommittee ferrets who were running loose these days, making Americans abroad uncomfortable. The office's well-kept files would help her get a picture of what they looked like in action in Paris. It was after embassy closing hours, but perhaps they worked overtime. She dialed the number but got a recorded message saying that the press attaché's office was closed till Monday.

It was after six, and it was a hot weekend. She hoped they were having a long, cool drink somewhere nice. Then she said, "Merde," and she felt better.

***

Penny and Vladek were away till next week on a visit to the Austrian Alps to keep Vladek and their little boy, Mark, within spitting distance of Czechoslovakia. After that, they would go for another two weeks to a village on the Côte d'Azur to keep themselves tanned and coddled in Western decadence, as Vladek put it.

Vladek might have known someone among the murky byways of exiles in Paris, someone who knew someone who knew all the agencies that might have displayed interest in Lane's breakaway family many years ago—an interest that was being revived now in Paris, or so it seemed. Marisa felt uneasy, uncomfortable, and a little apprehensive.

Summer weekends in Paris were by way of being suburbs of Limbo.

If this had happened in New York, someone would have left the hall light on.

She picked up the phone at her desk and again called Aaron Kaminsky, her patient New York colleague, hoping for his kindness and the comforting sound of his voice. He picked up the phone on the second ring, and she breathed freely. She felt a little guilty perhaps but reassured.

"Now, I know you will think I'm badgering you, and I suppose I am, but this Patricia Conway is really worse than I imagined. I don't know for sure why—it is tenuous—but I feel edgy. Please let me tell you about the beginning."

He must have been sitting comfortably, because he did not interrupt once. Then it was her turn to sit back and listen.

"Okay, okay, you're right to be intrigued, if that's the word. Her husband is Michael Conway. He works for HUAC's army of private agents doing Senate investigation takeouts in New York, out of an office here in the city: Acme Investigations on Upper Broadway, in the west seventies. They've been routine private-eye operatives since 1945, when they got out of the army. Conway and Burke, the partner, were MPs in the army, so it figures.

"Somehow, they connected with a couple of McCarthy's goons, and they hit on this odd story that goes back to around the end of the war, about a traveling salesman who may or may not have been smuggling drugs in from around the Florida coast. Now, wait for this: the rap was on him, not on his wife, who was moderately hooked on world peace but nothing much else. Not a case of spying at all, just drug smuggling. Got that? Okay, now listen.

"In these circles, world peace is a Communist plot. You have to understand the subtext here. Okay? So you have the New York version of world tension on one side, with Senator McCarthy saving us all for Wall Street, and the dreamy left indulging in wishful thinking among folk singers and poet dreamers straight out of Woody Guthrie and John Steinbeck's hobo trains on the other.

"That peacenik cast changed once the 1930s turned into World War II. Idealists, dreamers—you are too young to know about all that. But you can look it up. I can send you some stuff that will give you an idea of the mood.

"Now this Conway crew come in on the ham-fisted postwar wave of anti-Communists, which is why I was putting off calling you till Monday or Tuesday, because for the moment, I can only give you a mood piece outline without many facts or names and addresses. But this much is clear: it was the husband, Seymour Berger, who was doing real things, not the lady you described so vividly as wearing hats and talking utopia to her colored maid."

Marisa was speechless. *Seymour?*

Lane's father was an absent presence in her memory. He was a traveling salesman who traveled far—to Cuba, for instance, and maybe even Mexico. She recalled that he also went to the Bahamas.

That was exotic, she remembered thinking at the time. The Bahamas were British, or were they? Lane had reported that her father was surprised they all spoke with an English accent, like Leslie Howard. Marisa remembered wondering then how an English accent had survived in what were, after all, American waters.

That was the sort of trivia her mind accumulated, she mused, but then she also remembered that he'd once sent back loud, frilly, long samba dresses for the girls, which they'd hung on the curtain rod in Lane's room to show off to the others. *And who were the others?*

She tried to force her mind back to a long-ago afternoon when she'd come home from St. Catherine's with a couple of girls from her class whom she hardly knew. As they'd gotten off the bus, she'd seen Lane on the sidewalk, heading for her house, trundling a big package with colorful stamps all over one side of it. Marisa had looked at it and said, "It looks like an invitation to a party," as it was so gaudy with stamps.

They'd started chatting, and Lane had said on the spur of the moment, "Why don't you come in and see it? It's from Brazil. It's a couple of samba dresses for me and Sissy."

Marisa and the other two girls, near strangers, had gone to see the dresses. Lane had put on some Carmen Miranda records and brought out Cokes while they admired the samba dresses and dreamed of Brazil.

Marisa, trembling, sat back now and wondered what that incident meant. She had forgotten it totally.

Her heart thumping, she gave a clipped version of the incident to Aaron and promised to dynamite her memory in a search for other bizarre trivia threatening to drown her presently.

Aaron Kaminsky laughed and said, "My wife and I are thinking of paying you a visit in February. It's for her birthday and Valentine's Day and who knows? Maybe Lincoln's birthday too. I gather you will be back on the job, and we can celebrate almost everything at once. Will your husband enjoy it?"

"My husband will be delighted almost as much as I will be. I hope this creepy stuff will be over, though. It is making me nervous. What am I supposed to make of my former best friend, Lane? Her parents turn out to be a mix of Al Capone and the Rosenbergs. And now they vanish off the board when the Conway vigilantes come into view here in Paris? What am I supposed to think?"

He paused. When he came back to her, he sounded gentler and less excited than he had been before.

"Leave it with me. The answer is the House subcommittee, if indeed there is an answer. It could also just be that a couple of sleuths of the McCarthy persuasion are trying to make points on overtime.

"It might be that one of those hoods McCarthy hires as private investigators has hit on something that he thinks he can cash in on. If I were a betting man—and I'd love to be one, but I can't afford it—that's what I would go with. A little freelancing here, some old scores settled, and who cares what happens in faraway Paris?"

He paused again, as though he were giving her time to digest his words. Then he said seriously, "Stay away from it,

Marisa. I'm asking you that as a Dutch uncle. Stay away as of now. We will talk again next week, and please tell Milo the whole story, including the samba dress, on Monday. We'll pick it up then. I am very serious. Stay away. Have a nice weekend instead. Take care."

She was more than shaken now. She went up to the roof, thinking of what she should do and wondering where Riccardo might be. She was supposed to meet Patricia at the Closérie tomorrow afternoon. She sat down at the round white table and thanked the good Lord for the nice weather. The lingering sun seemed to be protecting her from evil.

The next day, however, she was less sure. She slept till late morning. It was a heavy sleep that left her feeling numb and apprehensive upon waking. She saw Riccardo's note on the easel—a big sheet of red wrapping paper with a note tacked to its center. He was out for a walk, he told her, so she could sleep for all three of them. The message was adorned with childish *x*'s for kisses.

He goes out for little walks on his own all the time, she thought, not sure she wanted him close right now anyway.

He was at sixes and sevens lately, with the prospect of having his house upside down for weeks to come, which daunted him more than he would admit. More so, the curious aftermath of his show, his first exposure to a major Paris art audience, was affecting him.

He had shown work in Genoa and Milan in group exhibitions and in Vienna once in an impressive grouping of young European artists called die Neue Europa, where several critics had mentioned his work as promising without knowing anything about him personally. He prized that enormously.

His Paris show had been well attended and well received, even by critics hostile to abstraction in general. However, there was something in his work that antagonized critics who did not find grace in the movement toward abstraction. *These critics would probably have shot down the impressionists,* Riccardo thought as he strolled through the Latin Quarter, *had they lived in the same time zone as Monet.* Yet he could not dismiss them altogether.

Their antagonism was almost personal, which was hard for him to understand, because he did not know any of them personally. It had to be something in the way he went about doing what he did, something that was seen as arrogant on his part.

He was anything but arrogant, yet he seemed to have been viewed as such by people who either could not see where he was going or did not like the path he was taking to get there.

The criticism disturbed him because it got in the way of viewing his work silently, the way he viewed it himself.

Now, after the show, he was trying to make sense of the reception he had received, with which he was reasonably at ease.

No one was throwing tomatoes at him at least.

He was deep inside himself these days, though, and felt remiss in not being more available to Marisa and the massive joy she brought him with the progress of the baby.

At that moment, he was strolling around the Latin Quarter aimlessly, in the maze of streets not far from the Shoe House, enjoying the warmth and the way the sun changed the colors of Paris charmingly. He headed home.

Perhaps he would take her for a ride on a Bateaux Mouches to watch the sunset.

Before he got to the house, he stopped to buy her a bouquet of carnations, flowers she was particularly fond of. She said she'd grown to love them because of Hemingway's attachment to Spain and the bullfight, their scent, and especially the fact that she thought Riccardo looked like a bullfighter, when he was not swooping around on his dolphin. Her fanciful notions of him gave him no end of pleasure, though they were light-years away from the way he saw himself.

He rang the bell and let himself in, in case she was up on the terrace, which she was. He met her at the door to the terrace and waved her back, offering her the bouquet as a peace token for his frequent absences.

She was pale, he realized. She shook her head and burst into tears. He took her into his arms, shocked and alarmed. "*Ma che cosa*, Carina, *que cosa*? What is wrong?" He led her to the chair by the table and pulled another one close for himself. "Shall I call the doctor, Carina? Does something hurt?"

"No, no, I am fine, and the bambino is fine. That's not the problem."

She sat back in the chair and told him about Patricia Conway, what Aaron Kaminsky had told her, what she had remembered, and, particularly, the appointment she had made with Patricia for la Closérie des Lilas that afternoon. Her voice tapered off when she saw his face.

"But you don't think you are actually going to go? To meet her in a café when she probably has goon squads waiting in the bushes?" He was aghast.

She stiffened, remembering the only other time she had heard him use that phrase—when he was describing what had happened to his parents at the hands of a Mussolini goon squad.

Of course, there was no comparison, but in his eyes, any move that put her in danger was abhorrent. He got up and made for the stairs. "I am calling Mario, and then I am calling Nonno for the name of the capo he knows at the Quai d'Orsay, who takes care of people like him."

He was furious, she saw, outraged that his family would be threatened. She felt dreadful for giving him even a hint of such a possibility, but she sat back and let him get on with it. Riccardo was already calling Mario, who was in Paris, staying at Giorgio's while doing some research at the Italian

Institute that might or might not end up in a contract to lecture there the next term.

Therefore, he was in Paris, just waiting to be called to the rescue. Giorgio was around too. Marisa gave a nervous little laugh and imagined the posse the four of them would make at a table on the terrace of the Closérie, with background music by Ennio Morricone. *Where is Rosselini when you need him?* she said to herself.

However, there was a chill underneath her lighthearted vision. Who were these threatening private detectives, and what was their margin of movement in France? They had none, she told herself coldly. They were powerless there, and any move to make a public fuss involving Marisa was nonsense. Yet she could not dismiss Aaron Kaminsky's insistence on her staying away from them.

"All right then," she called out to Riccardo, "we will stay put. Perhaps Mario would like to come over, or else we will go to Giorgio's, where I will tell everyone all about it, and Anna will calm us down with a pesto. It is now almost four," she added as he came back up to the terrace. He looked dark and angry.

He was carrying a tray with two mugs of Earl Grey, and she could see a package of *petits beurres* sticking out of his pocket. *There is a time for everything,* she thought, relaxing and taking the cookies from his pocket. "Thank you, my love. We can now calm down."

Mario arrived a few minutes later with a big bottle of Coca-Cola and several glasses in his hand, not being a tea drinker despite peer pressure. He sat down quietly and said, "To begin with, I know very little about our Marisa's New York life beyond the fact that it was near the George Washington Bridge and there was a French cloister that raised unicorns. What more can there be?" he asked.

They laughed, and there was something in his eyes that reassured Marisa and let her breathe again. He would make sense of all this, and his presence alone was reassuring. Slowly, Marisa told them both about Lane and her parents' bizarre flight from their home on the day her own father had died. She explained how she'd stumbled around the edge of the river by the railroad tracks below the well-lit paths that joined the street and its houses.

She did not have to mention her mother, and neither Riccardo nor Mario prodded her for any more information than what she offered.

Mario asked her about Lane, though, as she was then and as she was now. He asked about their extravagant flight from New York and their quiet present in Estoril.

At first, she was not going to mention her uncertain sight of a body by the river on that terrible night, because it was tenuous. Yet to leave it out might be foolish, because her sense of it was too persistent for it to have been nothing. There had to be some explanation.

She told them that the reason for the flight of the whole Berger family was accepted at face value. It had been odd, but odd things happened, and New York was the world capital of odd things, as the janitor in the Berger building put it.

"That was one chapter," Marisa said. "But then the sore loser of the senior play at St. Catherine's, Patricia Conway, suddenly turns up here with a husband who is a private detective specializing in Communist suspects as seen by American Senator Joe McCarthy, whom Europeans view as an aberration."

"What could you ever have done that they suddenly want to talk to you?" Riccardo asked calmly.

"No one was interested in me, really. I was just bumbling around, almost in the way. Incidental, if you like. Also, I got the lead role in the senior play because the teacher was being nice to me and because Patricia had a squeaky voice.

"On that dreadful night, though, I was just stumbling around the street by the park because it was the awful day my father had died, and I don't know. I was looking for someone to hold on to. I was looking for someone to help me.

"But when I went to their house, all the Bergers had vanished. I was in shock. The whole family had run away. My father was dead on the couch, and the Bergers had fled out of my life. It was like a body blow to not find them at home, where they had always been.

"So I just left their building, going—almost running—down through the scrub to the river, where I used to love to be. And I thought I saw a body. But I wasn't sure, and I wasn't really frightened; I was more like repelled. So I took a skimpy path and got up to the street and back to my house and went to bed and cried. That is what happened to me on the day my father died. Nothing else.

"Maybe the body was really there. Maybe I really did see it. Who would it have been? And who would give a damn about my having seen it? I wasn't a reliable witness. And anyway, if it was there, why was it not reported in the press or talked about in the neighborhood? Why was it kept secret?"

She shivered. Riccardo rushed to her side, knocking the empty tea mug to the floor and making Mario jump.

All three laughed at themselves in relief.

"You must not get upset. Otherwise, Riccardo will end up breaking all the dishes," Mario said quietly as he picked up a dead tea bag and waved it back and forth daintily.

The doorbell rang. Then it rang two more times. Riccardo went to the roof's edge and looked over. Astonished, he whirled around and said to Marisa, "It's Milo." His eyes were wide with surprise. "On a Saturday?" he added, making for the stairs.

"His day for trout?" said Marisa.

Milo came puffing up the steps. Riccardo followed a few minutes later, carrying a basket of glasses, two bottles of

San Pellegrino, a bottle of white wine, a corkscrew, a box of grissini, and a delicious Santini sausage Severina had sent with Mario recently, wrapped nicely in a napkin. A sharp-pointed knife stuck out of his shirt pocket.

He looked like a pirate.

Marisa put her arms around Milo's neck, and they all talked at once. Milo's arrival decanted all their unspoken questions as to what exactly they were into.

Milo sat down corpulently and took a well-deserved sip of the spritzer Riccardo handed him.

"I had a long talk with Aaron in New York last night, and we both decided something had to be done about this nonsense today. Aaron is a cool type usually, but he really got worked up by the Conway man. Seems that Conway is an ardent follower of the senator, plus Father Coughlin and a bunch of other choice liberals, and he runs a little army of freedom-loving private eyes who bust strikes and student rallies and the like for a modest fee. They specialize in storming picket lines."

Milo made a face that spoke volumes.

"Okay," Marisa said, "so they are Fascist hoods, but what are they looking for in me? Or with Lane and her family? And why now, especially? Why now? And what are they looking for?" she said, half rising from her chair.

Riccardo was standing behind her chair. He put his hands on her shoulders and gently pushed her down again, as though he were putting her back into a bottle.

Milo looked at the couple and found them irresistible, as he had from the beginning. He nodded and took a sip of his drink. "That is why I'm here and not there on my day for trout. Now listen, and take notes if you want. It is complicated.

"Let's begin with Mr. Berger. He is a traveling salesman in surgical supplies? He is. His territory is around the Caribbean, isn't it? It is. So one day, in the course of his mooching around the beaches down there, he picks up a sideline in a variety of recreational powders, just to round out his Band-Aid-and-talcum-powder salary at the end of the month. It is the Depression, remember. Ends of months were often painfully thin. A little extra would be welcome.

"That's not hard to set up in the islands, you know. The stuff is easy to find. It's going cheap even. Cocaine? Opium from the poppies? Marijuana in everyone's backyard? The drugs are light, pack easily, and pay a helluva lot better than corn plasters. And their price goes nowhere but up. He wonders why he didn't broaden out earlier—poor soul."

Milo made a funny face and shook his round, balding head. "But we are talking about Seymour, who is not your average daredevil gambler. Is he? No, but he's a smart cookie with a quick eye watching the world going through a brutal depression. Now, listen, if it hadn't been for the Depression, he wouldn't have taken a crazy chance like this. But he does, and it works. He is not greedy; he doesn't push. It is just a nice little sideline for his family. And it all goes well during the war years too. Okay? But—and there is always a but—as soon as the peace treaties flow down from heaven, the whole structure of the local drug trade as it had been before and during the war drops with a bang and splashes all over the ocean floor.

"That particular game changes from top to bottom. The old Mafia, which the navy had chased out of business, is back in place in the islands, and they instantly put the heat on the crop of freelancers who popped up while they were playing patriots. Okay? Good. Now listen to this scenario: Seymour is a freelancer, nothing more. The big guys hear about this little Band-Aid salesman who sneaked into their islands when they were away in the army or in the clink, whichever, and they don't like him one bit. They want him out.

"But Seymour must have made friends down there under the palm trees, because somehow, he is tipped off that either the Mafia or the narcotics squad or both are on his tail.

"But just then—listen to this; the timing is amazing— someone else on another desk coincidentally decides he should look into Seymour's crazy wife's collecting funds to rebuild Stalingrad or some such place they would rather leave in ruins.

"And that particular someone gets the idea that he can get hold of Seymour through his wife—subpoena her first on Commie charges and then arrest him as an accessory, even before they get their material together on his drug charge. It's a stroke of genius. That way, no one knows about his little drug scam, which—now, listen—allows one of their crew to just step in and take it over. It's a way of eliminating the interference Seymour had unwittingly made on their territory. They were playing both ends of the street. See?

"Seymour was crowding them out, okay? So they send their neighborhood operative, Charlie Conway, to bring him in for questioning through a summons for her, the missus, not him. The real NYPD cops are looking for him, and the HUAC, the McCarthy hoods, are looking for her.

"Seymour lets the whole scene play out before he decides what to do. Now, he's no Zorro; he's not going to make a move till that third summons-serving cop comes into his living room. Charlie is alone, and in fact, he is on his way home after serving his summons, whereupon Seymour follows him out, and going down those rocky bits at the edge of the park, he shoots him.

"He likes guns, remember? He knows that the body will be found without much trouble the next day. But not before.

"So he decides to pack up his wife and daughters, including his wife's hats, and he beats it. Out of the country.

"He was about fifty, you must remember. Just at the edge of everything. What are the chances? Either he is still young enough to pull it off, or he is too old and loses across the board, taking his wife and two girls with him. But remember, he was in the infantry in the First World War, in the trenches. After that, this is easy—wouldn't you say? He chooses the Zorro option, and he does the second most amazing thing in his life: he runs away en famille.

"The first most amazing thing was when he decided to become a freelance drug dealer in the Caribbean while he was selling bandages to banana pickers. Howzat for a story line?"

Milo, who had seen Europe crumble under the Nazis and who had come riding back into liberated Paris with General Leclerc and the US Army to reclaim it, sat back. Milo, the Paris veteran who knew the entire script, watched his young friends gaze at him in amazement.

For a second, they were silent, just staring at him as though waiting for more.

Then Marisa said, "And the story ends there? Mr. Berger doesn't remember his own name, from what Lane says." Marisa stopped there. "On humanitarian grounds alone, he is home free. No one would sit still at extraditing a senile old man to appear before a Senate hearing. Not even Cohn and Schine would try that one. It would dent their reputations. They like being feared but not ridiculed."

Mario burst out laughing. "*Si non e vero e ben trovato*," he said, and they all nodded.

"Senile as a fox, I'd bet," Marisa said in a low voice with an admiring little smile.

"Except that the whole bunch of Bergers have already shipped off to Brazil to be with the other daughter," Milo said. "There is no extradition in Brazil, I fear. Who is going to bother? It would be a bad gamble for McCarthy. Badgering an old man, a First World War veteran, on wacky charges of drug running in the islands that ended up with a dead cop in a New York park? No."

Marisa, shaking her head as though to clear it, said, "But I am curious about what Patricia wanted for real. Maybe just to get back at me for stealing her part in the school play?"

"There is that," Milo said, "but I think the other reason is that the cop Seymour shot in the park was her father. He must have worked out of that local precinct. You forgot that?

"Oh yes, by the way, that Carmen Miranda flouncy dress? That would have had a good pound of cocaine in its seams, you know. Maybe the envious Patricia remembered the dress, and someone put it all together into the full jigsaw puzzle. It fit.

"It is Saturday afternoon in New York too, and Aaron was going out to the island for a swim with his wife and twins. They have a place not far out on the island on Breezy Point, which is home to a bunch of writers, poets, and retired bootleggers. It's awful, but he loves it." Milo sat back and finished his drink, which was warm by then.

Marisa felt a wave of disbelieving laughter well up inside. "Breezy Point is where Peter and I were sent every year for our two weeks at summer camp. The postman's kids' summer camp."

Riccardo and Mario looked at each other and marveled at how this whole adventure seemed to fit into the five boroughs of New York. Marisa's mind followed the same thread, but her eyes were abruptly flooded by visions of Peter swimming in the always-cold water, his strong legs outstretched, splashing the sea into foamy wavelets to make her laugh.

How far I have traveled, she whispered to him in her mind, wishing desperately to believe he might know what was going on that day on her Paris roof, with a fragmentary spray of the Atlantic alive in the background, keeping him close to her.

"But why badger me?" she asked quietly. "They must have known I wasn't in touch with Lane. Everyone in the neighborhood then knew I was not in touch."

"Yes, well, you are being logical there. The Conway crew would not follow your logic. The dead man was Charlie Conway, Patricia's father. You might not have seen him at all that night in the failing light, you know. It's surprising you saw as much as you did. And you were so scared by what you saw that you kept embroidering on it ever since. Okay? You have the full picture of that part of it? Surprise victim number one: Charlie Conway.

"That sticks in their family craw. And that's what is behind the stubbornness in getting Seymour Berger after all this time. It was the daughter. She wanted Berger to pay for his death—and for giving his snooty daughters samba costumes when she had nothing of the kind. She is getting back. Jealous, mean, nasty—that's what she was and still is.

"But they have been removed from the picture. The disappearance of Charlie Conway has been resolved. They can't do much about putting Seymour in the clink, because it is too late, and he is in his own private clink forever. Anyway, that's what his family claims. From Brazil at that. So the case is closed. For good."

Everyone was silent. After a minute, Marisa bent forward, studying Milo. Then she asked quietly, "What have you done with them? Have you had the Conways deported? You couldn't have, Milo. Could you?" She was sitting up straight now, wide-eyed. "Did you?"

Milo, the guy who liberated Paris along with Hemingway, the American all the French boys in blue trusted more than they trusted each other? How many of them owed him favors that went way back? Milo the miracle maker?

Of course he could do it—and he had.

He smiled at her benignly with his eyes full of affection, as though he were applying for a job as Santa Claus.

"Ask me no questions, and I will tell you no lies. Didn't you learn anything in school?" He got up, took her in his arms, and said to Riccardo over her head, "And they won't come back again either. End of story." Then he handed Marisa over to Riccardo as if she were a precious package and said, "Take good care of her."

He let her go with a sweet kiss on the cheek. Riccardo put his hand on Milo's shoulder and said, "It will take me years to figure out what was in these people's minds. It is like *Medea* on the Hudson. But thank you for doing what you have done for Marisa. She calls it ironing out the wrinkles. I think they are lethal and considerably more than wrinkles. You have been fantastically kind and brilliant in figuring out all this insanity, which has everything in it but Sydney Greenstreet and Peter Lorre. Think of it. And on your day for trout!"

Mario had dashed downstairs, and he now came up with a bottle of champagne, four pretty Venetian flute glasses, and another Santini sausage in his pocket.

They sipped the wine and watched the sun slowly fading over Paris's fabled roofs, changing colors and inventing new ones.

"Your new and improved Shoe House will be perfect for the baby, Riccardo. Won't it?" Mario said.

"Oh yes," Riccardo answered, distracted, looking first at Mario and then at Marisa. "Until he goes to Harvard at least."

✷✷✷

The real world slid back into their lives after a while. They retrieved a schedule from chaos, and days resumed their usual colorings. For the Bastille Day long weekend, they took the train down to Genoa, where they looked around at the white ships on the quays and chose one they might like to cruise on. They ate ice cream in crunchy cones, feeling as though the summer had been a long time in coming.

Marisa's tummy was progressing nicely; it was round enough to make her feel proud but not yet uncomfortable.

They took the boat to Santini, where everyone was waiting for them, including Giorgio and Anna, who had taken three weeks' vacation—leaving the Latin Quarter to starve, according to Riccardo.

Anna had transformed into a suntanned version of Magnani, straight dark hair included. She bloomed in her own setting.

"Everyone is happy at the beach. That is why Italy has so many of them," Riccardo observed.

There in the sun, the Rinaldi heir began to wriggle. Riccardo put his hand on Marisa's tummy and was so moved that he thought his own heart would stop.

"Nonno, *ho fatto una vita*. I have made a life." His child was real, with a heart that beat under his open palm.

Don Carlo brought up the question of names for the baby and was greeted with a chorus of groans.

"Surely there are enough names in the Rinaldi and Corso families to find something that sounds good in

English and Italian and French? Like Giuseppe or Mafalda, for instance."

They were lying on striped towels on the beach near the house. Marisa was golden but not as golden as Riccardo, who looked like a waffle covered in maple syrup, she proclaimed. He had a trick of gleaming under the sun.

"What name do you prefer, then?" the happy ancestor asked.

"She is into antiquity. She wants to call him Arion," Riccardo said.

Don Carlo looked surprised.

Riccardo said, pained, "I want to call him something different from all the family names. He is a new person coming into a different world. He is his own self, not a reflection of our lives. But Marisa has gone one step further. She wants to call him Arion, the fish boy—the boy on the dolphin. Can you imagine?" He groaned.

Marisa had been quiet during this discussion, her eyes half closed, lying cozily on her towel with a makeshift pillow under her head. Don Carlo grinned at her, knowing she was looking at him and waiting for his opinion. "Arion? Well, it is interesting. Not everyone will know he is an ancient Greek, mind you. But that should not be a problem in the Latin Quarter. Arion? Hmm. Not bad."

Riccardo turned over onto his stomach, his nose leaning on the sandy towel. He sneezed, so he turned around again, defeated. Then he sat up, frowned, and looked out to Corsica in the distance.

His grandfather laughed happily. "You used to do that when you were a little boy—look out to Corsica. Well, I am afraid it is still too far, *carino*. You would really need a dolphin to swim that far."

Marisa stretched out her tan legs and wriggled her toes, making the sand fly off in a little cloud. "We should wait to see what she looks like, and then we will decide. I rather fancy Cunégonde for the moment."

She would never forget the looks on their faces when they heard her. They blurted out, "A girl?"

"We don't have girls in our family," Riccardo said. "But you know, it would make a change, wouldn't it? And she could always learn how to cook." He ducked when Marisa threw a handful of sand at him.

Riccardo continued, now coated with wet sand that looked like bread crumbs on his belly. "Arion is not so bad, come to think of it. There won't be another like him. If you call out Luigi on this beach, you will have fourteen little boys running up, expecting lemonade. And if you call out Arion, what happens? The fourteen Luigis will come anyway, but to steal his lemonade because he has a booby name. Except no, not him. He will be too tough for that. Mario will show him how to do judo when he is six months old."

Riccardo suddenly sat up and studied both of them with a slow smile that soon infused his whole countenance. He took a breath and said, "I have something most important to tell you. Now, listen. Mario will have a little boy at the same time, a few weeks apart. He called this morning and told me that everything is all settled. You know his beautiful Monica from the emergency room in the Milano *ospitale*? Well, he told me that *la dottoressa* and he will be married in two weeks' time. So our new little boys will have company for each other. But we all have to go to Milan for the wedding. She says it is her marriage too." He shrugged. "You know what the Milanese are like. So we must go to Milan, but it is not so far after all. And Monica is a very pretty Milanese."

He looked at them and smiled at their surprise.

Don Carlo's eyes filled with happiness. *My Mario too?*

"That was what all the whispering and conspiracies were about downstairs today with Severina, Anna, and the baker's wife, who will do the cake," Riccardo said. "Monica and Mario will be married in two weeks' time, and Marisa will be *la dame d'honneur* at the wedding ceremony, and I will be *monsieur d'honneur.* Anna and Giorgio and the whole Mario tribe will be there too. Like a gypsy camp in front of the cathedral in downtown Milan.

"And then in February, Mario begins a two-year contract at the Instituto Italiano in Paris, so the babies can learn all the essential things together—walking, talking, and punching all the other bambini in the Luxembourg Gardens. In Italian, of course. *The Green Hornet: Second Generation*—I am selling the film rights tomorrow. Is that not news?"

Mario, still dressed in city clothes, had come up behind Riccardo and heard the last few words.

"You are too late. I told them yesterday," he said, and Riccardo jumped.

Mario stripped off his shirt, showing how often he had been swimming that season.

"Make sure you have trunks on. I wouldn't want Marisa to have a shock now," Riccardo said in a stage whisper, whereupon Mario, who was now down to only his swimming trunks, dropped all his clothes onto Riccardo's head.

Marisa adored it when they behaved like ten-year-olds. It resonated everything she felt about sibling love—everything she had shared and lost and was now rebuilding with Mario and his tribe.

She studied Riccardo as he lay under the sun, his body graceful and at peace. She was thankful to all the gods on Mount Olympus for having put him in her path on that bright November day a lifetime ago.

He was her anchor, her fragile rock—the boy on a dolphin in her care.

***

The baby boy weighed just seven pounds and had long legs, an oval face, and the tiniest of aquiline noses. Marisa leaned back and gave thanks. He cried out in a perfect Italian tenor.

Riccardo kissed his love and whispered, "You have made this a patch of heaven. You know that, don't you?"

He watched the little tear well up in her eye as she nodded in response.

All came to know the beautiful little boy with the unusual first name as Patch. The nickname skirted the problem of the name Arion nicely. He was a few months older than Riccardino, Mario and Monica's little boy, and the children ruled the same sandbox as well as the donkey rides in the Luxembourg Gardens, just as their fathers had done on Santini in a time of exile.

Mario and Monica decided to stay in Paris for a while—to round out their career experience, they said too seriously for anyone to believe them. Don Carlo was often on the ground floor of the Shoe House or in the Luxembourg Gardens, enjoying the company of his two great-grandsons, who made him think back on his own young days as Lucca's papa, when Lucca was a graduate student in Paris, and Veronica was his young, clever, and exceptionally beautiful bride.

Lucca had been a meteor in his long life, and Veronica had been the star he had not succeeded in nurturing into old age with him. However, Riccardo was his universe, his beloved work of a lifetime.

Now Riccardo's and Mario's little sons played noisily in the sandbox, speaking mostly in Italian but sometimes yelling at each other in French or gently saying in English, "Nice boy. Nice boy." They made Don Carlo wonder if there might be some hope for the one-world dream he had aspired to for so long with little success anywhere beyond the children's playground.

He enjoyed watching his Riccardo's paintings grow increasingly sure and Mario's reputation flourish as one of the new historians, and now, as he watched over the two little boys in the Luxembourg Gardens on a sunny afternoon, hearing both of them call him Grandpa to his delight, he could only nod and say, "*Grazie mille* for inviting me in."

Printed in the United States
By Bookmasters